It is the height of the Roaring Twenties – a fresh enthusiasm for the arts, science, and exploration of the past have opened doors to a wider world, and beyond...

In the emptiness beyond time and space alien entities known as Ancient Ones writhe hungrily at the thresholds between worlds.

In Arkham, the people feel in their bones that something is different. Something feels wrong.

A dread tide draws fear and terror along the Miskatonic River, and when it reaches Akham, nothing will ever be the same again.

Only a handful of brave souls with inquisitive minds and the will to act stand against the horrors threatening to tear this world apart.

Will they prevail?

ARKHAM HORROR™

The
FORBIDDEN
VISIONS
of LUCIUS
GALLOWAY

The Drowned City, Book One

CARRIE HARRIS

ACONYTE

First published by Aconyte Books in 2024

ISBN 978 1 83908 310 5

Ebook ISBN 978 1 83908 311 2

Cover art by Martín M Barbudo.

Printed in the United States of America and elsewhere.

9 8 7 6 5 4 3 2 1

ACONYTE BOOKS

An imprint of Asmodee North America

Mercury House, Shipstones Business Centre

North Gate, Nottingham NG7 7FN, UK

aconytebooks.com

To Emily Cooperider and Jen Fick.
For putting up with bad writer jokes and
random freak outs every week for years.

PROLOGUE

Abdul Alhazred hadn't visited the Monastero di Camaldoli in over a hundred years, but he remembered the place in vivid detail. The quiet bustle of the monks, their all too trusting natures. Over simple suppers of bread and cheese, Brother Giacomo had tried very earnestly to save his immortal soul. Now the good brother was nothing but dust, while Alhazred maneuvered his motorcar down the bumpy, overgrown path toward the abandoned monastery. He glanced to his left, eyes glittering in the fading sunlight, eager for his first glance at his destination. A gap in the trees revealed the pale husk of a building broken by the dark gaps of its empty windows. An ominous visage, perhaps, but the sight brought a rare smile to Alhazred's lips.

Today, his centuries-long quest would end.

He pulled the car to a stop next to the green-robed figure of an acolyte waiting patiently in the growing gloom. She remained motionless, head bowed, as he unfolded his long legs from the passenger carriage. He stood, and the incessant late day twitter of the forest cut off abruptly, small creatures nearby sensing the presence of a predator. An eerie silence settled like a blanket over the hermitage.

"Acolyte," he said, his deep voice cutting through the tense silence. "Is it done?"

She straightened, but her eyes remained glued on the ground between their feet, telegraphing her reluctance to meet his gaze. A wise girl. Perhaps she would last longer than usual.

"So he says, but he won't let us look at the pages," she replied in crisp English. "His grasp of reality grows weaker by the day. It's difficult to say whether his work has improved or been rendered completely incomprehensible."

"Has he lit any more fires?" he inquired, suppressing a sigh of annoyance.

"Not since we moved him here. As you suggested, the solitude has done him good, and it's made it easier for us to control him."

"Take me to him."

Tucking her hands into her sleeves, she bowed again, deeply, before turning to disappear into the building. Leaves and animal droppings dotted the hard packed floor, and light patches on the plastered walls outlined the spaces where priceless art once hung. But he spared no attention for such materialistic things. He was focused on different and more lasting rewards. He swept through the halls without sparing a single thought for their sad state of decay. After all, even death may die.

The acolyte produced an iron key from the depths of her robe, inserting it into an ancient lock set into a heavy stone door. It opened to reveal a set of pale stairs descending into darkness. A torch set into a sconce at the top emitted an insufficient, fitful light.

Alhazred arched an eyebrow.

"He screams when the sunlight touches him," she explained. "We thought it wise to move him belowground to keep him working."

"Interesting," he said. "Wait here."

He removed the torch from its holder and descended into the darkness alone. Something rustled in the black, its small weight skittering over his foot, but he continued on without pause. The staircase emerged into a long hallway punctuated by the black yawn of open doorways. A dry, musty smell hung in the air, the scent of ancient secrets long forgotten. At the end of the hall, light outlined the shape of a single closed door.

He strode toward it, crunching the bones of long-dead things beneath his shoes.

The chamber beyond was walled in hard packed dirt, reinforced with ancient timbers. An attempt had been made to sweep the floor clean of detritus, and a small cot and a wooden desk had been placed inside. A lantern hung from a hook on the high ceiling, well out of the reach of the room's occupant, who sat at the desk, staring in blank raptness at the papers clutched in his hands.

"Is it done?" Alhazred asked in fluent Italian as he stood in the open doorway.

Cristiano Savastano came to himself with a start. Just a few months earlier, he'd been a vital young academic who soaked up dead languages like a sponge. Alhazred knew the type well – hampered by his lack of funding, Cristiano had been all too willing to ignore the dubious provenance of the manuscript in exchange for a steady paycheck. He'd thrown himself into the translation with eager abandon, and Alhazred had left him in the care of his acolytes as he attended to other matters.

The intervening months had not been kind to Savastano. His hair and beard had grown into gnarled, matted masses that nearly swallowed his face save for the burning embers of his wild eyes. Dirt and blood crusted the edges of his fingernails. His clothing was in poor repair, one sleeve burnt clear away to expose a mass of healing blisters.

"I've done it!" he replied, thrusting the wadded mess of papers at Alhazred. A sheet escaped from somewhere in the middle and floated lazily to the ground. "I've done it."

Alhazred firmly quashed his rising excitement. He recognized that expression of dazed, vacant horror; Savastano's mind had brushed up against a power it could not comprehend. His worldview had been shattered, its safe limits broken beyond repair. The Book did that to people. Even he could not unravel the meaning hidden within some of its passages, and he had written it himself. A few key sections evaded him despite his best efforts; he had tried to read them over and over again only to find the words sliding out of his grasp, leaving a blank space in his mind. Perhaps he had tripped upon some magical barrier, but it remained invisible and impenetrable.

But the prohibition laid on him did not appear to extend to others. This boy had seen the true purpose of the Book, even if his puny mind couldn't comprehend the full meaning of the power contained within its verses. Perhaps he had penetrated the veil that Alhazred himself could not. Perhaps he had succeeded where countless other recruits had failed.

Alhazred began to flip through the uneven pages, scanning the neat writing. He wanted to be certain that the document was completed before concluding their business. That aggravating mess with the Turkish academic had taught him not to assume such things; he would not be handed a stack of blank pages again. It had been forty years, and he still seethed over the gall of it.

As he flipped through the manuscript, the neat writing became jagged, the words abandoning their neat lines as they sagged across the page. He frowned, progressing onward. The words became harsh slashes etched so hard that they tore the paper. Toward the ending, they devolved even further into childish scribbles, the jagged marks devoid of meaning or thought.

"I've done it," repeated the translator.

Alhazred wanted to throttle him with his bare hands. All that time wasted once again! He would have to start all over with another translator. One made of sturdier stuff than the last few. Someone who could give him more to work with than this... this rubbish! He glanced down at the manuscript once again, marveling at its shortcomings. The lines shifted as his eyes tried to make sense of the markings. Hm. Perhaps there was something to be gleaned here after all. He tilted the page. Was that a few symbols of Yithian? The one right after looked Akkadian. Perhaps exposure to the Book had unlocked an answer this child's mind could not fully translate, in languages he had never heard.

Alhazred knew them all. He could identify characters from across the breadth and depth of space-time: in a short five-page excerpt, he spotted Naacal, Scythian, Cimmerian, and Voormish. But they translated into a mess of random syllables and words, and no matter how he tried to reorder them, no meaning became clear. Perhaps this simpleton had indeed glimpsed the depths of reality as he'd hoped, but he'd been unable to translate the truth onto paper as Alhazred once had.

The project had failed once again.

"I've done it," said Cristiano.

Alhazred dropped the worthless scribbles, favoring the man with a charlatan's grin.

"Yes," he said. "You have. I shall have to pay you."

The translator made a garbled noise, staring up at the lantern with eager longing. Alhazred followed his gaze, cold and calculating.

"You want this, don't you? Something deep within you cries out for release," he observed.

"I've done it," whispered the boy.

His voice cracked. Big, fat tears began to roll down his cheeks. If Alhazred had a heart, it would have gone out to him. But any ability to empathize had been squeezed out of him long ago.

"Let me show you something amazing," he said.

His shadow began to extend questing tendrils up the walls.

The crisp stench of burnt flesh followed Alhazred out of the cellar. The acolyte wrinkled her nose as she sampled the air, betraying the first hint of nervousness he'd seen from her yet.

"Shall I send for buckets?" she inquired with hesitation. "Or does the whole place need to burn?"

"He'll burn himself out shortly."

She blanched. For a brief moment, he considered pointing out to her that Savastano had opened the lantern himself, spilling the oil onto his smiling face. The translator had been so untethered from this reality that he didn't appear to have felt a thing. But Alhazred decided against offering this reassurance. Fear was the most powerful of motivators, and he needed her to be very motivated indeed.

"Come," he said, sweeping past her. "It is time to consult the list. I trust it's been updated."

She scurried to keep up as he strode down the hallway, swallowing her visible discomfort.

"Yes, of course. Although I must warn you, master. The pickings are becoming rather slim." He stopped in his tracks, staring at her wordlessly. She froze, agitation rolling off her in waves. Her mouth opened, spilling out a desperate, breathless explanation. "The criteria are rather strict, and we've already exhausted nearly all of the qualifying candidates. But I've taken the liberty of creating a few auxiliary lists covering new ground. We might consider pairing someone with a skill at poetical analysis with a translator, and thereby spread the strain between two minds. Perhaps that might work?"

Her voice quavered at the end.

"Exhibiting initiative, I see. Very well. Pick your best candidates from these new lists and make the arrangements," he replied.

"Yes, master."

He put a finger beneath her chin, forcing her deep brown eyes to meet his.

"If this fails, I will hold you directly responsible," he said.

She nodded, her eyes wide. When he turned to leave, he heard the soft exhalation of her breath as she sagged against the wall, all the strength seeping out of her. Alhazred's teeth flashed in the darkness. This time would be different. He could feel it in his bones.

CHAPTER ONE

Water pattered steadily into the basin, and Lucius Galloway stared at it with unseeing eyes. The cracked porcelain of the kitchen sink had brought to mind the echoes of a dream he could recall as clear as day: the steady pound of water emerging from some unseen source to pour through the great maw of a massive Cyclopean dam dominated by inexplicable crenellations. The water fell in rhythmic spurts, the sound wriggling in his ears as if desperately trying to form words he could almost grasp. Its flow turned great waterwheels that swelled and deflated in a rhythm that mimicked breath. The river beyond stretched out across the great horizon, glinting beneath the fluctuating, sickly yellow sky. In the distance, the endless bulk of a city stretched its architectural tendrils toward the pulsating moon, as if–

"Lu!"

Whenever Rudi got upset, his French accent came roaring out. Normally, it was faint and thin, a ghostly reminder of a long ago past. Now the accented tones pulled Lucius out of his reverie. He jolted, overcome by an overwhelming unease. The sensation reminded him of the mid-night moments he bolted upright, sweating and disoriented from his latest dream, dizzy with the conviction that now reality didn't quite fit and he had somehow shifted an inch or two off center from the rest of the universe. He looked around their tiny Brooklyn kitchen, where every inch of wall space was crammed with shelves full of spices and pans, graters and shakers and gadgets he didn't know the name of. There was a reason Rudi did all the cooking while he was delegated to dish duty.

He had no idea how long he'd been standing there, lost in the fading memories of his nightmares. But they were just dreams. No need to let them ruin tonight. He deserved this moment. This celebration.

"Hello? You've been staring at that whisk for a full five minutes. I require an explanation so I can decide whether I should be worried or exasperated," said Rudi.

Lucius smiled over his shoulder as he resumed scrubbing the whisk. Even at forty-eight, Rudi was as handsome as ever. His black hair still held the same rakish curl, and his russet skin still retained its youthful glow. Perhaps he'd gotten a little wider around the middle, but his grin was just as impish, his style as debonair as it had been when they'd met almost thirty years ago.

That grin surfaced now as Rudi tapped him with a wooden spoon on the shoulder.

"I sure hope you haven't lost the ability to speak, mon beau," he said. "Just think: everyone comes to see the man of the hour only to find that he's been struck mute. The tragedy!"

Rudi struck such a melodramatic pose that Lucius couldn't help but chuckle as he turned off the tap.

"Sorry," he said. "I was woolgathering."

"Insufficient. I suggest a bit more groveling."

"I'm afraid that's not in my nature." Lucius dried his hands, pausing to peck Rudi on the cheek. "Sorry. I'm just not sleeping well."

"Is it … ?" Rudi stared at him, eyes wide and worried.

"Stress," Lucius lied. "Just stress. This prize is a lot of pressure. It'll wear off eventually."

Rudi slumped, the manic, determined glee fading away to reveal the utter exhaustion beneath. He'd been having nightmares much longer than Lucius, waking in the night with his heart pounding, dirt on his bare feet, and no recollection of having gone anywhere. They'd had to take safety precautions to keep him inside. That had been jarring enough, but over the past week, Lucius had begun to dream again too.

Could nightmares be catching? After all, people tended to be afraid of the same things: Pain. Loneliness. Death. To some extent, everyone was connected by some giant unseen web woven of fears.

A good idea, that.

"Have you seen my notebook?" Lucius asked.

The tense alertness drained from Rudi's body like someone had pulled the plug. The sight chased away the last of Lucius' lingering disquiet. They would be okay. They always had.

"Ah, so that's it. You're in the grips of inspiration again already? You just won the Howard yesterday. Give the other kids a chance," Rudi teased, jerking his head toward the living room. "It's on the mantel."

Lucius retrieved the commonplace book from its spot next to an ornate Brobdingnagian candelabra and sat down to record the idea before it trickled out of his head. In the kitchen, Rudi hummed as he pulled canapés from the oven.

"Would you stock the bar once you're done scribbling?" asked Rudi. "I haven't gotten the garnishes out just yet."

"I'll take care of it."

But Lucius sat for a moment longer, running his hand over the cover of his book, worn from years of use. The familiar buttery warmth of the leather soothed him. This book had been his home, his livelihood, his escape. The words he'd recorded in it had led him to a surprisingly successful career. In these pages, he'd found peace.

Tonight, he would celebrate that and leave the worries behind.

The party was in full swing, spilling out the front door of their apartment and into the hallway. Lucius would have worried about the possibility of noise complaints except for the fact that the downstairs neighbors had gone out for the evening, and the woman from the apartment next door stood smack in the middle of the entryway mat, deep in a heated debate about artistic patronage in the Renaissance.

"Perhaps art cannot be bought," her strident voice rose over the babble, "but painters don't live on air, darling."

Rudi was in his element. He dashed from group to group with a sort of manic delight, telling anecdotes, introducing strangers, and making sure everyone tried his infamous gelatin mold. He also manned the bar, mixing up mocktails decorated with flowers, fruit garnishes, and sprinkles of colored sugar. Although they did have a bottle or two of the real stuff tucked away for special occasions, there wasn't enough to wet the whistles of a crowd this size. Besides, the downstairs neighbors weren't as friendly as Phyllis, and one never knew when they'd come home. Better to err on the side of caution than risk a confrontation with the authorities. After all, tonight was supposed to be a celebration.

The man of the hour sat on the sofa, trying to pretend that his head wasn't pounding. He preferred smaller groups and quiet conversation, but the pleasantries had to be observed. His mother had drilled that into him from a young age.

"Manners," she'd said, "are our best refuge from barbarity."

He'd used that exact quote in his first published book of poetry, but Alice Galloway had died a week before his complimentary copy arrived. Despite this, he'd kept writing, trying to say something true about the world. One book had turned into two, and then to three and four. He scribbled constantly, took on teaching jobs where he could find them, wrote ad copy for a while when things got too tight for comfort. Finally, the tide had turned with his latest book in a rather surprising way. He still could not believe his luck. Lucius Galloway, award-winning poet.

His mother would have been so proud.

At the moment, one of his former coworkers from the ad agency was shouting at him about the book with a persistence that bordered on tediousness. The conversation was made even more wearisome by the fact that Lucius couldn't remember the man's name. He wasn't usually so forgetful; he really needed a good night's sleep.

"So I told him that he missed the point of the book entirely. *The Drowned City* says something real about our meaningless little lives," the ad man bellowed in a foghorn kind of way.

"Such a profound statement on life in the Big Apple. We're all drowning in our own ways, aren't we? I certainly feel like I am. Never thought I'd be stuck writing drivel about face creams and corsets all my life."

"Ads aren't so bad. I was happy for the work when I had it," replied Lucius.

"One has to pay the bills, doesn't one? Those confounded things never stop coming. Mark my words – once you have a family, it only gets worse. You were smart to remain a bachelor."

Lucius glanced at Rudi, who was smack dab in the middle of another of his stories and gesturing wildly with his hands. They met eyes across the room, and Lucius smiled.

"Yes, I'm quite happy with how all that turned out," he said.

He meant it, too. In his younger years, he'd been furious with the knowledge that he could never marry the one person who had ever made him feel whole. Some part of him would always be angry about that, he supposed. But beneath it all, he knew the truth. He was lucky. So very lucky.

Unlike the ad man, who seemed to live in a perpetual state of unhappiness.

"Well, speaking of families, I'd best shove off," said the man. "Ever since the kid arrived, the wife has been positively puritanical. If I'm out too late, I'll hear about it for eternity."

"Thank you for coming. I'm very grateful."

"Of course!" The ad man clapped him on the shoulder. "Just remember me when you're rich and famous, eh?"

Lucius promised to do so dutifully, although he still hadn't come up with the gent's name. As the frustratingly nameless fellow made his exit, Rudi approached with a white-haired academic type in tow. Lucius tried desperately to place this new face but came up empty for the second time in a row. It was a memorable visage too, with bushy muttonchops and a substantial nose. How mortifying. He stood, inclining his head politely.

"Lu, I'd like to introduce Professor Harvey Walters," said Rudi. "From good old Miskatonic University. We were students in Arkham together, back in the olden days. Harvey is the only reason I passed history and became the fine, upstanding citizen I am today."

"Is that right?" asked Lucius, bemused.

"Well, I was his tutor," explained Harvey, eyes twinkling. "And I may have dragged him out of a scrape or two."

"By my suspenders," added Rudi, chuckling.

"It's a pleasure." Lucius offered his hand, and Harvey shook it. "Although I'm not sure if I should thank you or blame you for releasing this reprobate on the world."

Harvey let out a bleat of a laugh.

"You were right, Rudi," he said. "He's funnier than I expected."

"Told you so," said Rudi, looking toward the door. "Now if you'll excuse me, I see that the Carmichaels are here, and they brought their yappy little dog again. I've told them to leave the thing at home; last time they were here, he climbed up on the table and ate every single one of the meatballs. Entertain each other for a minute?"

He squared his shoulders and charged off without waiting for a response, but Lucius was used to such things. He gave Harvey an apologetic smile and gestured to the sofa.

"Would you like a seat?" he asked.

"Don't mind if I do." As they settled in place, the old academic added, "I hope you don't mind my barging in on your party. Rather tactless of me, I know. But I couldn't turn your roommate down. If he's anything like he used to be, he would have made a scene."

"Oh, if anything, he's worse." The two men shared a laugh, and Lucius continued, "I'm happy you ran into each other. Are you in town long?"

"Just a few more days, and then it's back to work." Harvey ran a hand over his face, which suddenly seemed to have aged ten years. "I needed the break. It's been good to take a walk down memory lane. Remember a simpler time."

Lucius didn't know what troubles weighed so heavily on the man's shoulders, and he wouldn't have dared to be so rude as to pry, but he patted Harvey on the shoulder anyway.

"Life is never quite what we'd expected, is it?" he asked, taking refuge in generalities.

The old man rallied himself visibly, straightening his shoulders and forcing a smile.

"You can say that again. But enough about me. Congratulations on winning the Howard! That's quite an achievement. I've been wanting to ask: did you do much research? Some of those descriptions of the buildings in your poems struck me as positively archaeological. Quite detailed."

"That's kind of you to say, but no. It's all from my–" *From my dreams, Harvey. I thought I'd exorcised them by writing that book, but they've come back. And worsened, which has been a really lovely development.* "From my imagination," he finished lamely. "Which is the stupidest thing I've said tonight. I think I could use a break too."

"Oh it's not a problem. These things are exhausting, aren't they? Every time you turn around, another fellow wants to glad-hand you and ask what you're working on next. They mean well, of course, and it's nice to be supported, but I'd much rather hide," the old man said gruffly.

Lucius nodded. "Oh, I know exactly what you mean. I'm simultaneously grateful and also counting the minutes until it's over."

"So shall I shake your hand and ask you what you're working on next?" Harvey asked with a twinkle.

"Why buck the trends?" Lucius grinned. "I'm honestly not sure yet. I've gotten quite a few offers since the prize announcement. Visiting lecturer spots, fellowships, that sort of thing. I even have an offer from Miskatonic U. Rudi is pushing quite hard in that direction."

Harvey's white eyebrows shot up in alarm. "No, no, don't go to Arkham!" he blurted. Lucius' eyebrows climbed up his forehead in shock. The man sounded positively horrified. It hadn't seemed like *that* bad of an offer, but perhaps the administration was less supportive than it sounded.

"I haven't quite decided just yet," he said noncommittally.

"I'm certain you must have better offers," Harvey continued, recovering his composure. "Don't let sentimentality derail your momentum. Come to think of it, I've just heard of an opportunity that might be a perfect fit for you. An old friend of mine by the name of Helen Berringer is undertaking a summer project at Harvard and is looking for a writing partner."

"Harvard?" Lucius' eyebrows crept up his forehead. "I'm listening."

"Heh. I thought you would. She needs someone who can analyze poetry and access the stacks in Widener Library. Ladies are only permitted in that ridiculously tiny reading room when they're not shunted off to Radcliffe altogether."

"Ah, well. I may not be the best candidate then. I'm fairly sure

Black men are only allowed to use the library during certain hours."

"But you can get in. Damned fool rule if you ask me. Helen knows more words in ancient languages than I know in English, and you're arguably one of the decade's great poets. If anyone belongs in that library, it's the two of you. I'm of half a mind to write a stern letter to the provost, if only I thought it would do any good. Of all the closed-minded, ignoramus..." Harvey trailed off, muttering disconsolately to himself.

Lucius appreciated the sentiment, but he didn't want Harvey to waste his time. Change would come over slow seasons, as his mother used to say. There was no sense in getting het up over its laggard ways. It only made a man miserable.

"Well, I appreciate the sentiment even if I'm not the right fit," he said.

Harvey jerked out of his reverie.

"Don't write the idea off that quickly," he replied. "I still think you're the ideal candidate. Most gentleman scholars won't stoop to work with a lady, you know, and you didn't blink an eye at the concept. I don't think she'll finish the work without full access, and from what I understand, her patron is the silent but moneyed type. There won't be any help coming from that quarter. At the very least, won't you have a chat with her? I think you'd hit it off."

"I suppose it wouldn't hurt to discuss it," said Lucius cautiously.

He would not get his hopes up, but he had to admit that the thought of working at Harvard gave him a bit of a thrill. In the meantime, Harvey was excited enough for the both of them. He clapped his hands together with an inordinate amount of delight.

"Excellent! I'll put the two of you in touch," he said.

Rudi came galloping back toward them, his eyes bright with the latest news, and the conversation turned to other things. The party continued on with its dog dramas, spilled drinks, and small talk, and Lucius sat at the center of the tumult, his writer's mind shelving it all away for use in the unknown future.

CHAPTER TWO

"I'm beat," Rudi declared as he flopped onto the sofa.

The party had finally wound down, leaving behind a complete mess and a random pair of ladies' heels tucked in the corner of the kitchen. Someone would come back for them eventually. Lucius grabbed the dish bin and began to work his way around the room, retrieving discarded glasses and napkins and tucking each one away in turn. He straightened pillows and swept up bits of food. His methodical work took him back and forth across the room over and over again while Rudi made periodic promises of assistance.

"I'll get up in just a minute, I swear," he said.

"I don't mind," replied Lucius truthfully. "You did all the cooking. It's only fair that I handle the tidying up."

"Well, you are a saint among men, and I shall worship at your feet accordingly." Rudi sat up and made an attempt at arranging the end table. "I hope you enjoyed yourself. I know parties aren't really your thing, but you deserve to be feted."

"Honestly, it doesn't feel real. The prize, I mean. I went from scrambling for work to having people practically beg me to take on projects. I keep expecting to wake up," Lucius said, heading back into the kitchen with the final stack of glasses.

"It's about time everyone else appreciates your genius. As always, I'm ahead of the times," Rudi said, grinning.

"Hah. How about you? Did you enjoy yourself?"

"Oh, you know me. Life of the party. It was good to see Harvey again. It's been twenty years at least."

"Is he much changed?" Lucius settled down on the sofa next to Rudi with two glasses of water and offered him one.

"Thank you, mon beau." Rudi leaned over, resting his head on Lucius' shoulder. They sat in companionable silence for a moment. "Honestly, I barely recognized him. He loosened up after a while, and I could see glimpses of the old chap I once knew, but the years have not been kind to him. He's so… heavy."

"Age does that, I suppose."

"Not in the body. In the mind." Rudi sighed. "I'm not explaining it very well. Some of us don't have your knack with words."

"Oh, I know what you mean. I had the sense that the man is laboring under some great, crushing burden. It weighs on him."

"See what I mean?" Rudi threw his hands up. "It's unfair that you can throw out these bon mots and leave the rest of us scrambling to keep up."

"Ah, well." Lucius took a sip of water. "He offered me a job, too. Harvey, I mean."

"In Arkham? I keep telling you, Lu, you've got to see it. I can take you to all the old haunts. We'd have a gas."

"Not at Arkham, I'm afraid. It's with a friend of his at Harvard."

"As in *Harvard* Harvard? What's the job and do you have any need for a personal photographer? I've been practicing, you know, and I do love to travel."

Lucius chuckled. At the very least, the offer was worth entertaining just to see Rudi's obvious delight.

"His friend has been hired by some Harvard alumnus who donated some ancient Greek poetry to the collection and would like to commission a book about it. The idea is that she translates, I analyze, and we co-write the thing," he said.

"And you said yes while jumping for joy, I hope?"

"I'm not completely sold on it. The book would be more for use in academic circles, and I might be better served by writing something a bit more mainstream. Mainstream money is always better than academic money, you know."

"Oh, hang the money. I can cover rent for the short term if necessary. Uncle Pierre's inheritance might as well be good for something, considering that the man was a raging bigot. How long is this project supposed to take?"

"Just the summer."

"Then write the thing, put the Harvard feather in your cap, and move onward and upward to fame and fortune. You have to at least consider it! Why wouldn't you?"

"I said I'd meet with the translator. We'll see what happens after that."

Rudi clapped his hands, rubbing them together with relish.

"I'll buy the train tickets. Because if you think I'm not going with you, you're not half as smart as I thought you were," he declared.

In the wee hours of the night, Lucius swam up out of another elaborate dream of undulating roads through a watery landscape, roused by a rhythmic banging. For a moment, he flailed about in bed, stuck in the liminal space between reality and the dreamworld, uncertain of everything. Awareness came to him in slow stages. He was Lucius Galloway, and he was safe and dry in his bed, and something in the living room was thumping.

The mattress beside him sat empty, the covers thrown back.

Oh no. Not again.

He slid his feet into the slippers arranged neatly by his side of the bed and made his way through the darkened room without the need for a light. He'd made this late-night trek all too many times in the recent past, misjudging his location and barking his shins on the end of the bedframe. But now he'd become quite the reluctant expert.

In the living room, the faint light that trickled in through the windows threw Rudi's silhouette into stark relief. But Lucius already knew what to expect: yet another repeat of the nightmare parade. Rudi threw himself at the door, jiggling the handle, his breath coming hot and short in his panicked need to escape whatever crepuscular demons haunted him this time. He never made a sound during these twilight episodes, even though the repetitive impact must have been painful. His eyes had frozen open, wide and terrified, locked on some insubstantial horror.

Wham! Wham! Wham!

He couldn't get out. Every night, Lucius hid the key away in the central flute of the enormous candelabra on the mantel, locking them both inside. It was the only way to keep Rudi from sprinting down the street in his nightshirt.

Moving with slow deliberation, Lucius plucked a heavy blanket from the basket by the door. In his panic and confusion,

Rudi could get violent when awoken from one of his episodes. Lucius didn't take it personally, but the resulting scratches and bruises broke Rudi's heart, and he needed to be stopped or someone would complain about the noise. As two Black men living alone, they preferred to avoid such negative attention. So they'd come up with the blanket technique. So far, it seemed to be working well.

He threw the blanket over Rudi's head, smothering him in a bear hug from behind. With a gasp of pure fear, Rudi flailed to and fro, desperate to escape. The back of his head slammed into Lucius' cheekbone, bringing with it a flash of white pain. Lucius grunted but held on even tighter, straining his strength to its limits. He had a few inches on Rudi, but he had always been rail thin and never particularly inclined to physical pursuits, whereas Rudi had played cricket and tennis until his knees started acting up. This wasn't an equal match, but that couldn't be helped.

"It's just a dream," he crooned. "Just a dream. You're safe."

Rudi jerked, his head snapping up. Lucius twisted, hoping to avoid another blow to his face, but there was no need.

"Lu?" asked Rudi, his voice clogged with terror.

"I'm here."

Lucius threw off the blanket, wrapping his arms around his partner as he trembled. Rudi clung to him like he was drowning, his breath hitching as he tried desperately to regain control of himself. The sight made Lucius feel like he was drowning too. Sorrow clung to him, threatening to pull him under. He would give anything to fix this.

Anything.

"I'm sorry. I'm so sorry," murmured Rudi. "Did I hurt you?"

"Not in the slightest."

"I don't know what's wrong with me!"

"Wrong with you?" Lucius pulled back, planting a kiss on Rudi's forehead. "It's just a dream. There's nothing wrong with you."

Rudi clutched at the collar of Lucius' nightshirt, his gaze intense.

"They're coming more often now. Someday, I might really hurt you. I couldn't live with myself," he said. "I won't stand for it. I'll… I'll take myself off to an asylum before I let that happen."

"Don't be ridiculous. It would hurt me much more to lose you. I won't hear any more of that nonsense, you hear me?" said Lucius, stern.

They stood there for a long moment, embracing in the darkness.

"I love you, Lu. I'm so sorry."

"And I will always love you. Come on now. Let's get some rest."

Lucius led Rudi back to bed and tucked him in before settling back down himself. Before long, Rudi's breath slowed, and he fell into a much-needed restful sleep. Lucius badly needed the same, but he couldn't force himself to close his eyes. The flooded roads of the city in his dreams waited for him.

Not for the first time, he lectured himself about his irrational concern. What did he have to be so worried about? Walking down streets all night – even oddly disconcerting ones – was much more preferable to whatever dogged Rudi's sleep. Besides, nearly every creative he knew had vivid dreams from time to time. It was almost certainly a sign of his creative impulses at work. His muse, if you will. And it had worked! Those dreams had fueled an uncontrollable paroxysm of poetry, a fevered three-day span during which he had barely eaten nor slept. At the end of it, he'd been left with the full manuscript for *The Drowned City* and very little recollection of actually writing it. But his creative impulses had always manifested in strange and sometimes manic ways. That was nothing to worry about.

His reluctance to sleep almost certainly had more to do with Rudi's struggles than his own tepid dreams. After all, if he slept too deeply, something might go wrong. Rudi might sleepwalk out the window next time. They were only on the second story, but a fall from such a height could still be fatal, especially if Rudi remained asleep and made no attempt to save himself. Perhaps he should see about installing some bars. When the summer heat came, there would be no rest without opening the windows.

The logic all made perfect, rational sense. But he still couldn't force himself to close his eyes. He wanted to stay grounded in this city: New York, his forever home. He couldn't shake the feeling that at some point, he'd find himself stuck on the sodden streets of his dreamscape, unable to distinguish between fantasy and reality. What if one day he couldn't wake up?

The worries whirled in a continuous cycle through his mind until well after the sun came up. Finally, he fell into a fitful, inadequate sleep.

CHAPTER THREE

It was a bright morning in early June, and the train chugged into Boston, lurching and smoking with such fervor that it made Lucius a little sick to his stomach. He'd always been an uncertain traveler. Rudi didn't share his discomfort, and his excited chatter served as a welcome distraction. He threw the window open, letting in a gust of sooty air, and stuck his head out. After a moment, he pulled back in, a little grimier for the effort and grinning from ear to ear.

"I can see the station," he declared, pulling out his pocket handkerchief and scrubbing at his face. "Just a little longer and you can get your feet back onto solid ground again."

Lucius nodded, not trusting his stomach enough to speak. The lurching had gotten more pronounced as the train crawled into the station. The conductor apparently didn't believe in the concept of gentle braking; he periodically slammed them on without any warning whatsoever. The sickening start-stop was enough to make Lucius seriously consider walking home once he'd had his meet-and-greet with Helen. He wasn't sure he could handle this again.

"I'll just keep on prattling until we get there, shall I?" asked Rudi. Without waiting for an answer, he launched into a long recitation of his plans for the day. He'd mapped out a circuitous route around the city, hoping to photograph a variety of historical sites. "And don't forget that you promised to take me to the Union so I can finally try their oysters. I've phoned ahead to book a table for three, just in case you want to invite Helen."

"Very kind of you but please don't talk about oysters right now. I don't think I can take it," said Lucius.

"Sorry, sorry. You've gone quite green around the gills. My mistake. We're coming up on the platform now. One last gasp – *mon dieu*! How does the attendant stay on his feet with all this rolling about?"

Lucius spared a glance at the car attendant, who hadn't moved a muscle since they'd boarded the train all those long hours ago. Perhaps he was one of those wax mannequins Phyllis had photographed at the Tussaud in London. She'd tried to talk them into joining her, but he wasn't getting on a boat. The thought alone made him queasy.

Finally, the locomotive hissed to a stop, and as the smoke outside the window cleared, Lucius could see the sign announcing their arrival in Boston. Not a minute too soon. He launched to his feet, retrieving their luggage from the rack next to the still motionless attendant. Lucius couldn't help but take a closer look. Was the man sleeping with his eyes open, or did he consider it beneath himself to help a Black man with his bags? The conductor didn't even seem to blink, his eyes fixed on nothing but blank air. If not for the minute shifting of his prodigious mustache, he might not have been breathing at all. Slightly unnerved, Lucius tipped his hat as he pushed past, but the man made no reply to that either.

His lingering disquiet was soon smothered by his relief at disembarking onto solid ground. All around him, passengers rushed hither and thither, driven by unseen timetables and to-do lists. None of them seemed to share his urge to stop for a moment and relish the sensation of motionlessness. He paused, ignoring the glare of impatient passengers rushing for the doors, and took a deep breath of the smoky air. It clogged his windpipe, sending him into a paroxysm of coughing. Rudi patted his back, snickering all the while.

"Come on," he said. "Let's get you somewhere that you can breathe without chewing the air first. Where are we supposed to meet your Helen?"

Lucius coughed again, covering his mouth with his pocket handkerchief like a gentleman.

"Inside," he said, gesturing with the bit of cloth and nearly hitting a stout man in a bowler. "Beg pardon. She said she was disinclined to wait outside with the masses for fear of a riot."

"Oh no," murmured Rudi. "Sounds like she's the paranoid sort."

"Actually, the implication was that she might start the riot. I'm hoping it was a joke. There's the door, off to the right."

They wound their way through the tumult toward the doors, suitcases thumping against their legs. The crowd cleared quickly as people hurried to board or to leave the station, bound for parts unknown. Inside, the long benches were largely empty save for an indeterminate person swaddled in blankets, apparently asleep, a young family with three boisterous children, and an old woman sitting all the way toward the back that had to be Helen if only by the process of elimination.

She was older than he'd expected. From the looks of it, she had at least a decade on him, seventy to his newly won sixty. Time had turned her curly halo of hair pure white and crinkled her face. Tiny and bird-boned, she looked like a good twist might break her in two. But the eyes that peered up at him held no trace of elderly vacancy. She looked him over with a keen alertness that seemed to take him apart, examine all of the pieces, and then reassemble him in perfect order. This was a woman who would miss nothing. Just the sort of collaborator who would keep him on his toes. Perhaps this trip wouldn't be as much of a disappointment as he'd expected; he'd never gotten his hopes up when it came to referrals. All too often, the "genius" friend of a friend had turned out to be nothing more than a bag of hot air and flimsy concepts.

"Well, look at the two of you," she said in a raspy, whiskey-soaked voice that was so low it bordered on masculine. Hints of an Irish accent peeked out from time to time like a groundhog in its hole. "You're a vaudeville comedy sketch in the making, aren't you? You two couldn't be more opposite if you'd planned it. I'm going to guess that Mr Tall and Thin is Lucius Galloway, which would make Mr Short and Comfortable…?"

"Rudolph LaChappelle, at your service," Rudi said with a flourish and a bow. "My friends call me Rudi, although I suppose Short and Comfortable will also do. After all, if the shoe fits…"

"Hah! I love a good sense of humor. Helen Berringer." A wicked grin spread across the old woman's face as she thrust her hand out and shook Rudi's with relish. "I'd tell you what my friends call me, but I can't use that language in polite company. That must make you Lucius, then."

"Charmed," said Lucius, a bit overwhelmed with the force of her personality.

She gripped his hand with surprising strength, pumped it twice, and then released it.

"Now, shall we blow this joint, as the young people say?" she asked.

"I can take your suitcase," offered Rudi. "I'll catch a taxi and drop the bags off at the hotel. Meet me there when you're done."

Lucius nodded, handing over his bag with a murmur of gratitude.

"Good boy," said Helen. "No sense in subjecting yourself to any more dry academia than is absolutely necessary if you ask me."

"My thoughts exactly. Ciao! Enjoy your dry academia!"

With that parting shot, Rudi hefted both bags, flashed them a grin, and made his way toward the taxi stand. Helen looped her arm through Lucius', leading him inexorably in the opposite direction.

"I hope you don't mind taking a nice stroll," she said. "It's too nice a day to be cooped up in a car."

"I could stand to stretch my legs," said Lucius.

"Excellent. Let's head to my office, and I'll show you the mess I'm hoping to rope you into."

"Mess? It can't be that bad," he said, snickering despite himself.

She grinned. "Challenge accepted, my boy."

The mess was indeed that bad, in the most literal sense of the word. Helen's tiny corner office sat tucked away in a cramped corner of Fay House, an imposing mansion turned college building. She opened the door to reveal towering and uncertain stacks of papers and books covering nearly every available surface. A tiny space had been cleared at the desk to allow for someone to work there, so long as the person in question was as tiny as Helen. If he were to try such a thing, his elbows would knock over one of those stacks within the first five minutes. He wasn't a betting man, but that one felt like a sure thing.

Helen waved a hand airily as she led him inside.

"See what I mean? The place is a firetrap," she said. "When they said I could borrow a space for the summer, I didn't expect this. I'm told this office belongs to an economist. I sure hope she's better with numbers than she is with tidying up after herself. I've retained a research assistant who's supposed to help me arrange all the piles into a pleasing landscape starting tomorrow, but in the meantime, I thought we might build a castle out of them, just for fun."

Lucius chuckled, looking around for a safe place to sit. He could deal with a bit of clutter, but he didn't envy Helen one bit for having to navigate this rattrap. However could someone be so inconsiderate to loan out an office in such a state? At least she seemed to be keeping a sense of humor about it.

"How did you end up involved with the project?" he asked. "I'll just clear off this chair if you don't mind."

"Have at it." Helen sat behind the desk and waited for him to arrange himself on the leather armchair opposite her. His knees bumped against the desk; there simply wasn't enough room. But he did his best, setting his hat on his knee and pulling out his book in preparation to make any necessary notes. "So I got pulled into this thing about the same as you, I'd imagine. Pure luck! Right place, right time, and all that rubbish."

"That's not inaccurate," he demurred.

"I figured as much. There's not much of a story, but I'll subject you to it anyway. Right around the new year, Harvard got a substantial anonymous donation of historical books and other random ephemera. I'm not sure how much experience you have with that kind of thing, but gifts like that tend to come with stipulations. Some of them are even reasonable."

He let out a chuff of laughter.

"That sounds about right," he said. "And the requirements for this one?"

"I don't know them all, but the most important one – at least for our purposes – was to commission a translation for this particular manuscript. The word went out along the usual channels; you know how that goes. Most academics chatter like old biddies at a boarding house. I think I first heard about it from a friend at a lecture. Let's be honest: I'm not exactly in high demand these days. Not only am I older than Rip Van Winkle, but I'm a lady as well, and most folks assume that makes me a bit soft in the noggin. I assumed that if it was down to the likes of me, the project wasn't worth taking, but a woman's got to make a living. I figured I'd do the thing, collect my dime, and be on my merry way."

"But…?"

She folded her arms on the desk, leaning toward him with visible excitement. Her eyes sparkled.

"I haven't made it through the whole manuscript yet," she said. "I've only finished about a quarter of it, so bear that in mind. But I've never seen anything quite like this. It doesn't follow the standard epic or lyric forms that you usually find in ancient Greek. I'm no expert on poetry, but once you've done enough of these things, you begin to recognize the rhythm. You've got some sections in standard elegiac couplets and a few other recognizable bits sprinkled in there, but otherwise the whole thing goes off the rails. Perhaps you'll recognize the structure, but it's certainly different than anything else I've read from that time period."

"I hate to ask this, but are you sure it's real?" said Lucius.

"Trust me, my boy, I had the same thought. I showed it to one of the lecturers in archaeology, and the materials passed the initial sniff test, but that's only the beginning. That's when I decided to pursue this mystery in earnest. I made arrangements to stay here for the summer and put out feelers for someone with poetry chops. My thought is that there's a book in this. A full investigative exploration of this historical document. Is it real? Is it a fake? Are we just misinformed about its origins, or does it tell us something about ancient Greek poetry that will upend our understanding of the art form as we know it? It could be something special with the right partner, because I sure as sin don't have the skill to do this justice. I appreciate a naughty limerick as much as the next person, but any analysis beyond that is beyond me."

"So I analyze the poetry, and you translate?"

"And perform a full historical analysis of the document. Handwriting, allusions to geographical or astronomical phenomenon, paper composition, that kind of thing. I've got a few favors I can call in."

Excitement tickled Lucius' insides, but he held it at bay. She could be wrong about the manuscript's significance, but the possibilities couldn't be denied. Perhaps he might become a Harvard scholar after all. After so many years of struggle, it barely seemed like any of this could be real. Perhaps he was dreaming again? If so, it was not the kind of dream he wanted to exorcise. For once.

But the thought of dreams quashed the excitement before it could truly blossom. Rudi needed him. If they'd been married, it wouldn't have been a problem. Academic housing usually allowed for spouses to stay, even if the accommodations were a bit cramped. But roommates weren't accorded the same consideration. Quiet anger curdled his stomach as he considered once again how unfair it was.

"Could I take the manuscript back with me to New York if I decided to join the project?" asked Lucius thoughtfully.

"Afraid not. The librarians will only let us take five pages or so at a time. I'm not sure if that's a requirement of the bequest or them covering their arses since the thing hasn't been appraised yet. Either way, the work's got to be done here."

"That's a pity. I admit this idea could have some legs, and I'm cautiously intrigued, but I've got responsibilities. I'm not sure I could spend the whole summer here."

"Up to you. Opportunities like this don't come along for the likes of people like us all the time. Maybe they do for you, but this may be my last chance to do some work I'm proud of."

Her voice was as gruff as ever, but it wavered at the end. The determination and need in her eyes was all too familiar. He'd shared it for most of his life, and once the excitement over his award faded, he'd probably be back there again.

But his duties weren't something he could pawn off on other people for an entire summer. Sure, he could turn his writing class over to a friend. But who would talk Rudi down after one of his nightmares? Who would lock him in and smother him in a blanket to keep him from hurting himself? They couldn't afford a hotel for the whole summer. There would be no choice but to separate for the duration of the project, and he couldn't live with himself if something went sideways during his absence.

"I'll see what I can do," he said skeptically. "But I can't make any promises."

CHAPTER FOUR

When Lucius arrived at the Tarrington Hotel, he found Rudi lounging in the lobby, reading the newspaper with calm savoir faire. One of his friends from the Harlem poetry salon had stayed at the Tarrington once and highly recommended it, and that kind of word of mouth was invaluable when it came to travel safety. In this place, one could laze about and read the paper without concern. Not that Lucius had the time for it. He had to freshen up for dinner. The long trip had caught up to him, and he swore the train smoke had settled into the creases of his skin, because the scent followed him like a persistent specter.

Rudi spotted him over the edge of the paper, dropping it and smiling.

"There you are. How does it feel to be a Harvard man now?" he asked, drawing the vowels out in a comical attempt at a Boston accent.

"I wouldn't go that far," replied Lucius, sitting down opposite him. The armchairs were upholstered in faded fabric that didn't decrease their comfort. The seat enveloped him, easing the faint pain in his joints. At this rate, he might never want to get up. "How was your walking tour?"

"I got some lovely photographs, but enough about that! I want to hear all about the project. And Helen, of course. What a character she is. Not at all what I expected."

"Me either, to be honest."

"She must be good at her job," Rudi declared. "Harvey wouldn't back a nonstarter."

"She's a natural polyglot. We had a nice chat about the process behind learning ancient Akkadian. I'd never really put thought into how that would work. One can't exactly find a native speaker and learn from them, can they? And it's rather far removed from our modern languages. Fascinating stuff."

"If you say so." Rudi smiled. "And the project? What do you think?"

Lucius pulled his pocket watch out by the chain, thumbing it open, trying to buy time. He really didn't want to talk about it. Rudi would sense his disappointment, and he didn't want to burst that bubble just yet.

"I think that if we don't want to be late for dinner, I should freshen up," he replied.

Rudi frowned, folding the paper up entirely to give Lucius his undivided attention.

"You couldn't bluff your way through a hand of blackjack with a table full of toddlers," he declared. "What's wrong with it? Too much administrative nonsense? The document in question is some ancient shopping list?"

Although he tried to joke, the idea that they'd hauled themselves to Boston for nothing really seemed to bother him. Lucius decided to demur until he could find a suitable reason to turn down the offer. Under no circumstances would he admit that he'd decided to turn down all offers that would take him away from home for extended periods of time until Rudi's sleepwalking was under control. It was his choice, and Rudi needn't feel guilty over it, but that wouldn't stop him.

"I haven't seen it yet. Tomorrow morning, the library is open to both ladies and Black men, so we'll head over bright and early to take a look. I'm reserving judgment until then," he said.

"Hmph."

Based on his unimpressed grunt, Rudi didn't like that answer. He folded his arms with a mulish expression that Lucius recognized all too well. It didn't matter how good his excuse for turning down the project ended up being, Rudi had made up his mind that this project was a golden ticket, and nothing would convince him otherwise. The thunderclouds of an imminent argument hovered somewhere just out of sight. There would be no avoiding the deluge.

With a sigh, Lucius headed for the elevator.

The immense Corinthian pillars of Widener Library stretched to the heavens, and standing in front of the huge limestone edifice made Lucius feel quite small. Helen had stopped at the steps to allow him time to gawk, and she looked back at him now, smirking.

"Ridiculous, isn't it?" she asked. "You could level the rest of the campus and still house an entire university in here. Of course, I'm used to the smaller buildings at ladies' colleges, but as my old mam used to say, there's nothing wrong with small beer so long as it's beer in the end."

"My mother was known for her sayings too," replied Lucius,

tearing his eyes away from the building. "Although none were quite so colorful as that one."

"Well, we're Irish. Beer runs in our veins. Just don't tell the authorities, or they'll cook up some nonsense and arrest me for running an illegal distillery." She paused thoughtfully. "That was meant to be a joke, but now that I've said it, I honestly wouldn't put it past them. Crooks, all of them."

Lucius had what he considered a healthy distrust of authority, and it was his policy never to say such things aloud. Certainly not in public. So he smiled slightly instead.

"Is there a side entrance?" he asked.

"Oh yes. We inferior academics enter through the Reference Room."

She spoke without heat, taking refuge in humor. He'd never been very good at that kind of deflection. Sometimes he regretted that.

He followed her through the side door and into the library. A row of long tables sat before them, deserted at this early hour. Large oil paintings hung on the walls, labeled with tasteful brass plaques which he had no time to examine properly. Helen charged toward the door with what he'd begun to realize was her default single-minded assertiveness.

"The Radcliffe room is through here," she said, urging him forward.

They passed through a cluttered room strewn with packages tied up in paper and string and a single, harried employee who staunchly ignored their imposition. Then into the card catalog room with its massive rows of wooden cabinets, each of the narrow drawers labeled with neat handwriting listing its contents. Lucius stopped, his breath caught by the sheer volume of literature that these cards represented. Regardless of the final dispensation of their project, he would have to take the time to admire the collection properly. Something about the hush of so many books in one place made him feel at home.

"This is me," she said, gesturing to a door at the back. "We ladies must study in here, and one harried undergraduate brings us our requests from the stacks. It's rather cramped in there. I should have thought to ask if that would bother you. Men are permitted, obviously, although most wouldn't stoop so low."

He hesitated. "It won't bother me in the slightest. But some ladies might not appreciate my presence. I have no desire to offend."

"Ah." She nodded, taking in his unspoken meaning without need for further elaboration. "Let me poke my head in and see." She did so, emerging with a triumphant smile. "We're in luck. It's only Celia Bingham, and she's spent half her life gadding about Africa. Archaeologist, you know. I'll set us up, if you'll go to the rotunda and inquire for the Berringer manuscript. They've got it lumped in with the Widener bequest for the moment, until they find a more permanent place for it."

"The Berringer manuscript?" he asked, unable to suppress a grin.

"Well, they have to call it something, and the rest of these ingrates are too proud to realize what they've got. You can't just call it "the book," because if you haven't noticed yet, they have more than one of them here. Why shouldn't it be named after me, until we find some indication of title or author?"

"No cover?"

"It came in as loose pages. No title. And there are gaps. Every time I find another one, I tear some more of my hair out. But don't take my word for it. Sign out the first five pages and we can take a look together."

"Will do. Back in a moment."

Helen's directions led him to the correct desk without incident, and a harried student in shirtsleeves told him that the pages would be brought to the Widener Room as soon as someone could be spared to fetch them. The chamber, which sat at the center of the immense building, looked more like a personal study than a public space, and brass plaques next to most of the furnishings and decorations proclaimed them part of Henry Widener's personal collection. He stopped next to a lion pelt rug on the floor, the gap-mouthed skull frozen in mid-snarl, and marveled at its fangs. The place felt steeped in the past, history seeping from its walls; such a place could inspire him to write if only he had enough time to soak it in. It whispered to him of faraway places – wild savannahs and ancient ruins full of forgotten lore. He could imagine long and dusty days toiling away at the latest dig, retiring in the night to jot down notes at a foldout desk in the tobacco-smoke air of the workman's tent.

He stared down at the desk, lost in reverie, until the bang of a door made him jump. The undergrad in shirtsleeves – who had managed to locate a proper jacket somewhere but still had not bothered to button his collar – hustled in with a sizable manuscript bound in chapboard and string tucked under one arm. He hurried to the desk and plunked a clipboard down upon it.

"Sign on line twenty-seven, please," he said. "Which pages are you wanting today?"

"One through five. Although I was hoping to get a look at the full manuscript if it isn't a trouble."

"I've only got a few minutes," the student said in mournful tones. "Old Yarbrough sent over one of his miles-long request lists again, and the other runner failed to show this morning, so I've got to fetch all those books by myself. Whatever is he wanting all that for during the summer anyway? You couldn't pay me to read all that constitutional reform nonsense during the year, let alone over summer term."

"I promise to only take a moment," Lucius responded, signing the form and sliding the clipboard back.

"I'd appreciate it."

The young man hefted the manuscript onto the table where it fell with a bang. Air wafted into Lucius' face, carrying with it the dry scent of ancient paper. The chapboard cover was bland and generic, the putty-colored surface only broken by a label with a blank line for a title and a series of numbers beneath which probably correlated to some kind of cataloguing system.

Lucius opened the cover, interested despite himself. Although he had no intention of accepting this project, he couldn't help but imagine the ancient poet who must have penned these words so long ago. Although they were separated by time and space, they were bound by a kinship of meter and verse. Without works such as these, modern poetry might not exist, and Lucius would have been left penning pulp magazines or, worse yet, not writing at all. The opportunity to interact directly with such a manuscript made the trip worthwhile all on its own.

His eyes fell on the first page, the paper tanned tea-leaf brown and crumbling at the edges. The characters were scrawled in some sort of flaking ink, brown and crusty, the handwriting a spider-scrawl that tilted across the page. The unfamiliar characters swam before his eyes, reforming themselves into new arrangements. He blinked, willing the sudden and unexpected vertigo to lessen, and the world shifted around him.

The writing was strangely familiar, and for a moment, he couldn't place it. Then he remembered: he had seen it in the city of his dreams. There, he had sat before a rough-hewn desk in one of the immense cyclopean buildings, its walls rising like jagged cliffs that extended beyond the limits of his sight. On the surface of the desk rested a closed book. The cover had been bound in some irregular and uneven leather, the sight of which made goosebumps course over him in a slow and inexorable wave.

The book had opened of its own accord, the pages rustling as they turned themselves. He could glimpse the text within, flashes of the characters searing into his corneas. Crying out, he turned away, but they floated there still. He could not translate them; he lacked even a rudimentary understanding of what language they were written in. But somehow, he could sense their tenebrous power.

"Sir? Sir?!"

The voice startled him, followed by a hand that clapped down on his shoulder, frightening him to his core. The shadowy chambers of memory faded, only to be replaced with the bright glow of the Widener Room. The undergraduate runner shook him again, his voice high and alarmed.

"Sir, should I call for help?" he asked.

"No, no, I'm fine," said Lucius, his lips strangely numb. "So sorry."

"Are you sure? When you shouted like that, it scared me half to bits, and I'm not ashamed to admit it."

Lucius held onto the edge of the desk as if to steady himself. He was in the library, at Harvard, in Boston – a mental map of ever-widening circles of comforting familiarity. Awareness of his body returned to him in a rush, punctuated by the throb of his aching head. It felt as if someone had stabbed him in the eye.

"So sorry," he said, looking up at the worried student. "I used to get these sudden headaches as a child, like an icepick to the temple. It's been a while since I had one; I suppose it took me by surprise."

"Oh." The worry went out of the young man's shoulders like a leaky balloon. "My ma gets those migraines sometimes. She'll just sit there in the dark. Brains are strange things, aren't they?"

"They are at that," he said, trying to believe it.

Lucius pushed the book toward the young man, touching only the chapbook cover. He found himself reluctant to touch the pages themselves. Just a harmless flight of fancy. Nothing wrong with that.

"I'm sorry to have taken so much of your time," he said. "I'm not entirely sure how to remove the pages I need from the binding. Would you be so kind as to take them out for me? I can look at the rest of the manuscript another day."

"Yeah, I suppose I ought to get on with that pull list. Taking the pages out is easy; we've just wound the stack with string to keep them from spilling out all over the place. At some point, they'll have to decide whether to permanently bind the thing or keep the pages separate, but it'll do for now." As he talked, the student unwound the string, plucked out the pages, and set them on the desk. "And there you go! I'll just wrap this back up and be on my way."

"Many thanks," said Lucius. "Sorry again for the trouble."

"Don't mention it."

As the undergrad hurried away, he steeled himself, tensing as he reached for the corners of the pages. His fingers made the slightest contact before he jerked them away, possessed by a sense of lingering doom. Nothing happened. Embarrassed, he looked around, but the room remained empty, the door closed. There was no one to witness his ridiculous display. What was he afraid of? Paper? Was there even a term for that? Could one be papyrophobic?

His dreams had preceded this book's entrance into his life. There was simply no logical relation between them, and his residual fear had nothing to do with the manuscript and everything to do with the very real worry that Rudi would be furious at him for turning this opportunity down. But there was nothing to do about that for the moment, and it would be rude to keep Helen waiting any longer.

He tucked the pages decisively beneath one arm and headed for the door. At the very least, they could have a pleasant chat before he had to torpedo all of Helen's plans.

CHAPTER FIVE

"What do you mean, you're turning it down?" Rudi yelled, throwing his hands up over his head.

Lucius held up a finger before his lips, urging quiet, but Rudi didn't notice. He was too busy pacing in the space between the two twin beds of their hotel room. Three long steps to the ends of the beds, then three steps back. The endless back and forth was making Lucius dizzy. He squeezed the bridge of his nose, trying to ignore the throbbing pain behind his eyes.

"Well," Rudi persisted, stopping in front of him. "Do you intend to answer, or are we playing charades?"

"Please stop shouting."

"This seems like a perfect time to shout. Conversations like this are exactly what shouting was invented for!"

"I have a headache. Please, let's talk about this like adults."

The moment the words escaped his mouth, he wanted to snatch them back. But it was too late. Rudi jerked as if physically struck, breath woofing out of him.

"So I'm a child now?" he said, his voice icy.

"That's not what I meant. Rudi…"

"Then what exactly did you mean?"

Lucius took a deep breath, marshaling his thoughts. They didn't quarrel often, and when they did, it was usually in these short and intense bursts. One of them would misspeak, and hot words would be exchanged, and then it would blow over. It always did, but Lucius could see the hurt in Rudi's watery eyes. He couldn't stand it.

"I didn't mean that," he said. "I'm so sorry. I didn't sleep well last night, and I've had a headache all morning, and I'm not at my best. Please accept my apology."

Rudi sat down on the bed opposite him, sighing. Worried creases aged his face, making him look much older than forty-eight.

"I suppose I shouldn't have shouted either," he admitted. "Don't want to get us kicked out of the hotel."

"At least it would be an adventure."

Lucius meant it as a joke, but neither of them laughed. Rudi folded his hands, rested his elbows on his knees, and leaned forward, as if to communicate that he was ready to listen with every cell in his being.

"Okay," he said. "What's the problem? Is it Helen? I rather liked her."

This was the perfect time for Lucius to give his excuse, but he'd laid awake all night trying to come up with a legitimate one to no avail. There would be no way to get through this without hurting Rudi's feelings or lying to him outright, and Lucius couldn't bring himself to do that. They had always been truthful with each other, even when the truth hurt.

"No, I found her delightful," he admitted.

"And the manuscript? Is it a fake? Uninteresting? What?"

"No, the work seems fascinating. I didn't get to read much of Helen's translation, but the few lines she showed me could have been lifted straight from *The Drowned City*. If I didn't know better, I would have thought I'd plagiarized."

"So let me get this straight." Rudi's gaze bore into him. "The project seems tailor-made for you. Your prospective writing partner seems lovely. A summer's work at Harvard would put a feather in your authorial cap. The pay – it's not the pay, is it? We talked about that."

"There's a small stipend for living expenses from the anonymous donor, and I could live on campus, but that's all that's guaranteed until the book sells."

"That's enough! I'll cover rent, I already told you that. I don't understand what the problem is."

There was nothing to do but rip the bandage off. Lucius steeled himself and said the thing he'd been avoiding all this time.

"I don't want to leave you," he said.

Rudi barked out a laugh.

"Don't be ridiculous," he said. "We've been separated before. As I recall, a certain person refused to get on an ocean liner to France with me because he likes boats even less than he likes trains. At some point, I'm determined to take you to my hometown if it means knocking you unconscious for the duration of the trip."

"But you didn't have your nightmares then." Lucius held up a hand, forestalling any rebuttal before it started. "Hear me out. Those dreams are intense enough that you ran into the street how many times before we started locking you in at night? You can't hide the key from yourself. It's not that I don't trust you; I just don't see how anyone could manage this problem alone. If you got hit by a car because I wasn't there, I would never forgive myself. No project is worth that. I know it's not what you want to hear, but administration won't allow you to stay with me in scholars' housing. We cannot afford this hotel for the entire summer. You cannot ask me to abandon you when times are tough. I won't do it."

Rudi sagged, defeat written in the lines of his shoulders. He tried multiple times to marshal up some argument only to deflate once again.

"I hate this," he said finally.

"It's not your fault! You can't help your dreams."

Lucius meant every word. After all, he couldn't control his either. Although he wasn't willing to admit it aloud, the vision in the library had shaken him. It seemed like he had gotten a step closer to Rudi's late-night rambles, interacting with the world through the substance of his dreams. What if he'd taken the book but never snapped out of that waking dream? What if one day he became stranded in that chimerical city with no way to return to reality? The thought shook him more than he cared to admit.

"If you stayed, do you think I'd just go home by myself and pretend that everything will be fine? Of course I wouldn't! I don't want to be hit by a car either. I figured I'd go stay with my sister. She keeps begging me to visit Pittsburgh anyway," said Rudi.

"Does Caro know about the dreams?" Lucius asked cautiously.

Rudi didn't like to talk about them. He was terrified of being locked away in some quiet hospital, never to return again. To be honest, Lucius shared those worries. He would have no right to see Rudi if he were to be locked away. No right to make medical decisions for him as a spouse should. Officially, they were nothing to each other, when in reality, they were everything.

"Of course she knows. I can trust her. She'll tie me to the bedpost if she has to. All jokes aside, she'll handle it. We will handle it. So stop babying me and take the job, would you?"

"I didn't–"

"Enough. I'm hungry," said Rudi, his voice gruff. "I'm going to find a café. Are you coming?"

He would need some time to cool off. Rudi ran hot sometimes, and stressful periods tended to bring his temper to the forefront. Lucius tried not to take it personally and usually succeeded. But he could not shake his lingering disquiet as he slipped on his suit jacket and followed Rudi out the door.

The corner café was like every mom and pop place he'd been to in the city – with smooth vinyl booths, shining countertops, and the scent of onions in the air. Working men in coveralls clustered at the counter, scarfing down sandwiches and soups before sliding a few bills beneath their plates and dinging the bell over the door on their way back out again. From the corner booth, Lucius looked up from his club sandwich to see Helen sliding onto one of the stools at the far end of the bar. Rudi followed his gaze but said nothing. The meal so far had been a rather tense and silent one, but at least the food was delicious and the coffee hot.

"I'll invite her to join us," said Rudi, setting his napkin on the table.

Lucius cleared off a spot at the table with slowly growing excitement. If Rudi truly meant to go to his sister, perhaps he could take on this project with a clear conscience. Lucius Galloway, visiting Harvard scholar. His mother would have been delighted.

"Are you sure I won't be intruding?" Helen asked as Rudi steered her toward the table. "As my ma used to say, there's nothing worse than an uninvited guest, because they… well, maybe I'll leave the rest of that saying unsaid. I'm beginning to realize that most of her sayings aren't fit for polite company."

"You can't fool me," Rudi teased. "I've barely met you, and I already can say with utter certainty that you bring it up *because* it's scandalous."

"Well, it takes a scamp to know one," she said primly, sliding down into her seat. "'ullo, Lucius. Is your headache better?"

To his surprise, Lucius found that it was much improved. The coffee and fresh air had performed a miracle, or perhaps it was that his worries over Rudi had begun to ease. No matter what the reason, he felt like a new man and said so.

"Glad to hear it. After you left, I took the liberty of phoning around to Harvard administration. They've got a visiting scholars' room available for the summer. You're welcome to it if you're interested. You can take meals with the summer staff, whether you'd like to sit in the dining hall or take a plate to your room. It's damned lucky if you ask me. Radcliffe is clear out of space this late in the season, so I've had to bunk down at a boarding house," she said.

"A boarding house?" Rudi perked up, the frustrated miasma that had enveloped him ever since the argument evaporating into nothingness. "I lived in a boarding house for a year, before Lucius and I became roommates. Is yours the interesting kind of train wreck or the sad kind?"

"Not sure yet," she replied, unruffled. She paused to flag down one of the passing waiters for a cup of coffee and a ham on rye. "Which was yours?"

"*Oh là là*, the interesting kind for certain. Every week, there was a drama. If it didn't happen naturally, someone manufactured it. In the time I was there, we had a hand towel thief, a pastry thief, and a boot thief." He paused. "You know, we may have just been living with a kleptomaniac."

"My place isn't half as exciting as that, more's the pity," said Helen. "I think most of the dormers are summer workers. Lots of young folks. Haven't really had the time to talk to them much, to be honest."

"Well, keep an eye out for good stories. And hide your hand towels and boots just in case."

She grinned, leaning back as her coffee arrived.

"Pass me the sugar, would you?" she asked, patting Lucius' hand as he complied. "Are you sure you're better? You're awfully quiet."

"Just thinking about our manuscript," he replied.

"Our manuscript?" She brightened. "Does that mean you've decided to take it on?"

Rudi grinned, his whole face erupting with such relief that any lingering misgivings Lucius had evaporated in an instant.

"I think it has real potential," he said, "and I'd be pleased to work on it with you if the offer still stands. I'll have to arrange to pick up more of my things, but–"

"I can swing by the apartment on my way to my sister's," offered Rudi. "I have to pick up a few things myself. It's no trouble to ship you a trunk."

"And I'll take you up on the offer, Rudi. Thank you."

"Pas de quoi. This afternoon, I'll make all the arrangements. Caro will be delighted. She says I never visit, and I'm determined to make her regret complaining to me in the first place. She will rue the day."

Lucius chuckled. "You'll have to send her my love and condolences."

"Gladly."

"Excellent!" Helen clapped her hands together, rubbing them with evident relish. "Then we should be able to get started right away."

"I've been meaning to ask, what are the chances that the city in the stanzas you showed me really exists? Identifying it would be a real coup, don't you think?" asked Lucius.

Helen smiled.

"My dear boy," she said. "I like how you think. Something tells me this is going to be a very profitable partnership."

"And I say we toast to it!" Rudi crowed, lifting his coffee cup.

The porcelain clinked, and Lucius took a sip. Helen eyed him, mouth twisted into an impish grin.

"How heartwarming. So, is it too early to tell you to get to work, or should I let you savor the moment for a minute longer?" she said. The waiter picked that precise moment to hurry over, sliding a plate in front of her. She goggled down at the sandwich with comical dismay. "Well, that's ironic."

Lucius laughed. "Eat your sandwich first."

"Oh, fine. But after that, it's back to the grind. You should come to my office. Meet our research assistant. Move some papers."

"That sounds delightful," said Lucius.

He couldn't wait to get started now that he had nothing to worry about. Everything would be fine.

Lucius and Helen arrived at the office to find stacks of papers and books lining the hallway outside the open door. As they approached, a young woman came barreling out with yet another towering load in her hands, which teetered as she veered sharply to avoid a collision.

"Whoa!" she exclaimed.

Lucius grabbed on to the topmost papers, sliding them off the top before they had a chance to fall, and the pile made it to the ground without further incident. The young Asian woman who'd been carrying it turned, revealing a flushed face and a black pageboy haircut dusted with cobwebs. She seemed remarkably cheery despite her disheveled state.

"Thanks awfully," she said.

"Lucius Galloway, I'd like to introduce you to Dao Chuahirun, our research assistant," said Helen.

"Nice to meet you," Dao added. "You can call me Dottie if it's easier. Some folks have problems remembering it."

"Lazy bums. It's one syllable," said Lucius.

Dao rolled her eyes, her grin widening. "You're telling me."

"How goes the remodeling?" asked Helen.

"Oh, it's duck soup," answered Dao.

"I don't understand half of what you young people say these days. What does soup have to do with it?" said Helen, sticking her head into the office. "Oh, that's much better."

"That's what I said," Dao scoffed.

"I'm not sure this place has been unearthed since the fall of Constantinople, but we'll make do. Carry on." Helen gestured to the piles. "Do you have anywhere to put all this mess yet?"

"There's a storage closet upstairs. One of the other girls gave me a key. But she says we'll have to haul it all back down at the end of term or risk a complaint."

"I'm happy to help carry it all upstairs," said Lucius, shrugging out of his suit jacket. "Just let me put this down somewhere."

"No, no, I don't mind," replied Dao cheerfully. "Did you want me to try and find another desk, ma'am? There should be space for it now if you don't mind packing in like sardines in a can."

"Up to you," said Helen, looking at Lucius.

"I think we can make do without," he said. "As long as there's a free chair for me to occupy while Helen and I debate. But I imagine I'll do most of my drafting in the library or in my rooms if they provide me with a writing space. I like the quiet."

"Right-ho!" said Dao, sketching a salute. "Then I'll get back to work, unless you need something else?"

"After you're done here, please see about getting Mr Galloway one of those visiting scholars' rooms we talked about earlier. Thank you, Dao." As the young assistant bustled efficiently away, Helen turned to Lucius, baring her teeth in an excited smile. "And now let's get to work. I've sketched out a basic structure for the book that I'd like to get your opinion on, if I can find the dang blasted thing. I should have thought to stash it somewhere safe before Dao scrambled the place. If it's somewhere in those piles, I will warn you that I'll need a stiff drink to work my way through the frustration, Prohibition be damned."

"I'm sure it won't come to that," Lucius murmured. "Let me help."

"A-ha! Success!" Helen crowed, holding up the paper.

Their lively debate sucked up most of the afternoon without either of them realizing that the time had passed. With each passing hour, Lucius became more excited about the challenges in store for them, and grateful that Rudi had arranged things so that he could undertake this endeavor without regret. He felt so intensely lucky.

Little did he know that his luck would soon change.

CHAPTER SIX

The visiting scholars' room was larger than Lucius had expected. Beyond the door sat a small sitting area with a pair of armchairs separated by a little Colonial-style wooden table. An ornate carved clock and a few watercolors added a homey feel to the space. The door beyond led to a bedroom large enough to hold a bed, a sizable wardrobe, a writing desk, and a bookshelf stocked with a variety of classical volumes, most of which Lucius had already read. Still, they would be handy to entertain himself with at night. Perhaps he'd reread Poe again.

As he was scanning the shelves, Rudi excused himself to locate the facilities. The morning had been full to the rafters between checking out from the hotel, picking up the key to his room from Dao, and hauling all of their luggage across campus. Lucius settled into one of the armchairs and slipped off his shoes to rest for a moment. But he was too eager to begin his work – the delays had nagged him all morning. Every project stimulated this overwhelming initial excitement, where the rest of the world seemed to lose most of its color in comparison to the creative and intellectual puzzle at hand. But that would fade with time. It always did.

He closed his eyes, a couplet dancing through his mind. With time and study, the key passages would cement themselves in his memory, but for the moment, he could remember only these two lines. They ran through his mind in a ceaseless circle.

"That is not dead which can eternal lie,

And with strange aeons, even death may die."

The apparent contradiction in the lines fascinated him. In the first line, there was the suggestion of a deathless sleep, followed by the suggestion that death is, in fact, so inevitable that even death itself would eventually end. What a strange aeon that would be. What did it mean? One of them would have to do some research into ancient Greek funerary rites to make sense of it. Or perhaps Helen already knew something on the topic. She seemed remarkably prepared.

The click of the door announced Rudi's return. He nodded in satisfaction as he closed the door behind him.

"Quite a nice set up you've got here," he said. "Although there's a sign on the door to the bath saying that they'll be locked at eight. I wonder what ruckus the faculty has been getting up to at the ripe hour of 9PM. Quel scandale."

"I think I'll be quite happy here for a few months. Thank you for upending your life to help make it work. I know it's a lot to ask," replied Lucius gravely.

"Oh, don't mention it. I feel a little foolish when I think back to how I carried on yesterday. You had a point. But we've fixed it now, and Caro will stop nagging me about a visit, so it's a win all 'round." Rudi glanced at the softly ticking clock. "It's the right thing to do. Although I admit I'll miss your face. Who else will give me a hard time about my theatrics?"

"Caro, I suppose." Lucius squeezed his partner's fingers affectionately. "I *will* miss you, you know. I know I'm not the most demonstrative of people, but I really will."

"You have nothing to prove to me, mon beau," Rudi replied with a return squeeze. "After all this time, I had better know how you tick. Now, shall we head out? I don't much relish having to run with this thing." He gestured to his suitcase with distaste. "It's so heavy."

"Heavy? I wonder why…" teased Lucius.

"Of course you do. That's because *some* people insist on packing only the absolute essentials, which necessitates *other* people to bring everything else. Someone must be prepared for emergencies." Rudi put the back of his hand to his forehead, pretending to swoon. "It is exhausting, but it's a sacrifice I've got to make."

While he was distracted, Lucius grabbed the suitcase and made for the door, ignoring Rudi's sputtering protests. The two of them made their way to the train station, chatting the whole way. After all these years, they still enjoyed each other's company more than anyone else's. The separation would wear on them both, but it would be worth it in the end.

Helen met them at the station door. She held a small parcel wrapped in white paper and tied with string, and as they approached, she held it out to Rudi.

"Here you go, my boy. A little snack for the road," she said.

"Helen, you shouldn't have," he replied, planting a kiss on her cheek.

"Oh, I didn't," she replied. "I can't cook worth a damn. I got it off the Radcliffe kitchen. But I had to walk ever so far, and I'm positively ancient, so I suppose I earned the gratitude nonetheless, didn't I?"

"I thank you and your aching feet," he declared, holding the package tight. "I suppose this is it. I had best head in if I don't want to be stuck next to some screaming children or snoring businessman."

"I'll write," said Lucius, clapping him on the shoulder. They had made their more personal goodbyes much earlier, far from prying eyes. "Give my love to Caro."

"Yes, I'll–"

Rudi broke off mid-sentence, the color draining from his face like a tub with the plug pulled out. He clutched at his chest, staggering slightly. His eyes widened in his ashen face.

"Rudi?" asked Lucius, catching hold of his partner's elbow.

His heart skipped a beat. Although he was no doctor, he knew a heart attack when he saw one. He'd been there when one took his mother off to heaven, and the symptoms hadn't been all that different. The thought of losing Rudi the same way made his blood run cold, but this was no time for panic. Every second could mean the difference between life and death, and Lucius Galloway had never been the sort of man to panic under pressure. He wasn't about to start now.

"Come," he said. "Sit down on the bench over here. I'll help you. Helen, could you have the station porter ring for a doctor?"

She nodded, her expression grave, but before she could make it more than a few steps, Rudi's shaky voice halted her in her tracks.

"No need," he said.

Helen frowned in uncertainty, looking back over her shoulder as Lucius helped Rudi to the bench.

"I'm not so sure about that," she said in her gruff voice. "You look like someone walked over your grave."

"I'm better. Je vais bien," said Rudi.

But he sat down anyway, and when he pulled his pocket handkerchief out to wipe his face, his hand shook. Lucius sat down next to him, mouth dry with fear, and took Rudi's clammy hand in his own.

"I know you don't care for doctors," he said, setting aside the fear. Agitating Rudi might worsen his condition. "But I'm worried. Perhaps it would be wise to delay a day at the very least. We can find you a room and make sure you're well before putting you on a train tomorrow."

"Honestly, I'm fine." Rudi straightened, his voice a bit stronger. "Helen's right; it felt like someone walked over my grave. I've never experienced such a sense of impending doom before. Like my world was ending. I've never felt anything like it, but I'm much recovered now. Right as rain, in fact."

Helen took an uncertain step toward them.

"If you're sure…" she said.

Rudi's mouth quirked, a wry smile twisting his lips.

"I don't suppose you truck much with spiritualism, do you?" he asked. "Lucius thinks it's a bunch of hogwash."

"I could say the same, but I don't judge," replied Helen, looking toward the platform. "Are you sure you're recovered? If so, you'd better get on your train. The conductor is starting to herd the last folks on board."

"Yes, by all means."

Rudi patted Lucius on the hand before standing up. He exhibited none of the momentary weakness that had gripped him so suddenly, and the color had returned to his cheeks. If Lucius hadn't seen it himself, he wouldn't have thought anything wrong. A heart attack wouldn't pass so quickly, would it? He hesitated, unsure of what to do. Should he beg for a delay? He would be tempted if not for the fact that it would insult Rudi's intelligence again.

"Come on, Lu," said Rudi. "The train is quite crowded, and if it'll make you feel better, I'll have a word with the conductor. But I'm quite fine now, and you know how Caro is. If I miss this train, I'll never hear the end of it. Plus, I need to send your bags off before I head out to Chicago. I'm not going through the hassle of rescheduling that."

Lucius hesitated, but he could think of no argument to make against the proposition. Rudi wanted to go, and he was a rational adult who knew better than anyone else how he was feeling. Lucius wasn't willing to start another quarrel in the middle of the train station even if he could marshal an argument that would stick.

They said their final goodbyes quickly, and Rudi boarded the train, pausing to say a brief word to the conductor as promised. He turned to wave, as cheery as can be, before disappearing into the passenger car. Lucius and Helen stood there for another moment, but he must not have been able to find a window seat, because he didn't reappear.

A whistle announced the impending departure, and Helen tugged on Lucius' sleeve.

"Come on," she said. "He'll be fine."

"I know, but…"

"Fretting about it won't get you anything except perhaps a nice case of dyspepsia, so I intend to distract you shamelessly with work. It's ultimately a self-serving gesture, because I'm positively itching to get started."

"So am I," he responded, allowing himself to be led away. She was right. Rudi would be fine. He had to believe that, or he would have to chase down that train. "I've got a few thoughts on the structure you proposed. I suggest we have a sit down to discuss them, and then I'll get to reading. Something tells me this summer is going to speed by."

"More's the pity," she replied, looping her arm with his. "Lead on, Macduff."

The train began to chug away, belching smoke into the air, but Lucius' mind was too full of poetry to notice.

The next week passed so quickly that Lucius lost track of the days somewhere in the middle. He spent nearly all of his waking hours reading and note-taking, haunting the stacks at Widener Library and spending pleasant evenings in spirited discussion with Helen. They complemented each other well. Her quick energy energized him, while his quiet contemplation forced her to slow down and consider the small details. When he wrote to Rudi midweek, he had nothing but excitement to report. Yes, he'd dreamed nearly every night of ancient books and forgotten languages, but that was only to be expected given how he'd spent his days, wasn't it? In turn, Rudi sent reassurances about his continued health and a few amusing anecdotes about his sister.

Other than a few polite exchanges in the hallways, he spoke to no one beyond Helen, Dao, and the occasional library assistant. One night, he ventured out to the Harvard Faculty Club for dinner, an experience he didn't care to repeat. He knew no one seated at the long tables, and there was no way to judge which members of the faculty would welcome the appearance of a Black man at their elbow. The fact that he saw no one else who looked like him did not bode well for his chances, so he found a spot in the corner, dined hurriedly, and left before anything could occur to mar his otherwise pleasant experience on campus so far. After that, he took his meals in his room and found that arrangement much more comfortable, not to mention much quieter.

Over the past few days, full summer had descended upon New England, bringing with it a humid heat that clung to the skin in a most uncomfortable way. Yet one more reason to dine in his room, where his rolled up shirtsleeves would offend no one's delicate sensibilities. With the windows open, he often enjoyed a breeze. Widener sported some of the new air-conditioning units, but his building had no such luxury.

On the Friday, he stood at the window of his sitting room as night settled over the campus, bringing with it a welcome relief from the damp warmth of the day. The curtains fluttered as he stood there, admiring the long green stretch of manicured grass flanked by neat-trimmed hedges. The white columns of the building beyond – some dormitory, he thought – shone in the cold light of the moon. It shone bright tonight, overpowering the yellow glow of the lanterns dotted along the walking paths.

The entire campus was steeped in history, as if the pride of its students had soaked into the very stones. Every time he walked these paths on his afternoon digestive, he was surprised to find the buildings smaller than they loomed in his memory. They strained to contain all of the years of learning that had occurred within their halls.

It was a strong contrast to the streets of New York, which were just like the wind-up clock that hung in his mother's parlor until the day she died. On every hour, a procession of singers came tootling out on their little track while a few lines of Debussy's *Clair de Lune* played on a little music box cartridge from somewhere inside. The streets of New York had always reminded him of the circling singers moving in endless patterns, unable to break free. Beneath it all, the haunting notes of the past followed them in their never-ending hustle, a poignant reminder of all they were missing in their scrabble to survive.

Rudi would have said that this line of thinking was rather pessimistic, and he would have been right, but Lucius made a note of it in his book anyway. Perhaps when he had the time to write his own material again, he could make something of it. It all kept coming around to the idea that cities have their own lives, their own personalities. He'd explored those themes in *The Drowned City*, and he couldn't help but circle back around to them now, especially with the weight of the Harvard legacy all around him. There was also the mystery of the city in the manuscript, which intrigued him to his very core. He still couldn't decide whether he thought it was real or the same kind of fanciful dream channeling he'd done with his most recent book.

Regardless, he was glad he'd come here. The manuscript itself maddened and fascinated him in equal turns. Helen still toiled over the second half, but she'd largely finished with the first, and he had begun to wrap his head around its contents. The verses hopped from topic to topic with no apparent link between them, and he'd begun to wonder if they'd discovered some ancient poet's journal, where he jotted down ideas willy-nilly. Why else would verses about sunken streets be immediately followed by lamentations about stellar bodies, which then segued into a disturbingly complete description of fish entrails? It reminded him of his own commonplace book. Anyone flipping through its pages would marvel at the jumble of ideas all crammed into one space, just like this.

His task was to separate and categorize the pieces, and he had begun to see the shape of the manuscript as he dug into the translated pages. The work delighted Lucius to no end. So much so that he debated squeezing in a few more minutes before retiring for the night, but the pressure behind his tired eyes cautioned against that. So he stood at the window a while longer, basking in the cool breeze, before taking himself off to bed.

As soon as his eyes closed, he dreamed.

Images flashed before his eyes, and somehow he knew that he was in all of these places at once. He stood watching the water pound down from a massive Cyclopean dam, flooding the plain beyond. He walked the road to the city gates as the humped and misshapen forms of barely glimpsed creatures wove through the water to either side in endless patterns he could almost grasp. He hung from the gates as scraps of flesh which served as a long-forgotten warning. He walked the winding streets between impossible buildings like vast insectoid behemoths, looming overhead on insufficient legs. He stood before some immense creature, eyes opening and closing at random across the wide mass of its undulating body, its slithering protoplasm reaching up to caress his cheek. He stood before a desk in an immense room, staring down at an all too familiar book as its pages turned of their own volition.

Although the images twisted the mind, he felt no concern as he went about his multiple tasks, walking and watching and reading and witnessing everything that happened in the city all at once. Perhaps he was the city itself, an entity with some strange sort of self-awareness which lived through the eyes of its many inhabitants. He was at home here. He was home here. He was the home and the creatures who lived within it, and he did not want to leave.

Something is wrong.

The voice was tiny, nagging, dwarfed by the immensity of his surroundings. He stood at the foot of a chthonian skyscraper, wondering at its magnificence. He put a hand to the stone and could feel it sing. It had been pulled from the depths of the earth in liquid waves, freezing into domes and arches and effulgent tendrils. It was as if every element of human architecture, every advancement that ever was or will be, had been mashed together to create this one perfect structure of balanced chaos.

The whole city sang to him of waking dreams and living nightmares, of the history that was and the future that will be. It reverberated through his bones. This, more than any place he had ever been, was home.

This is a dream!

The voice was stronger now. It sounded like his mother. She'd never had much time for nonsense, not even when he was a child. *The world has enough nonsense all on its own, Lucius,* she would say. *There's no need for you to add to it.* But his mother was long gone. A part of the glorious history that fueled this place, built on the bones of ancients. The city-song cascaded over him once again, filling his mind with glory and delight.

What about Rudi? He needs you.

The glorious rhythm hiccupped as a shudder of worry ran through him, pulling him back to himself. He reached out with his city-senses, touching the mind of every being that inhabited this place, searching for the familiar comfort of Rudi's mind. But he was not here. He did not belong in this place. He could not sing the song; he would not be welcome.

To stay was to leave him forever.

For one horrible moment, he considered it, lulled by the melody that still tugged at his brain, before he yanked himself free with a snarl of defiance. Rudi had been the one constant in his life all these years, his heart separated from his body and made whole. Lucius could sacrifice anything else in his life and find contentment, but not this.

He was dreaming. Now that he was aware of it, he could feel the tendrils of this chimerical place wrapping around his body and trying to suck him in. Blind and boneless pseudopods emerged from the buildings, from the book in his hands, from the road beneath his feet, their insubstantial tendrils disappearing into his ears and slipping around the orbs of his eyes, taking over his senses. He pulled himself free, feeling the sickening slurp as the monstrous appendages released him, reaching for consciousness with the desperation of a drowning man. He had never been religious, but he prayed now, beseeching his God or his mother – any benevolent spirit – to usher him back to reality. The pseudopods reached for him, persistent in their need to draw him back into the web of the city-song. If he acquiesced, there was a very good chance that he might never escape. He would forget everything he'd lost. He'd forget Rudi.

Shrieking, he pulled himself free.

He was sitting in bed, sweat-soaked sheets pooled in his lap, the ragged end of a shout scratching at his throat. For a moment, he looked around in sheer panic, fear clawing at the back of his neck.

The shadows were wrong.

Rational thought descended upon him once again. It was just another dream. He was safely back in his room at Harvard, and although the nighttime shadows here had not yet become familiar to him, they posed no threat.

He collapsed against the pillow, limp with relief. Had he shouted aloud? Good thing that the room next to his still sat empty, the name placard blank. He did not have to worry about disturbing an immediate neighbor.

Shaking with relief, he poured a glass of water from the pitcher on the nightstand. Hopefully a drink would settle his nerves so he could get back to sleep. But his heart still galloped in his chest, gripped by a lingering terror. He'd had the same dream the night before, but the repetition hadn't loosened the hold it had on him. If anything, it made it worse, because a part of him wanted to slip back into the hands of Morpheus and follow the road to the singing city. It had a hold on him still.

But that was ridiculous. A dream might have a hold on his subconscious, but such an amorphous thing couldn't pose any true threat. After all, he always woke. The idea that one might be imprisoned there was preposterous; if he took those worries to a physician, he'd probably be laughed out of the office. Perhaps he needed to work less. Take a vacation. Destress.

After he finished this project, he would do that. He and Rudi would travel – motion sickness be damned – and they would have a lovely time. Bolstered by this happy thought, he lay back down, pulled the covers up over him, and was soon fast asleep.

CHAPTER SEVEN

The Harvard campus slumbered in the deep recesses of the night, late night parties long finished and last minute papers completed. No lights shone in the windows of the campus buildings; the walking paths sat silent and waiting in the darkness. Even the moon had gone to rest now, leaving the night animals to scurry in the deepening shadows, ears twitching and alert for any sign of danger. The veil between worlds grows gossamer thin in deep nights such as this one, creating a perfect pocket of time for clandestine dealings and secret pacts.

Abdul Alhazred sat at the desk in Helen Berringer's office, face illuminated by the half-shuttered light of a rather archaic lantern. Although discovery was unlikely at such a late hour, he preferred to avoid the unnecessary risk of electric illumination. Not that he feared the outcome if some unlucky undergrad happened to spot him here in this place he did not belong. He had no compunctions against taking the necessary steps to ensure secrecy, and in fact he had terminated so many lives over the years that at some point murder became a rather commonplace and tedious chore. Adding one more tick to his ledger of lost lives would mean nothing to him, but he was loath to waste even a single night in cleanup.

Throughout his long existence, hopscotching across the annals of time and space, he had always been driven. Driven to survive, to learn, to overmaster arcane powers that left most men reeling in horror. His search for knowledge had led him across the breadth of the universe, from the light-swallowing towers of Bel Yarnak to the Palace of Rainbows deep in the heart of Ilek-Vad. He had learned the music of the moon and the truth of what lies beyond death, puncturing the veil between the domains to return again and again to the land of the living, driven by an aching need that he could not name.

That same need gripped him now. It had pulled him from his bed through the darkened Harvard halls to sit here for hour upon hour, rereading material he had practically memorized. His eyes locked on the neatly handwritten pages spread before him; his hands clenched in his hair, barely registering the pain of his agitated tugging. Somewhere in this useless clot of words had to be the phrase that would unlock the secrets of his hidden memories. It had to be here.

Something had infested him. It touched him even now, at this very moment, a malevolent hand that gripped the nape of his neck. This was no physical sensation, no fleshy hand that gripped him like a mother cat herding her young. But over the past few years, the pressure had become undeniable. Sometimes it felt as if the pull might sever his spirit from his body entirely, leaving it to roam the land as some sundered and insubstantial ghost, doomed to lose himself over the slow stages of eternity. After thousands of years of existence, there were very few fates that could truly frighten him, but this one chilled him to his very bones. Tonight, the pull was uncommonly strong. His soul strained at the edges, loosening from its mortal cage. At some point, the pressure would become too much for even him to withstand.

The eternal man was running out of time.

Just a few hours earlier, as he had every night of these past few cursed months, he had awoken with a moment of crystal clarity. His past, present, and future all sat before him in a perfect Möbius loop of certainty, the knowledge of his great destiny setting his veins to thrumming. He knew his task in its entirety. He remembered *everything*.

Then it faded, the knowledge sifting inexorably between his clutching fingers. He knew where he needed to go to end this torment. He had found the hidden way long ago, encoding the instructions into the pages of his *Necronomicon* where they would be safe. He had seen too much knowledge lost when seekers fell, their minds cracking under the strain of knowledge beyond the limits of human comprehension. Such undertakings must be made slowly to allow the mind to open, but those fools had failed to heed his warnings to their own detriment.

But he had planted the seeds of his own salvation in these pages. As the needy tug of some unseen parasite grew within him, he had become increasingly more desperate, sneaking out to the office every night in the hopes that the day's words would provide the answers he needed to survive. He had read them so many times that the words melted in his vision, but he could not stop. He was compelled by an unnamed will greater than his own.

Once again, he forced his bleary eyes to start at the beginning, skimming over the useless analysis of poetical forms and rhythmic structures and diving headlong into an analysis of nighttime imagery. It was nothing but academic prattle. Nothing he needed. The failure grated at him, locking his jaw with a growing frustration.

The words "tenebrous stars" leaped out at him, and for a moment, insight flared like the sudden light of a supernova, obliterating everything within its path. He grasped at the memory, reaching out before him like he might take it in his hands and keep it from escaping him once again. But it slipped away with ichthyic agility, leaving him bereft.

"Damn you to the depths of the black lakes of Hali…" he muttered, seething as he gripped the paper and stared hard at the words, willing the memories to resurface. "Come back!"

But his brain refused to cooperate. The blank spaces refused to fill. He thought desperately about the phrase that had jolted his mind into action, turning over its potential meanings. Perhaps the gate sat beyond the bubbling pits on the dark star of Algol, or somewhere in the green depths of Xoth. But these logical machinations brought him no closer to remembrance than before. He could traverse the width and breadth of the universe on the back of this insufficient clue and still be no closer to his answers.

A sudden and insurmountable fury took hold of him, and he swept the desk free of papers. After all this time, all these years, to be betrayed by the failings of his own mind was too much to bear. He, who had tamed the shoggoth and befriended the mi-go, he who had found the fabled streets of the City of Pillars and bathed in its magic, he who had faced an Ancient One and lived to tell the tale, how is it that his mind could be broken? It could not be borne. He would not bear it.

Another tug at the back of his neck, another reminder that his fate called him, but he could not hear the words. Something had blocked them, some magic he could neither sense nor divine nor undo, despite repeated attempts. It would tear him apart, and there was nothing he could do about it. Nothing but wait on the insufficient mewlings of some simpering poet and the shoddy translations of an old woman who was good for nothing but worm food. It was insupportable that he should be brought so low! That this should prove to be his undoing!

Shaking with fury and fear, he launched out of the chair, tearing at the bookshelves, pulling down piles of papers and ledgers. A framed photograph fell onto the rug, the glass shattering. A shelf shook loose from its moorings, cracking in two as it struck the floor. He shoved the heavy desk across the room and scattered the contents of its drawers. Threw books against the wall, breaking their spines. Toppled a tower of volumes with a sweep of a scornful hand.

The smell of lamp oil finally brought him back to his senses. Somewhere in the midst of his tirade, he'd knocked the lantern onto the floor. Although he could not see from this angle whether the flame still burned, oil trickled onto the rug, leaving a greasy stain. For one seething moment, he considered burning the place down. But he could not. While the release might give him some temporary ease, he would pay for it later. In the aftermath of a significant fire, work on the manuscript would slow to a crawl or potentially stop altogether depending on the whims of the university authorities. He needed to speed the process up, not stop it altogether.

The doorknob turned, and the growing gap in the door revealed his acolyte, her expression tight with equal parts concern and caution. The young woman had accompanied him from Italy, and in their brief time together, she'd become accustomed to the wild whipsaw of his moods. Her obvious fear soothed him. At least some things in this world were going as they ought.

"See to this," he ordered, wiping sweat from his brow.

Her gaze skimmed the destruction; her lips tightened. She would have her hands full putting the place back together before the early morning people arrived for their daily work. But that would not be his problem.

"Yes, master," she replied. "Is there anything else?"

"No."

He looked down at the lantern, frowning. She hurried to pick it up, revealing the oil stain on the blue Oriental rug. For a moment, the irregular blotch rearranged itself into a familiar shape, a symbol whose meaning hovered just outside of his grasp. But the harder he reached for it, the further away it became. The stain was just a stain and nothing more.

He pushed past her, impatient to leave the site of his defeat. But as he crossed the threshold, he paused.

"Time is of the essence," he said.

"Yes, master. The translation is progressing at a good pace. There's quite a backlog of pages for Mr Galloway. Should I push him to produce faster?"

"It must be approached with subtlety lest he break like the others. Your Mr Galloway is a precious commodity; I suspect he has had some brush with the world beyond the veil. In my long years, I have learned to recognize the signs. He has the look of a man who expects at any moment to wake up from a long nightmare."

The uncertain tension in her expression eased just a little. She allowed herself a fraction of a smile.

"I thought so myself," she replied. "The literary world has approached his poetry as if it's an allegory about the life of the common man in a big city. But it feels … bigger somehow. Like he has seen some of the things I've seen. I know–" She broke off, her cheeks flaming. "I beg your mercy, master. I'm babbling."

"You aren't wrong," he said coldly. "But take care you do not become too familiar."

"Yes, master," she murmured, her eyes on the floor. "What would you like me to do?"

"Arrange a watch rotation. I wish to know where he is at all times. What he does when he isn't working, who he talks to. Have some of your fellow pilgrims strike up conversations with him. I want to know what makes him tick."

"I can have a daily report written up of his activities. Loved ones. Fears. That sort of thing?"

Her eyes rose hopefully, and he allowed himself one firm nod.

"You have picked up on my meaning," he said. "At some point, we may need to provide him with a bit of extra inspiration. You will make this possible. Remember: I ask much of you, but I will repay you. There are positions in the pilgrims which you may aspire to, with time."

She nodded, her eyes glowing with the mania of a true zealot. He pushed past her, the promise and her eager response already draining from his mind. After all, he did not intend to keep his word. She would serve him or be fed to the howling darkness, as so many pilgrims had before.

It was the natural way of things.

CHAPTER EIGHT

Sunlight streamed through the gap in the curtains, painting the wall in bright stripes. Somewhere nearby, birds twittered in a happy call-and-answer, filling the air with music. In his bed, Lucius flopped over, folding an arm over his eyes to block out the light, trying desperately to hold on to sleep. A long series of surreal dreams had made for a restless night, and fatigue clung to him with its grasping fingers. A bit more rest would set him to rights. But the early morning sun seeped in around his arm and through his eyelids, bidding him to wake up and face the day.

Strange. He'd been at Harvard for more than a week now, and the light had never woken him before.

He sat up, gripped by a sudden and inexplicable concern. The small bedside table upon which usually rested his alarm clock sat empty, the clock on its side on the floor. With a sinking feeling, he picked it up.

9:30AM!

Lucius Galloway did not sleep in. He woke every morning at precisely 6:40, and he had done so for years. The habit had become so ingrained that he needed no alarm. When he was ill or traveling, he would set one just in case the deviation from normalcy threw off his schedule, but he rarely needed it, and he certainly had never overslept in such an egregious manner. He threw off the covers, heart pounding, and hastened to ready himself. Thankfully, his nightly preparations served him well, providing him with a freshly pressed shirt and suit waiting on the hanger, shoes brushed and standing on the floor below.

He would have to skip breakfast, but there was a small coffee station on the floor of the faculty dormitory, and he paused long enough to pour a cup. The faint stirrings of a headache pushed at the backs of his eyes. Perhaps the strong morning tonic would set the world to rights again. He and Helen were due to review her comments on his first chapter, and he needed to be at his best, but his head felt like a balloon bobbing at the end of a long string.

Steaming coffee sloshed into the cup. He poured, sugared, and stirred before lifting the drink to his lips. His hand spasmed, pouring the scalding liquid down his vest and shirtfront and making him yelp in surprise and dismay. One of his fellow lodgers, a portly gent with a fashionably thin mustache, clicked his tongue as he fetched a mug from the sideboard.

"That's bad luck, what?" he said.

Lucius almost snapped at him. Yes, it was bad luck, and pointing that out added nothing helpful to the situation. But the gent's florid face exhibited nothing but amused sympathy. He'd meant nothing by the comment, as vapid as it might be. There was no sense in creating a fuss about it.

"Yes, sorry," he said. "I'd best run to change."

"Just button the jacket," said the gentleman, snatching a small pastry from the plate on the sideboard and stuffing the whole thing into his mouth at once. "Nah wah wi no ess."

"Beg pardon?"

The man swallowed and said, "No one will notice."

"Perhaps not. Good morning to you."

Lucius bowed his head in what he hoped was a friendly sort of manner before he hurried away with the half-empty cup still in hand. He drained its contents as he rushed back to the room. The trousers were fine, but he would have to re-wear his shirt and vest from yesterday.

From somewhere in the depths of his mind, Rudi sighed in exasperation and said, *Here's a wild idea: you could wear something other than the same three-piece suit every day, mon beau.*

It was an argument they'd had a million times before, an almost comforting one. The kind with no true heat behind it. Lucius had never been able to make him understand. Rudi had grown up under more gentle conditions overseas. In low light, he could pass as a white man, while Lucius had come out a deep brown that only got darker with age. Rudi was no fool – he knew the dangers they faced every day from bigots of all stripes – but he thought Lucius took his caution too far.

As Lucius gave the shirt a quick brushing, he thought back to the day his mother had gotten him his first suit for his sixth birthday. He hadn't wanted the stiff and starchy thing. He'd wanted a new baseball bat. But he knew better than to defy his mother, so he thanked her politely and put it on. She waited in the parlor, hands folded neatly in the lap of her housedress, her hair perfectly curled into gentle loops, feet crossed at the ankles. When he came out, rigid with discomfort, her eyes had lit right up in a way he'd never seen before.

Your clothing is your armor, Lucius, and don't you forget it, she'd said.

Then, her eyes sparkling, Alice Galloway had hugged him. It was the only time he could ever remember her showing any physical affection. She would exchange polite cheek kisses of greeting, and of course she saw that his needs were attended to. She poured over every report card and bandaged every scrape. But over the most difficult years of his youth, he'd occasionally wondered if she loved him – or anyone. Then he would think of the way she'd clung to him that day and the hurried brush of her hand over her eyes, and he would flush with shame.

She would have clucked her tongue at the wrinkles in his shirt, but it would have to do. His laundry had been sent out the day before; it would be delivered sometime this afternoon. It only needed to be a temporary fix.

His armor back on, Lucius went out to face the world.

The hallways of Fay House were uncharacteristically crowded when Lucius arrived, but he put it down to the late hour. By now, he was usually secreted behind a wall spun from manuscript pages and reference material, locked deep within the recesses of his thoughts. Rudi always complained that once he got to working, the building could fall to pieces around him and he wouldn't so much as blink. Lucius knew it to be true, but he didn't care to admit that out loud.

He climbed the stairs, flattening himself against the wall as a pair of dusty undergrads came thundering down with two large sacks of rubbish clutched in their hands, paused to let a cleaning lady with a broom and dustpan cross the hall in front of him, and finally reached Helen's door.

The office had been demolished. The desk sat askew on three legs, its contents dumped on the floor. Papers and books had fallen into crumpled heaps. Every last thing that had been on the shelves had been dashed to the floor. Helen crouched in one corner, where she had made some small progress in cleaning up the mess. As he watched in horror, she smoothed the pages of a leather-bound book before closing the cover and placing it on a small stack of recovered volumes.

"By God, Helen, what happened here?" asked Lucius, hovering in the doorway. "Are you okay? Was anyone hurt?"

She startled, knocking over the stack of books and letting out a curse. After a moment, the tension in her shoulders eased, and she sat back, clutching at her chest.

"Lucius, my boy, don't you go scaring an old woman like that. It's been an awful morning for sure." She frowned. "I was worried about you. If you didn't show within the next hour, I was going to send Dao to hunt you down."

"I overslept. My apologies, Helen. I didn't mean to frighten you."

She clucked her tongue, trying to wave it away, but he could tell that beneath the brusque exterior she was truly relieved. Her entire body seemed to relax. A wave of guilt clenched at his guts.

"It's all water under the bridge now, which is where most of these books can go. Look at this one. It's ripped clear in half!" She held up a fragment of what must have been a substantial volume, the torn binding trailing string into her lap. "Chuck this into the bag behind you, if you wouldn't mind."

He did as she asked before taking off his jacket and hanging it from the hook on the back of the door, which was still miraculously intact. Then he started on another pile of papers, flattening each one and collating them into a pile.

"What happened?" he asked again.

"Dang blasted hooligans. They destroyed two offices downstairs and three on this floor before the night watchman came to investigate the noise and scared them off."

"A random act of destruction, do you think? Or an upset undergrad?"

"I suppose it could be a student, but I'm not sure how many of our girls could rip a book in half. I'm thinking it's a protest against the women's school. You know how that goes: we little ladies shouldn't dare to think we have brains in our heads."

For a moment, her gruff voice was clogged with frustrated tears. Lucius knew exactly how she was feeling, but all of the empathy in the world still wouldn't make it right.

"I'm sorry," he said, and meant it.

Her pale eyes met his, and after a moment, she nodded.

"Yes, well… enough of that." She paused for a moment to collect herself, and there was no noise but the quiet shifting of papers as they each collected and collated. "I appreciate the assistance. Dao should be back in a few minutes with an empty bin. The two of us can take it from there, and you can head to the library to work."

"Heavens, no! Let me help," he protested.

"Mighty kind of you, but this is a two-butt office," she said, some of her usual arch humor creeping back into her voice. "I don't see how we'd all fit."

"Fair," he said, chuckling. Then his good humor was buried by a wave of growing panic. "Did you lose any of our work? I've got my notes for the first chapter, but I'd have to reconstruct the text…"

"First thing I looked for," she replied. "It's all safe in the one drawer that survived intact. I suppose I'll have to rethink my position on the presence of a higher power now."

"Hallelujah," he said, sagging in relief.

"Exactly."

A thumping in the hallway announced the arrival of Dao with the trash bin. She blew a stray wisp of hair out of her face and surveyed the mess, her eyes eventually coming to rest on Lucius.

"Good morning, Mr Galloway," she said. "Isn't this just the cat's pajamas? What a mess."

"Good morning," he replied. "It is indeed a colossal mess."

"Dao, if you can sweep up behind the desk, we can see what can be salvaged there. I'll take just a moment to confer with Mr Galloway," said Helen as she pushed up off the floor.

Ever the gentleman, Lucius stood hurriedly and offered her an arm. She took the assistance with an arched brow and a curl of her lip, and the two of them made their way outside. A pair of perspiring undergrads maneuvered a heavy bag of trash out the door of the office next door, keeping up a steady stream of invectives against the troglodytes who had caused such wanton destruction. Helen tugged Lucius down the hallway and away from the tirade.

"I hope this damned unfortunate setback doesn't sour your excitement for our project," she began. "It's really nothing to be worried about, just part and parcel of life at a women's college."

He snorted, unable to contain his amusement.

"Believe it or not, I've seen much worse in my time. My presence isn't any more welcome than yours in many academic spaces; it'll take much more than this to frighten me off," he replied. "No need to worry."

"Well, I'm sorry and relieved. Now, do you need anything from me before you go?"

"Just those manuscript pages, if it's not a bother. I wanted to revisit the section on the sun; I've found a new quote that suggests a rather advanced understanding of astronomical phenomenon which opens an entire new line of inquiry on the use of poetical forms as scientific record."

She perked up. "Oh? Pray elaborate."

"Let me write it first. Then you can poke holes in my reasoning as much as you like."

She let out a long suffering sigh.

"Very well," she said. "I'll be patient, but if the suspense kills me, you'll have to deal with the guilt. I'll fetch those pages."

In a moment, she handed them over to him along with his suit jacket, which he'd almost forgotten in his tired fog. She watched as he shrugged it on, frowning. As much as he wanted to ignore her expression of concern and make his escape, he knew she would ask questions about his late and disheveled appearance at some point. Best to get the uncomfortable conversation over with.

But to his surprise, she didn't comment on his near constant yawns. Instead, she said, "Do you play mahjong, Lucius?"

He blinked, taken aback by the sudden and unexpected direction the conversation had taken, but it took only a moment for him to recover.

"I've played a few times. It's quite the rage in our building," he said.

"You should come to my boarding house on Thursday and have a game. We play every week. There are some characters in the place that you should find amusing."

"Okay?" he replied, drawing the word out into a question.

She patted him on the arm.

"It's rare that I meet someone I don't want to punch in the face," she said. "Especially under stressful circumstances. I've been remiss on capitalizing on that. After all, we can't work all day every day, can we?"

"I'd be pleased," replied Lucius, smiling. "And I'll have you know that I intend to remind you of this conversation the next time you start pestering me for pages."

She laughed. "I expect nothing less."

CHAPTER NINE

On Thursday night, Lucius arrived at the Shady Glen Boarding House promptly at 7:00 as arranged. He carried a box of pastries from a local bakery under one arm, and his neatly pressed suit bore no traces of the coffee that had soaked into its fibers only a few days before. He looked surprisingly presentable for a man who had averaged two to four hours of sleep a night over the past couple of weeks. He hadn't had a night of unbroken, dreamless sleep since his first few days here. But life went on, and so did he. As he approached the door and rang the bell, he stifled yet another yawn.

Helen answered the door, her wide mouth splitting into a grin.

"Good to see you," she said. "Come on in. Our landlady was called out on some family emergency, so I'm playing hostess tonight. I'm afraid that means we're a bit shy on the eatables."

"Hopefully this will help then," he said, holding out the pastry box.

"Well played, Galloway," she said, taking it. "You've saved us. There will be no hunger pains or cannibalism here tonight."

He followed her inside, wrinkling his nose as the stale air inside hit him. It had a strong, moldy tang, the sharp scent of growing things left to rot. Its herby sting unsettled his stomach. The idea that Helen breathed that air all night angered him. She deserved high quality accommodations just as much as he did, and perhaps even more so due to her age and qualifications. But there would always be people who saw her as less than because of who she was, just as they did him.

He gave no outward indication of his queasy stomach, nor the way his heart went out to his hostess. She seemed not to notice the stench. For a brief moment, he wondered what could have caused such a smell and promptly decided that he did not want to know. The answer wouldn't be pretty.

Helen led him through the entryway and into a bright sitting room. At a single folding table sat Dao and an unfamiliar man with a shining bald pate and a ridiculous pencil mustache. In the dining room beyond, another game was already full, game tiles spread across the table. When he entered, both tables stopped to stare at him with such intensity that he began to wonder if there was something on his face.

"We've got a short table without Margie, so it's doubly good you came. You know Dao, of course, and this here is Marco," Helen said, indicating the bald man. "Have a seat, and I'll pour you a cuppa."

Dao nodded at him as she helped herself to a pastry topped with bright gelled raspberry. Marco offered his hand, and the two men shook and exchanged polite murmurs.

While Helen bustled about, Lucius took in his surroundings. The sitting room was comfortable but cluttered, with porcelain figurines and tattered doilies on every available surface. Decorative pillows in a riot of colors were heaped at the back of every seat. A collection of dolls sat on a table, empty eyes glittering as they stared at him. At least the people at the other table had gone back to their game, or he would have become quite paranoid. He tore his gaze away from the dolls' unsettling regard and accepted a coffee.

"Sorry about the aroma," Marco said gruffly.

"Beg pardon?" asked Lucius.

"I said I'm sorry for the smell. And the dolls. The doilies. Some days, I'd like to burn the whole lot of it to the ground."

"It's…" Lucius cast about him, searching for a polite but accurate adjective. "Quaint."

"I suppose." Marco frowned. "But I don't have to like it. A man shouldn't have to deal with such frippery. It's unseemly."

Lucius decided he didn't care for Marco. He seemed inclined to put too much stock in his trumped-up masculinity. Lucius had met many Marcos over the years, men who waited for an excuse to vent their frustrations upon the world with words or fists, and who would manufacture an excuse if one didn't come up on its own. He would have to be extra careful and steer the conversation away from any dangerous personal topics.

"I can see how you'd feel that way," he said in neutral tones.

"And to make matters worse, something's gone off with the pipes. Mrs Pitts has a fellow coming tomorrow, and I'm inclined to give them both a piece of my mind. I work hard! I don't deserve to live in a sewage house, and you can bet that I'll take the inconvenience out of my rent if something isn't done about it!"

Marco clenched his fist, his jaw growing tighter with every passing sentence. Lucius pasted on the polite smile he always employed in the presence of bigots and toughs as he tried to come up with some reason to head home early. Between the stomach-curdling air and the even more curdling company, he regretted accepting the invitation at all. Sure, the evenings had begun to get a bit lonely, but a solitary, boring night sounded positively capital compared to this.

Then Helen bustled over with a cup of coffee in one hand and a dishtowel in the other. She rapped Marco over the head with the towel. Marco seemed like the sort of man who wouldn't take that lying down, especially from a woman.

"Thank you for inviting me," blurted Lucius, trying to deflect attention away from the growing tension in the room.

Marco stood. He dwarfed Helen's tiny figure, looming over her like a vengeful god. His black hair and solid build stood in stark contrast to her pale frailness. He would snap her like a twig. But Helen had spunk, and she suffered no fools. She arched a brow at him and tilted her head as if waiting. At the other table, the players set down their tiles and craned their necks to take in the show.

"Well?" she asked. "Are you going to strike an old woman today, you lout?"

With an inarticulate snarl, Marco threw up his hands. He whirled on Lucius, eyes blazing.

"Do you see what I have to put up with?!" he exclaimed. "Women!"

Then he stomped out of the room, muttering to himself. They listened as his angry footsteps climbed the stairs. The slam of his door rattled the pictures on the walls, and then there was nothing but blessed silence.

"That's that, then," said Helen, sitting back down as calm as you please. "Honestly, it's probably for the best. I'm a damned poor mahjong player."

Lucius let out a tense breath.

"Is he always like that?" he asked.

"Oh, sometimes he's worse," said Dao. "He's a first degree lout, that one. Do you mind if I have another pastry? I'm positively famished."

"Please do," said Lucius. "If I take them back to my room, I'll eat them and be up all night with indigestion."

"Perhaps we can eat and take a nice stroll around the block. That sewage turns my stomach," said Helen, putting a hand to her belly. "I'm sorry. I would have rescheduled if I'd known the pipes went off."

"It really is awful. Are you sure you want to stay here tonight? We could book you a room at the hotel Rudi and I stayed at. It was quite clean," suggested Lucius.

Helen considered for a moment before shaking her head.

"Mighty kind of you, but if it's just one night, I think I'll hold out. If they don't manage to fix it tomorrow, I'll find somewhere else to bunk. What about you, Dao?" she asked.

Dao looked up from the plate of pastries, which she had been steadily demolishing. A dab of jelly stuck to the corner of her mouth. To Lucius' amusement, she didn't exhibit a hint of guilt over eating enough baked goods for an entire room full of people.

"Oh, I think I'll stay with one of my girlfriends," she said. "If you won't take me as awfully rude, I'll head up now and pack an overnight bag."

"Please do," said Lucius, his eyes flicking toward the stairs. "I wouldn't want to leave you here unattended."

No one mentioned Marco, but Dao nodded, her smooth curtain of hair swaying. Their eyes met, and he acknowledged the gratitude in hers with a nod of his own. Without another word, she bounded up the stairs.

"She's a good kid," said Helen gruffly. "Smarter than I sometimes give her credit for, but that's not entirely my fault. I don't understand three quarters of what comes out of her mouth, what with all the newfangled words the kids use these days. Sometimes I wonder when I got so old."

"Tell me about it. I swear 1890 was just ten years ago. It feels like it was yesterday, and I'm not sure I like that very much."

They locked eyes in a moment of perfect understanding before breaking out into grins. Helen let out a loud bark of laughter that elicited an angry stomp from above and an inarticulate yell from Marco. Lucius' amusement faded fast as he turned a concerned look toward the stairs.

"I'm not thrilled about these living arrangements, Helen," he said.

"Don't you get all het up," chided Helen. "I'm no damsel in distress, and I expect better from the likes of you."

"I'd be concerned for any friend in this situation," he replied. "It's not safe here."

"Oh, I suppose it's time to do something about it. This whole sewer issue has him riled up worse than I've ever seen. Mrs Pitts has been rumbling about turning him out. I'll have a word with her tomorrow morning and tell her I'll get a room with Dao elsewhere if she doesn't take action. If it's a choice between losing two lodgers or losing one – and an angry pest to boot – I'm confident she'll make the right choice."

"Just be sure he doesn't take his frustration out on you on his way out the door."

"Oh, I won't. I plan to spend most of the weekend out on my boat. If he's got a bone to pick with me, he'll have to swim out to me to get it." She paused thoughtfully. "You should come."

"Me? On a boat?" Lucius chuckled. "I get motion sickness. I'd hate to see what a boat would do to me. My insides would become my outsides."

"The water's supposed to be calm tomorrow. Give it a try. If you're not a fan, I'll have you back on dry land in a jiffy."

Lucius opened his mouth to refuse, but the hopeful glint in Helen's eye stopped the words in his throat. Her eagerness was palpable, and that fact made him see the whole situation in a new light. He'd taken her invitation to cards as a polite gesture from a coworker who had picked up on his growing sense of isolation, but perhaps he'd had it backward. She hadn't invited him today out of pity for his friendless state; she shared in his isolation. It made sense. He'd expected a weekly mahjong game to be bustling, an event where he could hide in the corner and slip away unnoticed, his social obligations fulfilled without too much fuss or bother. But Helen couldn't scrape up eight players. Her social circle was so small that she had been forced to invite Marco.

With that in mind, her persistent and repeated invitations made sense. The poor thing was lonely, and Lucius knew how that felt. To his immense surprise, he found himself agreeing to set off on her sailboat early the next morning. During that conversation, he may have neglected to mention that he did not know how to swim, but that wouldn't matter. He would set sail, vomit a few times, and return safely back to land with a story to tell. What could go wrong?

Late that night, he sat down at his writing table to pen a long overdue letter to Rudi, whose most recent missive had begun with a full paragraph chiding him for his short correspondence. Now, at least, he had things to report.

Dear Rudi,

*I'm sorry my letters have been so short! Up until now,
there really hasn't been much to talk about; I haunt
the library, Helen's office, and my rooms in a constant
rotation. At each place, I write, eat, or sleep – sometimes
for variety's sake I combine the activities, which explains
why I ended up wearing my coffee the other day. But the
project is going well. Helen is just as prickly as ever, but I
think she's pleased with our partnership, and I have every
confidence that we'll finish the manuscript before the end
of the summer. I've been writing so much that I think my
fingertips may be permanently ink-stained, but it is a
small price to pay for success.*

*You will be entirely amused to hear that I am going
boating tomorrow. I think Helen must be desperate for
company, because she wouldn't take no for an answer. So
I'll have something exciting to talk about in my next letter.
Otherwise, things have been fairly quiet. The office is all
tidied up, and there has been no additional vandalism.
The night watchman has taken to roaming the halls at all
hours as a deterrent, and I think I nearly gave the poor
man a heart attack coming out of the office late last night.
It is a good thing that Helen thought to introduce us, or I
think I would have had a hard time justifying my presence
there. But we simply exchanged a laugh and moved on
none the worse for wear, although I confess my heart got
quite a workout for a moment.*

*I would like to say that I'm shocked to hear that you
threw a midnight costume party, but it sounds like the
sort of ridiculous scheme you are famous for, and I'm
almost sad to have missed it! You are kidding about the*

chicken costume, though, I hope? Did you think to take
any photographs? I should very much like to see them.

As for travel plans, I do not yet know exactly when
we'll be done here, but if you'd care to meet me at the end
of the summer, we could travel on to Arkham then. I know
you're eager to reconnect with Harvey again after all this
time. I won't pretend to put much stock in spiritualists,
but we could also consult with the group you found if you
think it might bring you some relief with your nightmares.
But please, don't undertake that trip alone! I know you
will think me paranoid, but caution is never unwarranted,
and if you are to trust a stranger with your secrets, it
would be wise to have a friend there to back you up.

He paused there, the scratch of his fountain pen across the page
falling silent. Not for the first time, he debated whether or not
to tell Rudi about his own dreams. He could no longer convince
himself that they would pass, that he was just a stressed out
creative stuck in the grip of a fickle muse who tormented him at
night with dreams of drowning cities. He had a problem. If their
collective nightmares had been linked by some outside source –
some gas in the air or poison in the water – they would have
improved with the change of scenery. No, this was something
in the blood or in the brain, some sickness of the mind. He had
become even more convinced of it with every passing day, and
although the situation still rankled, the conviction soothed him.
He could combat any foe so long as he understood it. But how
would his partner take this revelation?

On one hand, the honesty might ease them both. Rudi would
feel less of a freak, while Lucius would be relieved of the guilt
associated with hiding such a significant revelation. But that

was the only advantage Lucius could see. Rudi already worried too much. He blamed himself for the stress his nightmares had brought to their relationship, and Lucius knew he would consider Lucius' dreams to be his fault too. How much more of this stress could Rudi's heart take? The thought chilled Lucius to the bone.

He tapped his pen on the desktop in growing agitation. Spilling the beans seemed less appealing the more he considered it, even though he had a personal preference for honesty. Rudi's guilt would likely make him even more determined to seek out that spiritualist group in Arkham. He'd first brought up the scheme in one of his previous letters, and Lucius had disliked the idea from the start. He abhorred spiritualists. Charlatans and grifters, most of them, preying on the hopes and beliefs of good, honest people. They would tell Rudi what he wanted to hear, take his money, and wave their hands around while intoning some superstitious nonsense. But Lucius couldn't say that without causing a row. Rudi always needed to come to these conclusions for himself, and although it was frustrating, Lucius could understand it. He didn't much like to be herded either.

No, it would be better to conceal this knowledge for a while longer. After all, he was holding up well under the strain. With enough coffee, he could stay awake and alert during the day, although he'd taken to snatching a brief cat nap after lunch. Just a half hour made all the difference in the quality of his work. He supposed he was becoming an old man now, and with time, those naps would stretch longer and longer into his days. But at least for now, he was bearing up tolerably well.

His mind made up, he concluded the letter with a few brief sentences and signed his name. Although they had agreed early on to put nothing in writing that would suggest the truth of their relationship for safety's sake, he always kissed the paper before putting it into the envelope, and he knew Rudi did the same.

He addressed the letter from memory before licking a stamp and tamping it down in the corner. A quick consult of the clock suggested that he might take a walk across campus to deposit the letter in the campus postmaster's box to save him the trouble in the morning. Hopefully the stroll would tire him out enough to snatch a few hours of restful sleep before his nighttime revelries inevitably began. He could only hope.

Retrieving his suit jacket from the hook, he shrugged it on and let himself out of his rooms, exchanging a friendly nod with the gentleman from the coffee station who boarded across the hall. Mr Badenhorst, according to the card outside his door. They ran into each other at the coffee service most mornings, although Lucius had only managed to spill on himself once. Still, Badenhorst brought it up every single time they saw each other in a dogged but failed attempt at humor.

"Heading to a party, are we?" asked Mr Badenhorst.

"Out for a walk to catch the air before turning in for the night," replied Lucius. "I'm afraid I'm much too old for late night revelries. My undergraduate days are long behind me."

"Too true, too true. Not enough coffee in the world for that, is there? Especially if you spill it–"

"I'm headed to the postmaster's," Lucius interrupted. "Do you have anything I can take for you?"

He hadn't intended to make the offer, but he just couldn't force himself to chuckle at the same jibe he'd heard so many times before. But now that it had been made, he would stand by it. It would be no trouble to carry another missive or two across campus.

But if anything, Badenhorst seemed alarmed by the prospect. His eyes widened, and he shook his head with much more gusto than necessary.

"No, no. Mighty kind of you, but no. No, thank you," he babbled. "I don't have anyone to write to."

Lucius sighed. Some people got like that when he was simply trying to be friendly. He always assumed that they didn't know many Black folks and worried about what might happen if they were seen associating with one. Of course, some were probably bigots themselves, but he'd gotten pretty good at spotting those and avoiding them from the start.

Although he always felt a vague unease when faced with this sort of friendly prejudice, he couldn't suppress his relief. At least he would no longer have to sit through the coffee jokes every day.

He nodded, pretending not to notice the fact that the other man had visibly begun to sweat.

"Fair enough," he said calmly. "Just thought I'd offer. You have a good night now."

Badenhorst nodded.

"Yes, of course. You as well," he said, before opening the door and slipping inside with a rapidity that suggested he was worried he'd be followed.

Such an odd person. Lucius stood there in the hallway for a moment, unsettled without entirely knowing why. Most folk didn't turn on a dime like that; either they were friendly and stayed that way or were antagonistic from the start. But it's not like he hadn't seen this kind of behavior before. Perhaps it bothered him because he'd been hoping against hope that Harvard of all places would be different.

He mulled this over as he exited the building and set off

across the campus. The sun had drifted down behind the trees and shadows stretched long upon the ground. The oppressive heat of the day had begun to give way to a pleasant summer evening. Breeze stirred the flowers planted in beds along the walkway and rustled the leaves in the trees. The comforting bulk of the university buildings lurked at every corner, their stolid presence advertising logic and solemnity, a history of academic excellence.

For once, the beauty of the campus escaped Lucius. He'd strolled across campus many times before, marveling at the fact that he had been welcomed here, that he could touch the buildings the great minds had inhabited and walk the same paths they'd walked. He'd imagined himself as a participant in an endless parade of great minds through this vaunted space, and the thought that he of all people belonged in that company had touched him. It was the intellectual community he'd longed for in his younger years, the kind his mother had always wanted for him.

But Harvard was not immune to the same problems that faced the rest of the world. He had always known that, but experiencing it firsthand still robbed the experience of some of its joy, and now he struggled to recover. If Rudi were here, he would have picked up on Lucius' growing melancholy and started telling his most outrageous stories. From the sounds of it, he would have more to tell when they next met. Lucius tried to imagine his partner dressed up as a chicken and couldn't help but chuckle, his unease melting away.

He climbed the steps to the postmaster's and deposited his letter in the slot set into the door, listening for the faint noise as it hit the basket inside. His errand safely completed, he took the long way back to his room, shedding his gloom in slow stages. From a young age, he had learned that holding on to negatives would only rob him of the positives. As always, it all came down to the lessons his mother had drilled into him. Sometimes it felt like she'd never left, and perhaps she never had. He would carry her proud memory with him always.

By the time he reached his building, he'd recovered from his temporary malaise. To his surprise, he found himself looking forward to tomorrow's expedition on the water. Although he fully expected his stomach to rebel, he enjoyed Helen's company. Like Rudi, she had a knack for saying the most ridiculous things and making them seem quite reasonable. The familiarity comforted him.

He climbed the stairs to his second-floor room, hoping that he'd managed to tire himself out enough that sleep would come quickly. Fatigue tugged at him, slowing his progress up the long staircase. He paused on the landing, remembering earlier days when he would have run up these stairs two at a time, driven by an innate curiosity to see what life would throw at him next.

A faint noise from somewhere up above him caught his attention. He listened for a moment but heard nothing notable. Just as he was about to continue his climb, the sound repeated. His keen ears picked up the quiet scuff of shoe leather against the ground as someone on the landing above him shifted their feet.

There was no law against standing in the stairway and plenty of legitimate reasons to do so, but Lucius couldn't deny his growing unease. Over the years, he had learned to trust his instincts, which had sometimes steered him out of dangerous situations in inexplicable ways. They screamed at him now.

Something is wrong. Do not go up the stairs.

He glanced upward, feigning casualness, but saw nothing. A slow slide toward the corner gave him a better vantage point. The long shadow of someone up above stretched down the stairs, but it was so warped and indistinct that it told him nothing about the person who waited there. It might be some random faculty member waiting for a late companion, or it could be something more nefarious. Something inside him suggested the latter. His pulse throbbed at his temples and fluttered at the base of his neck, blood pumping in anticipation of the need to run.

In his younger years, he might have felt some need to prove his bravery, but he had left that foolishness long behind him. As Shakespeare had said, "The better part of valor is discretion," and he had nothing to prove. He had no need to reassure himself that there was nothing to fear, no desire to determine for certain if his instincts played him false. He turned, his ears perked for any sign of pursuit, and began to ease his way back down the stairs. There was no movement from up above. He paused halfway down the flight, listening intently, but the silence was so complete that he almost began to question whether he'd seen anything at all.

Nonplussed, he descended to the bottom of the staircase and crossed the lobby to the other end of the building, nodding at the night watchman. For a moment, he considered alerting the young man to the presence of the lurker in the stairway, but what exactly would he say? Standing silently on the stairs was no crime. Any potential crisis had been averted.

To his relief, a pair of young, mustachioed researchers held the door to the other staircase for him, not pausing in their spirited debate of Mendelian genetics. Although he barely understood one word out of three, he listened with pleasure as he followed them up the stairs and onto his floor, where they stopped to argue over what seemed to be a point of serious contention.

As he passed them, touching a finger to the brim of his hat in polite apology, the blonder of the two gentlemen caught his eye and exclaimed, "I say, do you believe a word of this nonsense?"

"Sir, I believe I can honestly say that I don't understand a word of it," he replied.

Their laughter carried him down the hallway and to his door without incident. His key was already clutched and waiting in his hand. The door that led to the stairs where the lurker had waited did not move an inch as he let himself inside.

Still, he found that he couldn't relax enough to sleep until he'd locked the door and put the coat rack in front of it.

CHAPTER TEN

The next morning dawned bright and sunny, but after a long night slogging through the city of his dreams, Lucius struggled to awaken fully. He didn't manage to shake off the last vestiges of sleep until after he'd padded into the sitting room to see that the coat rack had fallen over at some point during the night. But the door remained closed and locked, and nothing appeared to have been disturbed other than a few papers that had blown onto the floor. The curtains were twisted with the wind; perhaps it had gotten truly gusty overnight? He wasn't sure, but he resolved to pay attention and keep his valuables upon his person just in case.

He dressed quickly. Some more modern gents might consider his boating ensemble to be a bit on the conservative side, but he couldn't imagine gadding about in a knit shirt or baggy flannels. No, he would arrive properly in white trousers and a navy boating jacket and do the thing right. By the time he tied his bowtie, he'd forgotten all about the disquiet of the night before.

To his relief, the coffee station was deserted when he arrived, and he helped himself to a cup and a pastry without incident. Then he took a pleasant stroll through the campus toward the docks, passing bicyclists and early picnickers chatting on the grass. Birds sang merrily in the trees, and all was right in the world.

He arrived at the docks right on time and was pleased to see Helen waiting for him in a long white dress and a hat decorated with a wide blue ribbon. She broke out into a smile as he approached.

"Are you sure you weren't pulling my leg, Lucius?" she said. "I'd swear you're a proper boatman from the looks of you."

"As God is my witness, I cannot tell a lie. I've never been on a boat in my life," he replied, putting a hand to his heart. "I bought this rig at a shop after you extended the invite."

"Good thing I'm here to fix that for you, then. We'll make a sailor out of you yet."

"I can't say I've felt like I was missing out," he replied in dry tones, eliciting a laugh from her.

"You'll learn. Now, come on and we'll show you the ropes."

She led him to the end of the dock, their footsteps echoing on the planks beneath them. Water lapped at the sturdy wooden pillars, setting a relaxing tempo that somehow eased the tension in his shoulders. The sun bathed his face, turning the inside of his eyelids red when he lifted his head to bask in the warmth. Here on the water, the growing heat of the day was eased by the gentle moisture of the breeze. Across the river, gulls cawed and wheeled. He took a deep breath of the water-tinged air and smiled.

"I feel the same way," said Helen.

"I like looking at it, but I'm honestly terrified of sailing on it," he replied.

"Let's take a look at the boat before you get your back up, shall we?"

He turned his attention to the watercraft clustered along the edges of the docks. There were so many of them – large boats and small ones, simple craft with open benches and fancy ones with leather seats and glistening chrome. Some had masts, others tilted beneath the weight of heavy motors. Lengths of rope were everywhere, punctuated with elaborate, puzzle-like knots. Their shapes fascinated him, pulling his attention away from the growing tension in his belly. Soon, he would be out on the water on one of these craft. He couldn't decide whether he was excited or terrified out of his wits.

"This is the *Damascus*," said Helen, gesturing to a smaller craft nearby. "I've arranged to borrow her for the day."

"I didn't realize these boats were available for rent."

"I don't think they are. I'm borrowing this one off a friend from the language department."

"Oh? Maybe you should have invited her to play mahjong."

"I would have, but she's just gotten married, and I didn't think she'd want to interrupt her honeymoon to come to my place and exchange barbs with Marco."

"Ah, Marco." Lucius shook his head, clucking his tongue. "How were things this morning?"

"I skedaddled before he was awake, and I don't intend to return home until well after he should be gone. I'm no glutton for punishment." She grinned briefly, the wind tousling her white hair, before turning back to the boat. "Now, the *Damascus* is a sloop, so she's light and relatively easy to maneuver. You won't have to do a thing, although if you feel like learning a bit, I'll be happy to teach you. I was out on the fishing boat with my da when I was a wee girl, and it's quite easy once you get the hang of it."

"Honestly, if I manage to make it out there and back in one piece, I'll consider it a triumph."

He eyed the boat. Although the water seemed calm, the craft rocked back and forth in a very alarming manner. He didn't know how he'd manage to get on board without getting tossed into the drink. The more he thought about it, the more his nerves grew.

"You really never have been on a boat before," Helen said, putting a reassuring hand on his arm. "I thought you were joking."

"No." He swallowed, his throat dry with nerves. "I'm terrified of them."

"Well, you don't have to do this. Although my ma used to say that the best way to deal with fear is to face it head on and screaming. Who knows? You might even enjoy yourself."

The temptation to leave gripped him hard, but something held him back. A boat sailed past, far out on the water, a pair of gents on board with their feet up and heads tilted back to enjoy the sunlight. He wanted to experience that, just once. Maybe he'd like it. How would he know if he didn't try?

"No, I want to give it a go, but not too far? So we can turn back if I can't handle it?"

"Fair account then. Come on aboard, and we'll get you settled. It's easy, see?"

Without even pausing to judge the movement of the boat, Helen stepped down into it. The small craft swayed alarmingly, but she stayed rock steady, her legs absorbing the movement, her expression placid. She grabbed hold of the mast and turned to him, holding out a hand.

"Simple as pie," she said. "All you need to do is grab hold of my hand and come on down. You can sit right here on this cushion next to me."

It did not seem simple as pie. He stared down at the bobbing craft, trying to time his approach. Should he step when it went up or when it went down? His stomach roiled. Helen just stood there, patient, her hand never wavering. If she could do it, he could. But his feet didn't want to move.

"Come on," she said, not unkindly. "The first step's the hardest."

Maybe if he sat down on the edge of the dock and eased into it, that might help. But that would be childish. Instead, he wrapped a hand around the pillar next to him, stretching forward with one foot, teeth clenched with nerves. As long as he held on to solid ground, he would be safe. The tip of his shoe touched the boat, but he could reach no further without releasing his grip, and that was the last thing he wanted to do.

"You're just making it harder on yourself now. Throwing yourself off balance."

He nodded, squeezing his eyes shut.

"Yeah," he croaked. "I feel rather foolish right now. Maybe this was a bad idea after all."

"Nonsense," she snapped. Something in the tone of her voice reminded him of the stern firmness of his mother. They shared the same intolerance for foolishness. "Let go of the dock, Lucius. Face your fears and take my hand."

He took one *shaking* breath in and did exactly what she said. For one tense moment, he wobbled off balance, but then her bony fingers closed over his and pulled him down to join her. His feet moved as feet tend to do, and he found himself standing on the boat without quite knowing how he'd managed to do it. It tipped back and forth, back and forth beneath his feet, but with Helen holding his hands, he found himself adjusting to the movement quite easily.

"See?" she said, flashing her teeth in a satisfied grin. "You're a natural."

The natural made it almost an hour before he began to get seasick. It turned out that he could tolerate boating in the calmer waters near the university, but once they entered the larger and more choppy area near Boston, his stomach rebelled. He paused mid-sentence and leaned over the railing, gripping it with damp hands as he vomited coffee and pastry over the side.

"Sorry," he said, wiping his mouth.

"No worries," she replied. "It's a bit rough here. If we head out a bit further, it won't be so bad."

"Sure, okay."

He gasped, clinging to the rail as another spasm gripped his guts. The nausea had come on fast. His stomach roiled and flipped as she bustled about behind him, fiddling with the knots or tugging on the sail or whatever she needed to do to make the boat go faster. Up until now, he'd been so distracted by the fact that he was actually sailing that he'd failed to pay attention to the mechanics of it. Now he was afraid that if he moved a muscle, he'd lose what little was left in his belly.

Helen kept up a steady reassuring patter as the boat rocked and creaked. They were making good time, this would all be over soon, and he would be able to enjoy himself again. He was a natural sailor. She hoped a little seasickness wouldn't turn him off the process, or she'd be driven to drink. He nodded whenever she paused, not trusting himself to speak. Frankly, he didn't dare move a muscle. He tasted bile in the back of his throat. The straps of his newfangled inflatable life preserver dug into his armpits.

Try as he might, he couldn't restrain himself. He leaned over the railing, spilling the contents of his stomach into the water once again. Acid stung his throat and clogged his nostrils. He watched as the lapping waves swallowed his vomit, erasing it from sight. If only he could wash away the lingering nausea.

The sun, which had been playing peekaboo from behind scattered, fluffy clouds, popped back out again, painting the water with bright rays. It glinted off something far beneath the surface, illuminating a long straight edge that reached toward the distant sky. Beyond it, he could just make out the outline of some large, ornate structure. For a moment, he wondered what it might be, but of course it had to be some sunken vessel. Who knew what the depths of the river would reveal, if someday the whole thing drained dry? These waters probably held a great variety of sunken relics.

His curiosity had distracted him from his queasiness, and although his stomach had settled to a slow and warning roll, he opted to stay where he was, scanning the depths. Small fish darted away from the hull, frightened by its bulk. Torn fragments of underwater vegetation floated by, undulating in the water. It was like an entirely different world down there. Then the bright sunlight faded once again, and all he could see was his own reflection.

"Feeling better, captain?" asked Helen. "Or should I turn this thing around and deposit you safely back ashore?"

"You were right; it is better out here. I'm not quite ready to move, though. I'm afraid I'll break the spell," he replied.

"Fair enough." He could hear the smile in her voice. "I'm not sure you're ready for the open ocean, and in a boat as small as the *Damascus*, we'd be tossed around like beans in a bottle anyway. But we can head past the city and take in the view."

"I'd enjoy that."

Once again, the sun crept out from behind a billowing cloud, and once again, it glinted off the shape of something far beneath the surface. The outline was familiar: a long length of what might have been a mast which led down to the inexplicable jumble of shapes beneath. A busted ship, perhaps? Strangely, he noticed exactly the same shape beneath the water just a few minutes earlier.

"Did we turn around?" he asked. "Are we headed back?"

He turned to look at her, the last vestiges of seasickness vanishing beneath a wave of curiosity. She threw back her head and laughed uproariously, the cords of her neck sticking out.

"My friend, you have a lot to learn about boating if you think we turned 'round," she said. "I haven't moved a muscle. The boat won't turn by itself, without my hand at the boom or rudder. If my da had heard that one, he would have laughed so hard he'd split in two."

He gave her a sheepish grin.

"I suppose it was a stupid question, but I just saw something beneath the water, and then I saw the same thing again. I thought it was a sunken ship, but what are the chances that there would be two identical wrecks so close together?"

"Slim to none, I'd say." She frowned in thought. "Are you sure it wasn't floating debris? On occasion, something'll break loose off a passing vessel, and the pieces don't always sink to the bottom right away, especially if the river is busy. The boats churn everything up."

"I don't think so. It looked to me like a fairly sizable structure, but I didn't get the best look at it. Maybe I'm mistaken."

After a moment's consideration, she said, "I don't like it. I'm sure there are plenty of sunken vessels all up and down this river, but you shouldn't be able to see them. It's much too deep here. If your 'sizable structure' is close enough to the surface for you to see, it's a hazard, and someone ought to be told. We're fine in a small boat like this one, but a larger craft could bottom out on it. I haven't heard anything about any recent downed vessels, but I haven't read the papers over the past few days. Been head down in that manuscript and trying to avoid my neighbors."

"Tell me about it," said Lucius, thinking about the man from across the hall at his lodgings. Both he and Helen had had poor luck when it came to neighbors. "If you'll turn around, I'll see if I can't spot the wreck, or whatever it is. It's fairly big, so as long as you can get us to the right area, I think I could find it again."

"Right-ho," she replied. "Sit tight for a moment."

At first, Lucius wondered how she would manage to backtrack. The wide expanse of water looked all the same to him, and hunting for something beneath the surface felt very much like searching for a needle in a sunken haystack. But she took the time to fetch a compass and a sheet of paper from a small metal case attached to the deck. After making a few quick scribbles with a stub of a pencil, she tucked the lot of it safely into the pocket of her jacket.

She answered his look of inquiry with a lift of her chin.

"It's overkill, maybe, but it'll bother me all night if we don't figure this out. I don't like loose ends. So I'll just graph out our search, and you'll pretend that's perfectly reasonable, eh?" she said.

"I'm curious too," he said. "I think it's a brilliant idea."

"Ach, well. I'm a paragon of unrecognized brilliance."

He chuckled, turning back to the water as she performed her sailor's magic once again. The boat shifted with a creaking of

the mast and the heavy flap of sails. The motion of the craft
changed as they turned, the small vessel tilting to and fro. He
grabbed onto the railing again, his grip firm and determined.
He would not allow his tendency toward motion sickness to
distract him from his task. He badly wanted to see this mystery
solved.

The sun glinted on the water, momentarily blinding him.
Tenting a hand over his eyes helped a little, but still he squinted,
tilting his head this way and that as he scanned the depths. A
fish flitted by, and he nearly raised the alarm in his excitement.

"Almost there," said Helen. "Or my best guess, anyway. We
should be close if my calculations are correct. Do you see
anything?"

"I don't think so."

But as soon as the words were out of his mouth, the sunlight
caught on something too far off in the murky water to be seen
clearly. He leaned as far over the railing as he could manage
with his feet still on deck, gripping the railing with all his might.
Excitement and nervousness vied for dominance within him.
He could smell the water; spray hit his face. But the answers
were too close to let his fear overpower him. Even if his buried
treasure was nothing but river debris, he couldn't resist the
opportunity to play pirate, just for a moment. After all, there
was no harm in it, and Helen seemed just as intrigued by this
puzzle as he was. For once, he'd have a wild story to tell Rudi
instead of the other way round.

Something hit the boat with a hollow thunk that reverberated
through the entire craft, eliciting a shocked cuss word from
Helen. Wood groaned under the sudden strain of arrested
momentum. The deck heaved beneath his feet. His wet hands
slid on the railing. His heart skipped a beat, panic filling his

veins with cold horror. He overbalanced, grasping at the slick wooden rail, desperate for salvation. The water glittered as if beckoning him in. It no longer seemed peaceful. After all, he could not swim.

Wham!

With another mighty heave, the boat shook him free, launching him airborne. Time stretched like taffy. Although it couldn't have been more than a second or two, it felt like he had an eternity to contemplate his fate, to anticipate the icy shock of immersion, to regret the choices that had brought him here. The strap of his life jacket smacked him in the eye, making it water. He needed to blow it up, but he had no time ...

The water swallowed him. There was an eerie roar in his ears, the sound of distant motors on distant boats. The river pressed on him as if eager to find a way inside, and he kept his mouth clamped shut despite the intense urge to scream. Panic addled his senses; he looked around wildly through the greenish blur, trying to figure out which way was up. His eyes stung. There was no air. He needed to breathe, needed the warm touch of the air on his face. *There was no air.* He thrashed about with futility, desperate to inflate his lungs. His chest burned. Was he truly going to die here? Where was Helen? Surely she ought to come to his rescue, unless she'd been thrown overboard, too. Still, she would come after him once she realized he'd gone under.

Or she would have, if he'd mentioned his inability to swim. But he'd avoided it out of pride, and now it would kill him. The certainty of it settled in his bones with a cold finality. He would drown here, and he could blame nothing but his own foolishness.

A cool blanket of fatigue overtook him, inexplicable but undeniable. His struggles eased. This wasn't such a bad way to die. He needed to rest after all that flailing. A few bubbles escaped his mouth, winding up past his eyes in endless spinning patterns. They were so beautiful. He stared at them, transfixed…

Something moved in the depths, undulating toward him with surprising speed. Perhaps Helen had come to his rescue after all? Or could it be a shark? Was that possible, so far up the river? He had no idea, but it did not matter. Even the possibility of a shark attack failed to rouse his oxygen-starved brain. But still, he watched, suspended in the frozen state between life and death.

The thing that swam up to him was no shark. Nor fish. Nor human. It was something he had never dared to imagine, some obscene amalgamation of all these natural creatures, twisted and morphed into a being that was terrifying in its familiarity. A creature shaped like a man should not possess such large and amphibious eyes that bulged and swiveled in their deep sockets. Those webs did not belong on long, deft humanoid fingers. The wide, frog-like mouth gaped at him in a hungry leer, exposing row after row of jagged, shark-like teeth that gulped down his deathlike peace and left nothing but terror behind. This unnatural thing was going to eat him, or perhaps do something even more unspeakable, something he could not contemplate.

It would make a sacrifice out of him.

He had no idea where that thought had come from, but he knew down deep in his bones that it was true. It reached toward him, and he shook out of his frozen reverie. There was no air left in his lungs, but still he struggled, desperate to move, to flee, to fight. Something. Anything. He would do whatever it took to get away from this abomination.

With a pang of shock, he realized that a group of the unnatural creatures had surrounded him. Where had they all come from? Beneath him? Behind? It did not matter. The touch of their slick scales sent shudders through him. His life slowly trickled away, the strength ebbing from his muscles. But his mind remained all too aware as the things took him by his arms and legs, dragging him into the inexplicable depths. He could not see the bottom. They dragged him down and down and down. His head lolled, the tether holding him to his body growing as thin as spider silk. But something unnatural anchored him to this mortal coil, maintaining his life despite the torturous lack of oxygen. The pain was immense. If it went on much longer, he was quite certain that it would break him. Locked deep inside his mind, he screamed, but his traitorous form remained limp and unresponsive. Try as he might, he could not move. His body had ceased to become a home. Now it was a prison.

A yellow-green glow deep beneath them drew his attention. Some immense structure rested there, and with a pang, he recognized it. He'd seen it from the boat, although how he'd managed to spot something so deep beneath the surface made no sense. It was the very top of the tallest building, tipped with what looked almost like an empty flagpole. Maybe a mast. The city beneath it seemed to have grown more than it was built, with inexplicable humps and tendrils glowing with phosphorescence. The buildings reminded him of his dream-city. If he hadn't known better, he would have thought it the same place. His captors led him toward the tall building, croaking in their obscene tongue, which was somehow audible despite the noise-dampening water. The words were clogged with consonants and strange croaks that his mortal mouth could never have replicated, and he understood not a word.

An altar sat at the base of the tall building, studded with spiny growths and slithering with tentacles which emerged from somewhere in the darkness beneath it. They undulated as his abominable captors drew him near, reaching out to receive him. The touch of their suckers somehow reached deep down inside him, sucking out all light, all hope. The thing that touched him was no octopus nor any other natural sea creature. He could sense the mind behind the tentacles, vast and unknowable and filled with a bottomless hunger. Nothing would ever satiate this being. If it devoured everything that had ever existed, it would still not be enough. He could sense it.

The tentacles wrapped around his wrists and ankles, and the disgusting fish men released him, retreating with a rapidity that suggested fear. Locked within the recesses of his mind, he thrashed and fought as the inexorable, horrific appendages drew him toward the altar, but his body remained limp and unresponsive. Would he remain alert through whatever horrible fate awaited him? He could not bear it. Although he wanted more than anything to survive this inexplicable abduction, it seemed like the most he could hope for was a quick end.

He had the sinking feeling those prayers would not be answered.

The tentacles lay him atop the altar, its sharp crenellations digging furrows into his skin. A needle-like spine poked him in the ribs. He could feel every gouge even though his body refused to respond to his commands.

One of the tentacles rose above him, its tip wrapped around the hilt of a knife. Eerie green light glinted off the ornate blade. The sight of it froze his mind. In a moment, those hooks would plunge into his flesh, ripping it to shreds. The warped batrachian creatures that had brought him here would feast on whatever remained; his blood would stain the water. No one would ever know what had happened to him. He would simply disappear as if he had never existed.

Rudi. If he would miss one thing, it would be Rudi.

The knife swung down.

CHAPTER ELEVEN

Pinned to the length of an obscene underwater altar, Lucius could do nothing but stare in abject fright as his tentacled captor stabbed at him. The tip of the knife glinted in the glow thrown off by the phosphorescent things that lived deep in the inexplicable depths. This was his last moment, and he could do nothing but watch as the end of his long life came for him. It seemed like he ought to take this time to reflect on his existence or to regret the loss of the things and people he'd loved. But there was no room for conscious contemplation. Gibbering horror filled his mind.

All around him, the fish creatures released a garbled, ululating chorus that made his ears shiver. They raised webbed hands, swaying in the throes of manic worship.

A hand grabbed him by the collar and yanked him upward. The restraining grip on his limbs vanished; the pressure on his back immediately eased. Gone was the city, the altar, the worshipping fish-things. The frozen lock on his body faded, and he was hauled, gasping and flailing, up into the air. The blessed air! He took in a great gulp of it, filling his burning lungs. Then he was deposited in a shivering, dripping heap onto the deck of the boat.

Helen crouched over him, worry crinkling her face.

"Damn fool!" she exclaimed. "Are you trying to drown yourself?"

"I…" he gasped, unable to find the words to describe what had just befallen him. He could not bear to even try. "I can't swim."

She jerked upright, alarm suffusing her features. He stared up at her, confused and aching, trying desperately to sort out the contents of his jumbled mind. But he could think nothing other than: *I'm alive. I am alive. I, Lucius Galloway, am still alive.*

Helen opened her mouth again, preparing to launch what looked like one hell of a lecture. But his bruised psyche could take no more. He rolled onto his side, dripping and shivering, and laughed until he cried.

Sometime later, Helen deposited him on the armchair in his sitting room, swaddling his still-shivering form in blankets. He was dry now, although he could smell the river on him. It was a wet green scent, not entirely unpleasant, but it brought back memories he would rather not consider, so he tried not to breathe it in too deeply. Eventually, he would sit down and try to make sense out of what had happened to him, but for now, he wanted to revel in his continued existence. After today's events, he could not take a single breath for granted.

"Warm enough?" asked Helen, tossing another blanket atop him.

He had been strangely chilled since she had pulled him out of the water. None of it made sense. According to her, he'd only been under for less than a minute, floating just beneath the surface. But that was impossible. The descent to the sunken city altar had taken much longer than that. His mind clamped onto the mystery, worrying at it, until he shoved the thoughts away once again. He was too exhausted to unravel the situation now, and the last thing he wanted to do was worry Helen further. She wasn't the fussing type, but concern radiated off her in waves.

"Much better, thank you," he said, forcing his voice into a bright cheer he did not feel. "Please don't worry. I'll be sweating properly in no time."

"Let me know when that happens so I know when it's safe to beat the tar out of you," she replied with a frown.

"I'm sorry," he said. "I didn't mean to frighten you."

"Yes, well…" She cleared her throat, looking around for something else to focus on. Her hand shook as she brushed hair out of her face. He'd rattled her badly, and the realization filled him with shame. He should have been honest with her about his lack of swimming ability. Look where his pride had gotten them. He opened his mouth to apologize again, but she cut him off with an impatient wave of her hand. "Enough of that. I saw a coffee service outside, and I could use a cuppa more than anything. I'll bring you one too."

"That would be lovely."

But she was already out the door, slamming it behind her with perhaps more force than was necessary. He sat there, huddled in a pile of unfamiliar blankets in an already warm room, and tried not to think about anything. Before too long, she was back, juggling a pair of steaming mugs.

"Looks like it's fresh. I'm more jealous of your digs with every passing moment," she said, the lightness in her voice as thin as paper. "Maybe I'll start sleeping on your armchair."

"You deserve it after hauling me out of the water. I really am sorry, Helen," he said, taking the proffered coffee from her and cupping his cold hands around it.

"What in the Sam Hill happened?" she demanded, sitting on one of the footstools and turning to face him. She leaned forward, elbows on her knees, to stare him dead in the face. "Explain."

Lucius took a deep breath, marshaling his thoughts. He couldn't afford to betray what he'd seen, not without some time to unpack his thoughts about it. Perhaps the whole event – from the aquatic man-things to the underwater city – had been a hallucination brought on by lack of oxygen to the brain. But he could not be sure. Right now, he was still too shaken for true rationality.

The best course was to put her off, at least for the moment. After all, if he confessed – *fully confessed* – she'd think him mad.

"I'm sorry, Helen," he said. "I should have told you that I can't swim. I've always been afraid of the water, and I thought this might be a prime opportunity to face that fear. I handled the whole thing very poorly, I think. I hope you'll accept my sincere apology? Frightening you like that wasn't sporting of me at all."

She grunted, leaning back and sipping her coffee, her avid eyes not straying from his face. But this didn't bother him. He'd spent years learning to weather Rudi's stormy moods, and he understood very well that sometimes people with intense passions needed a moment to marshal them. So he waited and took a drink of his coffee. It burned the roof of his mouth, causing him to cough.

"You okay there?" asked Helen, stiffening.

"Hot," Lucius wheezed.

A ghost of a smile flitted across her face.

"Coffee often is, you idiot," she said fondly.

The reappearance of her sharp humor was better than any apology. Today's events could have irrevocably broken their strong working relationship and growing friendship, but the friendly jibe suggested that wasn't the case. Lucius relaxed ever so slightly. At least he could strike one item off the long list of things he needed to worry about.

"Touché," he replied, chuckling.

They sat in friendly silence for a long moment. Warmth returned to Lucius' hands in slow stages, the heat of the cup seeping into his skin. He was comfortable and dry now, and if not for Helen's company, he could have fallen asleep sitting up. After all of the excitement, his body craved rest. After all, he wasn't a young man any longer.

"My da's people are Scottish," said Helen out of the blue.

"Oh?" asked Lucius. "I beg your pardon – I thought you were Irish?"

"I grew up in Ireland with my mam's people. Come on, Galloway, try to keep up."

"My apologies," replied Lucius, lifting the cup to his lips to hide his grin.

"Anyway. My da used to make the pilgrimage back home every five years or so, and more often than not, he'd cart us along with him in the back of his wagon. What a miserable trip that was. If you strung up tarps to keep the rain out, it would just go 'round. I'm surprised we didn't drown." She paused, clearing her throat awkwardly. "Sorry. Making a drowning joke right now is a tad tactless, isn't it?"

"It's fine," murmured Lucius. "Pray, continue."

"Well, my da's people live on the shores of Loch Ness. It's way up north, y'see, in the Highlands. Beautiful land when it's not pissing down with rain. Somehow, the green is greener up there. I've never been able to explain it, but it's true."

"Sounds lovely." Lucius leaned his head back against the chair, closing his eyes as he pictured it. "I've never been, of course. You've seen how well I do with boats. As much as I love the idea of travel, I'm a homebody by necessity. It takes something special to dislodge me from my home and my routine."

"Well, I'll take that as a compliment that you came here for the summer, whether you meant it that way or not," said Helen, preening.

"My lips are sealed on that front," teased Lucius.

Helen threw back her head and let out a bark of her deep-throated laughter.

"Well, then, I just won't ask, you rascal," she said. "Anyway, it's a lovely place, Loch Ness. If you ever do manage to make it over the pond, it's worth the trek. Some of the prettiest water I've ever seen. Attracts a lot of those amateur photographers."

"Rudi would love it, then. He's somewhat of a hobbyist. He's got a lovely eye for it too, if you ask me. My photographs never turn out how I picture them in my head, but his seem to capture the spirit of a thing as well as its outlines, if that makes any sense."

"I know precisely what you mean. If it makes you feel any better, I'm with you. I'm an indifferent artist at best. I enjoy looking at it, but I've never been very good at producing any.

As a young girl full of romantic fancies, I was quite put out by that fact."

He chuckled, sipping his coffee. It had quite cooled by now, and the bitter liquid slid smoothly down his throat.

"For some time, I desperately wanted to be a singer," he admitted. "So I understand all too well."

"You have the voice for it," she said. "All low and melodic. What kept you from it?"

"Practicality, I suppose. I decided that I wanted something a bit more stable to support myself with and settled on poetry," he said, unable to keep a straight face.

Helen roared with laughter once again.

"I'm astounded by your level-headedness," she said when she could talk again. "So practical."

"The heart wants what it wants, I suppose." He smiled. "Have you been back to the lake recently, or are all your people gone from there?"

"Actually, I took myself off for a holiday before I came here to work on this project. There was this one fellow there who was out on the water all day and all night. He claims – and I feel compelled to state that I never once believed him – that there's a monster living in the loch. Naturally, no one believes a word of it, so he's determined to capture the thing in a photograph so no one can gainsay him any longer. Apparently, the poor chap has been at it for a couple of years now."

"Perhaps his monster has already perished," said Lucius, amused. "I'm not entirely familiar with the standard life expectancy of sea beasts."

"Nor I," said Helen. "I suppose there are worse hobbies than sitting out on the quiet water every morning with a camera, but the poor fellow is batty. We used to tell stories about the creature in the loch when we were kids, but that's just it: they're children's tales. The Highlands are full of legends. Of course, no one really believes in selkies and kelpies anymore."

"I'm sorry, I'm not familiar with selkies and... what did you call them?"

"Kelpies. Killer water horses. And selkies are pretty ladies that use their magic skins to turn into seals. It's a load of superstitious hogwash."

"Right."

Lucius' good humor faded as he thought about his fish people. Those ought to be superstitious hogwash too, but what did that mean for him? He could swear that he'd seen them, plain as day. Where was this line of conversation going? Had she seen them as well? It almost sounded as if she'd seen something and was trying to talk them both out of it, but that was preposterous, wasn't it?

"My point is that I'm inclined to look for a logical justification for these sorts of phenomena," Helen continued. "The area is full of vegetation, and in the right light and at a distance, I might see a perfect arrangement of branches and leaves and think it a giant head too. Besides, if some giant sea creature did live in that lake, more folks – reputable adults – would have reported seeing it. But all we've got is one git with a camera, a lot of time on his hands, and still no photographic evidence."

"I agree," said Lucius, his stomach sinking. He valued Helen's good opinion, and with every passing moment, he became more and more determined to keep his strange experiences to himself. From the sounds of it, she wouldn't believe him. "More often than not, there's a rational explanation for even the most unusual of situations."

"I'm mighty glad to hear you say that, because I've got an important question to ask you."

Helen stared at him, her pale eyes blazing out from the depths of her wrinkled face. She had never looked as old as she did now, but her strength and determination hit him with an almost physical force. If he reached out toward her, would his hand be repelled by the sheer force of her will? It was the kind of eldritch nonsense that he usually laughed at when he read it in the pulps, but at this moment, it felt very real indeed.

"What do you want to know?" he asked, his voice weaker than he wanted it to be.

"What in the hell ran into our boat?" she demanded.

CHAPTER TWELVE

A chill settled over the sitting room, defying the bright summer sun that streamed through the windows. Lucius wanted to burrow into his blanket and hide from this discomforting conversation, but cowardice had never solved anything, and that wasn't about to change now. He had no choice but to face Helen's inquiry head on.

"What do you mean?" he asked, forcing his voice to firmness.

"Just what I asked," she piped back tartly. "What did we hit out there on the river? It struck the hull hard enough to knock you over the side, and at first, I assumed that we'd hit whatever you spotted. A wreck of some sort. But it had to be fairly close to the surface, and I saw nothing."

"Maybe it sank after we struck it?"

To his immense surprise, some of the coiled tension eased from his shoulders despite the uncomfortable direction this conversation had taken. Helen was clearly wrestling with some of the same questions he'd asked himself. Perhaps she wouldn't judge him after all. Perhaps he wasn't as alone as he'd felt.

She shook her head, lips pursed in something like discontent.

"But that's no good," she said. "To generate that kind of force on the water, our mystery object either has to be sizable or stationary. Maybe both. Or it would have to be moving so quickly that it would have displaced the water, and we would have seen it coming. So that explanation's no good either. As soon as we made impact, I went looking for what we'd hit, because I was worried it had breached the hull and we were going to be up the creek without a paddle *or* a boat. I saw nothing. Something that big, I should have seen it."

He tried to think back, but his memory of the whole event was so muddled that he didn't trust his recollections. Where did the true memories stop and the hallucinations begin? He couldn't be certain, so he had no choice but to disregard the whole lot and consider the situation from a theoretical standpoint. What might explain this strange experience?

"Could we have drifted away from … whatever it was that we hit?" he asked after a long moment's thought.

"No," she said with obvious confidence. "I was trying to hold her steady so you could look for your buried treasure or whatever the heck it was that you spotted. On a windy day at full sail, sure, I'd buy that explanation. But not this time."

"So it had to be mobile. Is the river deep enough for some aquatic creature to come up from beneath …"

He faltered, the memory of the strange ichthyoid creatures rising unbidden from the depths of his memory, stirred up by the topic of conversation. They had surrounded him before he could so much as react. Perhaps they had hit the boat, but that would lead him to a conclusion that he did not want to contemplate. It would mean that they hadn't been a hallucination at all. They were real.

But the equations still didn't add up, no matter how hard he tried to make them work. He couldn't have been dragged down to the depths of the river to some subaquatic city. Helen had reached right in and pulled him out. If he allowed himself to believe in the fish men, then he had to believe in the rest, and no matter how he turned it around in his mind, none of it made sense.

The contradictions unsettled something deep inside him. It felt as if he was sliding down a slippery slope, grasping frantically for some logical purchase but finding nothing to slow his fall. He did not want to see what awaited him at the bottom. He could handle anything so long as he could understand it, but perhaps some things defied understanding. What could he hope to do then?

Helen still stared at him, her mouth curling into a frown. He schooled his face to stillness, but it seemed the damage had already been done. She had realized that there was more to this situation than he'd let on. She placed her coffee cup on the side table and sat back, folding her hands across her belly.

"Explain," she said simply.

There was no sense in lying, and to his surprise, he found that he wanted to hear her take on all of the strange happenings over the past few months. So he took a deep breath and said, "I can make neither heads nor tails of this, so I would welcome your perspective on what has been happening over these past months. I am sure there must be some logical explanation, but I've been hard pressed to find it."

"We make a good team, my friend," she said, the hard edge leaking out of her gravelly voice. "If there's more of this nonsense, you should have brought it to me sooner."

"And risk you thinking I'd lost my marbles? It was a risk I wasn't willing to take. But after today?" He blew out a long breath through pursed lips. "I suppose that changes things."

"Tell me, then," she said.

After taking a moment to marshal his thoughts, Lucius complied. He endeavored to tell the story without frills or editorializing, sticking to as factual a narrative as possible. He started with his nightmares and general paranoia. That part was easy. When he got to his fall off the boat and the things he saw there, he could not deny his discomfort, but he forced himself to carry on without censorship. He would lay this thing bare and hopefully in the process exorcise its demons. At the least, it felt good to get the whole sordid mess off his chest. Regardless of what happened next, he would no longer have to carry this burden alone.

Helen listened without comment, her eyes half-lidded and her hands steepled in front of her mouth. She said nothing as he continued his narration except for one moment when she asked him to repeat a phrase he'd mumbled out of embarrassment. Calling them "fish men" seemed entirely inadequate.

"And then you know the rest," he concluded. "I'm quite interested to hear what you think. I know there must be some rational explanation for the lot of it, and I can brush off quite a few things myself. The stress of Rudi's dreams made me follow in his footsteps. Once I became worried about it, that only intensified the problem. I went to bed every night dreading the possibility I might dream, so of course my subconscious delivered. But my logic fails me when I get to today's happenings. I'm more than willing to believe that the whole thing was a hallucination – the creatures, the city, all of it. But something hit the boat. If it wasn't my amphibious captors, what else could it be?"

Their eyes met. In Helen's, he saw a familiar desperation, a flailing about for the security of logic in new and uncharted waters.

"God help us, I don't know," she replied.

"Exactly."

A not-uncomfortable silence settled over the room. He felt wrung out like a used dishrag, all of the debris flushed clean. She hadn't disbelieved him outright or brushed away his questions as hysterical rubbish, and he felt bolstered by the fact that her questions mirrored his own. At the very least, he would no longer have to worry that he was overreacting. The situation disturbed him for good reason. Somehow, that realization made it easier to face the problem anew.

"You know," she said slowly, "as a person of logic, it's rational to believe that there are things in this world we cannot perceive. Our human bodies have their limitations, and history has shown that time and time again as progress reveals more of the natural world to us. Just think of how we knew so little about the makeup of things before the invention of the microscope."

"Certainly, but I'm not sure that solves our problem. Whatever we hit wasn't too small to be seen. Far from it."

"I'm simply defining the playing field. That there are things in this world that we cannot perceive, but they do have a logical explanation behind them. We simply haven't found it yet."

"'There are more things on heaven and earth, Horatio, than are dreamt of in your philosophy?'"

The corner of her mouth quirked. "Now don't you bring Shakespeare into it. We'll get so wrapped up in a quote war that we'll never make any progress on this puzzle at all."

"Honestly, that might be a relief. I'd rather forget the whole thing altogether."

"I would too," she replied, "but I'm not sure I could let it go. It's the kind of thing that haunts a person, isn't it? But maybe that's just me. I like things to be tidy."

"I'm much the same, but I don't know where else to go from here. What kind of specialist do we call in? Should it be a marine biologist to identify a new species of fish man? A spiritualist, to banish my bad dreams? Or do we need a priest to exorcise the entirety of the Charles River of the foul demons that live in its depths?" he asked, overcome by a wave of unexpected humor.

"Don't you dare call up one of those muckety-muck spiritualists," she shot back, relaxing visibly. "What exactly are they going to do to help? Send your soul off to vacation in the tropics?"

"Well, regardless of what happens next, at least we'd have solved my travel problem."

"Looking on the bright side. I like that."

"And if we're moving souls about, I'd like to stash mine in a nice middle-aged body."

"Not a young one?" she asked, cocking her head.

"I think a surfeit of youth would tempt me to foolishness. Middle age seems the most logical choice, doesn't it? Young enough that my knees don't hurt so much but old enough to know better than to tempt fate too badly."

"Not me," she said, snickering. "I didn't realize what I had when I had it. I'd like a do-over, if we're placing orders with the Almighty."

They kept on bantering for the rest of the afternoon, steering away from the difficult and still-unanswered questions and sticking to the safety of old anecdotes. The respite eased some of Lucius' lingering tension. As with any other tangle, sometimes setting it aside and coming back to it with fresh eyes helped. He had no doubt that the answers would come, now that they had established a true partnership.

It had been a long time since he'd truly relaxed, so he allowed himself to bask in it, just for a little while.

Shortly before the dinner hour, Helen excused herself to return to the boarding house and see whether Marco had, in fact, been kicked to the curb. If not, she would need some time to make alternate sleeping arrangements. Lucius made her promise to shout if he could be of any assistance, and in return she kissed his cheek.

"I'm glad you didn't drown today," she said.

"Thank you again, Helen," he replied.

After she left, he took himself off to a remarkably early bath. His skin had dried with the peculiar sheen left behind by natural bodies of water, creating a taut, unnatural feeling. It would do him good to wash off whatever had been left behind by that traumatic experience. The bath was hot and steaming, and there were no signs of any strange creatures anywhere in its depths. Once he was clean and dressed in a fresh suit, he detoured to the dining hall to fetch a dinner plate, intending to spend the evening with a bit of Shakespeare. He and Helen had snuck a few more quotes into their conversation, and he was thinking that a night of relaxation lost in the Bard's work was exactly what he needed. He hadn't yet picked a play, but he was determined it would not be one of the tragedies. He'd had enough melodrama to last him for a very long time.

Plate in hand, he began to climb the stairway toward his room. From somewhere up above him, a door boomed, and as he looked up, once again, he saw the creeping tendrils of a shadowy figure on the landing. The light and the angle of the stairway combined to create a monstrous outline with too many limbs and a bulbous countenance. The unnatural figure brought to mind his underwater excursion; although it didn't look anything like his scaled captors, there was always a chance that it could be something *else*. Something much worse. A momentary chill crossed over him, but he pushed it away with firm determination. As Helen had said, some things might be inexplicable, but that did not mean they did not have their own laws by which they were governed.

On further reflection, perhaps he was embellishing that quote, but he liked the spirit of it anyway.

So he climbed the stairway without pause, ignoring the accelerating pitter-pat of his heart. As he turned the corner, he craned his neck, unable to resist the need to see what was coming toward him as soon as humanly possible. The stout figure of Mr Badenhorst looked up at him with a guilty glint in his eye, hands cupped around something he didn't want to be seen. A cigarette, perhaps, or some illegal hooch? Lucius didn't care. Frankly, although he wasn't the biggest fan of the man, who seemed to run hot and cold in inexplicable turns, Lucius could have hugged him in thanks for being so refreshingly normal.

He doffed his hat with his free hand as he climbed past.

"Good evening, Badenhorst," he said, pleasantly enough.

"Galloway," grunted Badenhorst. "Dinner in your rooms tonight, eh?"

"I've been burning the midnight oil a little too much. I think it's past time I took a night off."

Badenhorst nodded, stepping aside so Lucius could get through the hallway door. As it closed behind him, a prickle on the back of his neck alerted him to the fact that he was being watched. Badenhorst's eyes tracked him until the door eased shut. Lucius found it strangely reassuring. He had no problem with fear or danger; he'd faced plenty throughout his life, and he was confident in his ability to evade or diffuse as needed. But the unknown and unknowable shook him to his core, because he could not prepare for something he didn't understand. That made him vulnerable in a way he could not accept.

Badenhorst did not exactly welcome his presence here. Perhaps he harbored some secret prejudice against Black folks, or perhaps Lucius had managed to offend in some other unknown way. It didn't matter. Lucius knew how to handle that sort of thing; he'd been doing so all his life. Although he wished the world was more accepting, at least he recognized this problem. In a way, the familiarity comforted him, as crazy as it was to admit it. The world spun round with all its glories and all of its faults, familiar in its complexity.

Now that was a lovely turn of phrase. Lucius paused in the hallway to write it down in his commonplace book before letting himself into his room, feeling more relaxed than he had in ages. Perhaps at some point, he would put it all down in a letter to Rudi, but he thought not. Such stories were better told in person.

In the shadows of the tree across the quad, a dark figure watched his window, but for once, Lucius never looked out. He read his book, went to bed, and did not dream for the first time in a very long spell.

The dark watcher remained there all night, undetected and undisturbed.

CHAPTER THIRTEEN

Lucius found himself whistling as he collected his latest chapter into a neat stack and placed it into his briefcase. Ever since his strange experience on the river almost two weeks earlier, the writing had been going particularly well. He now had enough distance from the whole sordid affair that he could joke that perhaps he ought to try a near drowning the next time he suffered from anything close to writer's block. Helen had found that one particularly amusing. She'd laughed so hard she choked.

The briefcase snapped shut. He placed his hat on his head, brushed a piece of lint off his trousers, and let himself out to face the day. Nothing could dampen his good spirits, not even the wet slap of the air, which promised the most uncomfortable of humid days. Not even the glower of Badenhorst from the coffee station as he passed. Apparently, the man was having one of his bad days. As long as Badenhorst limited himself to angry mugging, Lucius honestly couldn't bestir himself enough to care.

He crossed the quad, exchanging pleasant greetings with the people he passed: a pair of women in smart dress and fancy headgear chatting about their lovely brunch; a young scholar, tie askew, sprinting pell-mell across the grass with panic in his eyes; a grizzled academic with muttonchops and a distant, thoughtful gaze; and a workman in stained coveralls who stood off the path in the grass to allow him to pass. They returned his greetings with polite words of their own – with the exception of the sprinting academic, who was breathing too heavily to be understood – and once again, he was struck by his immense luck. Not many people could say that they'd worked a summer at Harvard. He had gotten too distracted by his worries to truly appreciate it before now, and if he didn't set himself to rights, the whole thing would be over, and he would lose his chance. Rudi liked to say he was a pessimist, and Lucius had always taken issue with the label. But perhaps there was something to it after all.

Speaking of Rudi, Lucius owed him a letter, and he had been putting off the writing of it. If he wrote, he would have to decide once and for all whether or not to make any mention of his underwater experience. Early in the week, he'd held out hope that he'd be able to unravel the mystery of exactly what had transpired before putting the tale down on paper. But he and Helen had revisited the topic a few times to no avail, and she had even taken the boat out again on Friday, sailing back and forth over the area where he'd gone into the drink, searching for some sign of wreckage. He'd turned down her hesitant offer to bring him along, admitting without embarrassment that the idea of getting in a watercraft ever again frightened him near out of his socks. Thankfully, she hadn't pushed the matter, and instead had drafted Dao to accompany her. But after hours of searching, they'd returned without having discovered anything remotely helpful.

Yesterday had brought a somewhat playful message from Rudi demanding a return letter soon and threatening a phone call or even a visit to verify that he still breathed. Although Rudi had joked, his concern was clear. Lucius would have to put pen to paper that evening, but for now, he could delay the decision a while longer and enjoy the lovely summer day unfolding before him.

When he arrived at Helen's office, he found her bent over the desk with Dao by her side, murmuring over a set of manuscript pages. He rapped on the door, hat in his hand, and sketched a bow in greeting.

"Good morning," he said.

"Good morning, Mr Galloway," replied Dao, showing off her dimples.

"Lucius! There you are! We were just talking about you," added Helen.

"I'm not that late, am I?"

"No, no, not at all. Please, join us in this expansive and luxurious chamber, and we can get to work."

The joke made him snort as he hung his hat on the peg. If he had one true complaint about this whole process, it was that their small project team of three had no comfortable location in which to collaborate. The research carols at Widener were off limits to some members of their party, and there was no larger office or conference space available at either Radcliffe nor at Harvard despite Dao's repeated inquiries. They could all testify to the number of empty rooms they'd seen, gathering up layers of dust only disturbed by the cleaning staff. But they'd been repeatedly assured that these spaces were in use, and there was nothing available that would suit their needs. Lucius found it unhelpful to leap to accusations of prejudice every time a negative situation presented itself, but he had to admit that he had his suspicions. It mattered not in the end. They still had to make do.

They were left with the option of cramming into Helen's office, squeezing into Lucius' sitting room, or tucking away in a corner of the women's reading room at the library. Two of these three options lacked sufficient seating, while the third required them to conduct all of their business in a near-inaudible whisper to avoid disturbing the other academics. Last week, Dao had made a joke about having more room to work on the boat, and Lucius' aggravation over the whole situation was so terrific that he might have agreed to try it if he hadn't been so terrified of ever setting foot on the water again.

There wasn't enough room for all three of them behind the desk, so he remained on the other side, scanning the upside-down documents strewn out before them.

"So, how's it looking?" he asked.

"I'm pleased as punch," replied Helen. "Dao's finished the proofreading on the first two chapters. We've got a couple of bits for you to sign off on in red, if you've got the time today."

"Gladly."

"Then I'll tackle the final, and I'll never have to type up pages and pages about fish guts ever again. Won't that be swell?" asked Dao, grinning.

By now, Lucius was used to her cheeky comments, so he took no offense. Instead, he smiled in appreciation of the consistently high spirits she brought to their little team.

"If you call them 'ancient divinatory rites,' it sounds a lot better," he said.

"It's fascinating work, Mr Galloway," she admitted. "But after about the tenth time, the varnish tends to come off even the nicest turn of phrase. It's nothing personal."

"Well, I've got something new for you to put into the mix." With some maneuvering, he managed to edge his briefcase onto the corner of the desk and produce the new manuscript pages from within. "I've finally managed to smooth out the rough edges on the chapter about religious imagery, and I think it's ready for your review."

Helen took the pages eagerly from him, squinting at the words.

"Is my handwriting truly that poor?" asked Lucius, alarmed. "I thought I wrote it quite neatly."

She flashed a grin at him without lifting her eyes from the page.

"I think it's less about your writing and more about my unwillingness to wear spectacles," she admitted. "But don't tell anyone I said that."

Dao snorted but said nothing.

"Your secret is safe with me. I'll get those changes reviewed right away," he said. "Then I think I'll tackle the chapter on overall narrative structure. I've read through the notes a few times, and I think I've got a couple ideas on how I might add to them."

Helen appeared more uncertain than he'd expected. She frowned, drumming her nails thoughtfully upon the desk.

"Are you sure you want to tackle that next? I was thinking it might be smarter to finish off magic or architecture next. They'll be much longer, and I'm not too keen on burying Dao with too much to type right at the end of the summer. I don't mind helping out a bit since my scribbles will be done long before yours will, but those longer pieces will still take quite a while to finish up properly," she said.

"I beg your pardon," replied Lucius. "I hadn't thought of that. I'd offer to lend a hand, but I don't think I'd do much good. I'm quite slow when it comes to those things. There's a reason I handwrite all of my own material and pay for the typing of it before it goes to my editor."

"We're not taking it personally, Galloway," said Helen, the corner of her mouth turning up. "Although if you insist on keeping the schedule as is, I fully intend to end every night by making a full report to you regarding the pain in my poor hands."

"Do you intend to type the hand-pain report too?" asked Lucius. "That strikes me as a step in the wrong direction."

Helen barked out a laugh.

"You dog. You seem so quiet and well-mannered, but Dao and I know the truth of it," she said.

"Now, don't start that, or I'll regret my decision to switch the order of my chapters," he replied.

"Ah, well. I suppose I'd better content myself with that win. Shall we reconvene late afternoon, then? You're welcome to stay, but I don't think you'll relish sitting on the floor while Dao and I trip over you every few minutes."

"I'll see you then," said Lucius, accepting the sheaf of pages Dao handed over with a nod of gratitude. "I'm looking forward to hearing your thoughts on the new work. There's some interesting stuff in there, I think."

"Looking forward to it."

Lucius retrieved his hat and briefcase, made his goodbyes, and set off to return to his rooms. Before he reached the stairs, Helen called his name, stopping him in his tracks. He turned to see her charging down the hallway with a speed and ferocity that stood at stark odds to her tiny, withered frame. Years ago, she must have been a force to be reckoned with.

"Should I be worried?" he asked as she drew close. "You seem a woman on a mission."

"Well, I am. I almost forgot to tell you. I got you a present," she replied.

"A gift? You shouldn't have."

The polite saying rose automatically to his lips, but the sentiment couldn't have been more in earnest. The thought that she had gone out of her way to do him a kindness touched him. His mind whirled, already trying to think up some way he might return the favor. Perhaps a new set of mahjong tiles? He had no idea where to purchase such a thing, and he wasn't particularly familiar with the shops here in town. He would have to look for a gift shop on his lunchtime stroll.

"Don't be too impressed," she said, chuckling. "I didn't spend a dime. But the opportunity presented itself, and I took it. It seems tailor-made for you."

"Oh?" he asked, taken aback. "Well, it's kind of you to think of me regardless. What is it?"

"I got you a free swimming lesson."

Lucius had heard the idiom "his blood ran cold" many times, but to his recollection he'd never experienced the phenomenon firsthand. A chill ran down his arms, the cold penetrating him to the bone. As far as he was concerned, he could go the rest of his life without immersing himself in water any deeper than the bathtub. He could live an eternity without setting another foot on a boat. What did he want a swimming lesson for? His parents had never learned to swim, and clearly, they'd made a wise choice.

Memories of the warped underwater creatures floated at the edges of his mind, threatening to unsettle his nerves even further. With firm determination, he pushed them away. He had no desire to rekindle those frightening memories. Everything had been going too well for that. Perhaps the lesson would do the same, although he had to admit that he did not like the idea one bit.

Helen watched him, her bright eyes seeming to see right through the polite mask he maintained through force of habit. She patted him on the shoulder.

"I know it will take a remarkable feat of will to attempt it after what happened on the river," she said, "but that's all the more reason to do it. And it's just a pool, not open water. You'll always be able to stand up. I thought that might set your mind at ease."

He forced himself to nod.

"I suppose it makes sense," he said faintly. "I wouldn't have to worry about a repeat of whatever happened that day if I knew how to save myself."

"Exactly. If you don't want the lesson, I'll cancel it, but I couldn't pass up the opportunity. The new boarder who took Marco's room is a swim instructor. When he said he was looking for new clients, I told him about you. He'll give you a lesson for free if you're willing to provide a statement for his promotional pamphlets, and I'm sure we could get more out of him if you wanted to go again. He needs the publicity."

He cleared his throat, an uncomfortable thought rising to his mind.

"I'm not sure I'll be welcome at the pool," he said. "Did you tell him that I'm not white?"

She looked startled. As open-minded as Helen had been, it was the sort of concern she didn't have to trouble herself with. But at least she didn't insult him by arguing.

"I didn't, but I don't see how it could be a problem. I'm not sure what Eugene is, but he's not lily-white himself. I wasn't impertinent enough to ask him for his pedigree," she said.

"You don't say?"

Lucius found himself intrigued despite himself. None of his family nor his friends had ever learned to swim. Rudi claimed to enjoy sea bathing, but on the rare opportunity he'd had to try it, he had never ventured out past his waist, and only in calm waters. The idea that a Black man might not only be able to swim but also be skilled enough to instruct others delighted Lucius to his core. Of course, this Eugene might not be Black at all, but what if he was? That was something Lucius wanted to see. The excitement of the idea banished some of his fear. Not all of it by any means, but enough that he could accept the offer with grace.

"I'm going to be honest with you, Helen," he said. "I'm not sure how long I'll stay in the pool. I'm a bit more nervous than I'd like to let on. But I appreciate you thinking of me, and I'm willing to try it so long as I won't offend anyone if I terminate the lesson early. I'm honestly not sure how well I'll tolerate it."

"Very fair," she answered. "We'll have to find you a bathing costume or whatever the young people call it these days. I'm sure Dao will bring us up to speed, as it were."

He snickered. "Whether we like it or not. But yes, I'll see if any of the shops have anything. I'd think my chances must be good this time of year. If not, I'll have to send away for something and have it sent here."

"I can ask Eugene as well. Perhaps he knows of some rental scheme. Not everyone owns bathing suits, so there must be some sort of provision made for them. Once we've got you squared away, I'll make the arrangements."

"Thanks again," he said, trying to mean it. "I'd best get to work. See you this afternoon?"

"You betcha."

She sketched a salute, turned smartly on her heels, and charged back toward the office with her usual momentum. Shaking his head in fond exasperation, Lucius continued on his way. She was a character for sure. Now if only she'd stop trying to get him drowned…

CHAPTER FOURTEEN

Not a week later, Lucius found himself in the dressing stall of the private club where Eugene taught his lessons. To his immense relief, the place sported two pools, both of which were in good repair. The larger of the two had a better placement on the grounds, with beautiful landscaping and good sun, and that was where the bulk of the club members spent their time. The smaller and less impressive pool had been unoccupied when Eugene had shown him around. There would be no one to take offense at their presence, nor to laugh at the realization that a sixty-year-old gentleman was terrified of the water. Normally such things didn't bother him, but he was already keyed up enough. It would be better to avoid any additional stressors.

He stared at the orange wool of the bathing costume and wondered – not for the first time – how he'd gotten here. Once Helen had decided that he needed a lesson, she'd pursued the idea with dogged determination. She'd found him the bathing costume, arranged for the date and time, and practically ferried him to the door of the club. He had the feeling that if not for her sense of propriety, she would have stood on the edge of the pool and shouted instructions at him. She probably still harbored some feelings of guilt after the accident on the river. This would be her way of ensuring that such a thing never happened again, and he could understand it, but he wished she might have found some other way of absolving herself. The last thing he wanted to do was to appear in public in this unsightly costume. Perhaps he was being old-fashioned, but it was his firm opinion that the last thing the world needed was a glimpse of his ankles.

But this lesson would be good for him. If he did not get into the water today, he might never do it again, and he had no desire to let himself be overmastered by fear. Even if he did not learn how to swim today, it would be a victory to get in the water. Rudi would be thrilled, but Lucius hadn't had much time left to write letters after long days spent with the manuscript. Perhaps after this triumph, he would make the time.

His lips firmed. He was made of strong stuff, and he would see this through, ridiculous bathing garb and all.

A few minutes later, he let himself out of the changing area with his cheeks blazing. Without his customary suit, he felt vulnerable and exposed. His knees looked strangely old. In his youth he would have welcomed the opportunity to strip off the confining suit and embrace the freedom of lighter dress, but things had changed. He had changed, and he didn't care to be reminded of that every time he looked down at his legs.

Eugene waited near the pool gate, trim and stylish in his swimming woolens. He was a svelte young man with a thin Rudolph Valentino mustache. His light brown skin glowed with health, and muscles bulged along his exposed biceps. This was a man who probably never wanted for romantic prospects. But instead of being all swagger and ego, he seemed the sort of fellow who would be blind to his own charms. His gentle smile hinted at the presence of an old soul.

He bestirred himself as Lucius approached, clutching a towel like it possessed some remarkable life-saving qualities. Eugene's eyes flicked down to the towel and the white knuckles of Lucius' hands before lifting again.

"I'm not sure this is the best idea," said Lucius. "I'm too old for this. You know the old idiom – you can't teach an old dog new tricks. They say that for a reason."

His nervousness made him babble. He clamped his mouth shut, trying to preserve the ragged threads of his dignity. Beyond the fence, the water glistened and rippled, the pool a serene and unbroken expanse. Such a ridiculous thing to be afraid of. How humiliating this whole ordeal was. He wished he'd never come here.

But if Eugene judged him, it didn't show on his face. He folded his arms, muscles rippling, and leaned against the gate with an enviable casualness.

"You know," he said, "I was terrified of the water up until a couple of years ago."

Lucius arched a brow. "You?" he asked.

"My little town didn't have a pool where I was welcome. Whites only, you know. My friends and I, we snuck in there late one summer night, determined that we were gonna have our chance to swim. I jumped in and went straight to the bottom. By the time my friends fished me out, the caretaker of the place had set his dogs on us. I didn't think I'd ever swim again, but here we are."

"I'm glad you found that opportunity, but I'm afraid it's much too late for me, old chap. I've got a few more miles on me than you do. And ..." Lucius hesitated, but Eugene didn't seem like the type to judge. He might as well leave it all on the table. "I have dreams."

Although it was a simplification of his problems, it felt true. For the first time, he realized that all of his problems, all of his nightmares or visions or whatever one wanted to call them, had something to do with water. The streets of the drowned city. The creatures in the river. Heck, the sight of a running faucet or a rainy evening often preceded one of his stressful episodes. Was that it? Did all of his problems stem from a deep-seated fear of the water? The explanation both dismayed and relieved him. If that was the case, he could finally put those demons to rest today. He could sleep undisturbed. He could let go of his late-night worries about his sanity. What a relief that would be!

"Would you like to banish those nightmares for good?" Eugene asked, seeming to read his mind. But maybe it wasn't anything so improbable. Maybe he truly understood because he had been in Lucius' shoes not so long ago.

"I'd like to try," replied Lucius, his voice uneven. "But I'll warn you that I'm frightened out of my wits. I didn't realize quite how scared I was until this moment. I mean, I knew it was an issue, but I honestly feel sick."

"Let's go and sit on the side of the pool. We'll put our feet in and talk about what the lessons would entail. You don't have to get in until you're ready, I promise."

Eugene opened the gate and held it for Lucius. With a deep breath, Lucius stepped through. The air stung his nostrils, sharp with whatever chemicals maintenance put in the water to keep it so clean. The long rectangle of the pool stretched out before him, the tiles running along its edge tinged yellow with age. The space was simple and utilitarian, with a concrete slab, a small handful of chairs in dubious repair, and the empty pool. It lacked a lifeguard to laugh at his fear and screaming children to swim by him, splashing and teasing. It was the perfect setting for a lesson, but he still hovered by the edge, unwilling to sit down and immerse his feet.

With a gentle hand on his shoulder, Eugene urged him down. The younger man put his feet into the water, and Lucius followed suit before he could think twice about it. The cool water enveloped his skin, driving away the clammy heat of the summer day. This wasn't so bad. It was like a nice refreshing bath. If only he could stay safely here, he would be fine.

"The first lesson is devoted to getting you used to the water," said Eugene. "We'll touch it. Stand in it. Move around in it. I won't ask you to go anywhere that you can't touch. You'll always be able to stand up, and you'll always be able to get out if you truly need to. But I believe you can do this."

"I just have to stand up in it?" asked Lucius, his heart hammering inexplicably. "I don't have to swim?"

"You don't have to swim. If you want to try picking your feet up once to experience what it's like to float, I'll help you. But you're not required to do that." Eugene smiled. "To be honest, most new students say that's their favorite part. It's frightening at first, but there's nothing like the sensation of floating."

Lucius nodded, trying to slow his rapid breath. But Eugene proved to be a patient instructor, engaging him in conversation about the new book with what appeared to be genuine interest. He asked intelligent questions about poetical forms as he led the way to the stairs and stood on them. They descended the steps into the water together as Lucius explained his writing process. By the time Eugene admitted that he'd always wanted to be a writer, they were standing in the waist-high water.

"There's no time like the present," said Lucius, his eyes locked on Eugene's face. "And it's never too late to follow your dreams. I didn't publish my first poetry until I was almost forty."

"Really? What did you do before that?"

"A little of this and a little of that. I taught for a while. I did typesetting for a newspaper. I worked in an advertising agency. I knew I wanted to be a writer, but I had no idea how to go about it, so I found any work I could that had to do with words and hoped it would be enough. Of course, it never was."

"That's where I am. I have no idea how to go about following my dreams," admitted Eugene. "It's frightening."

"Sometimes you just have to take the leap. By all means, do it smart. Being destitute sounds inspiring and bohemian, but I've seen what it does to people. It's not pretty."

"It's all about taking the risk, I guess. And speaking of risks, you do realize you've been standing in the water for a good few minutes, don't you?"

Lucius nodded, a pleased smile flickering over his face. Of course he'd noticed; the water licked at his skin, deliciously cool. The firm pressure of it against his body was odd but not unpleasant. When he moved, it tugged against him, turning every motion into a liquid ballet. He swished his hand through it experimentally, watching the water ripple peacefully in his wake. This was not so bad after all. There was nothing to be frightened of here. Although his heart still fluttered at the idea of venturing out into the deep end, he could say that he'd faced his fears today. Despite his initial reluctance, he felt better for it.

"Very well done. Let's walk around a bit. Get used to it. You'll see that the rope marks off the deeper areas, so as long as we stay on this side, we'll be able to touch the bottom quite easily."

The two of them walked around for a short while, and Lucius' confidence grew by the second. He no longer needed to stare down at his own feet, nervously alert for any signs of danger. Instead, he glanced around the small courtyard where the pool was tucked. Beyond the chairs and the fence was a row of scraggly trees, boughs drooping under heavy branches. The dappled shadows waved and twisted on the ground as a gentle wind ruffled the trees. There was a flash of shadow there, a human figure standing somewhere out of sight. For one chilly moment, Lucius was convinced that they hid there, specifically to watch him.

He shivered.

"Is the water too cold?" asked Eugene. "I find it refreshing myself."

Lucius shook his head, standing on tiptoe to try and get a better look at the hidden figure that had produced the shadow. For all he knew, it was just some statue, or a gardener, or some club-goer waiting for a friend. He'd been seeing things just like the man convinced about the monster in Loch Ness. His paranoia really was ridiculous when he thought about it logically. He turned his back on the shadowy figure with resolution and took a deep breath.

"No, it's not too cold," he said. "What's next? I'm ready."

"Next, we put our faces in the water," replied Eugene. "This can be frightening for some people, so we'll do it in stages."

Lucius watched as Eugene demonstrated the whole process, explaining what to do and why to do it. Nerves gripped at him, but he shook free of their grasping hands. He was tired of being afraid. At his advanced age, what did he truly have to fear? He'd lived a long life and survived all sorts of hardships, and he was tired of jumping at shadows. He would put his face into the water, and he would survive it, and then he'd take himself out to a nice dinner. Perhaps Helen might be available to accompany him. Good food and good conversation were exactly what he needed.

"Now it's your turn," said Eugene. "Remember, just blow out. You can't inhale the water if you're blowing out."

Lucius leaned over. The water enveloped his face, and he blew out as instructed. The bubbles tickled his cheeks. Exhilarated, he sprang back up into the warm air.

"That wasn't so difficult after all," he said.

"No, but the fear of the unknown is real, isn't it?" said Eugene. "It can hold us back from so many things."

"Do we have much time left? Can I try again?"

"Honestly, we should have been done about five minutes ago." Eugene grinned. "But I don't mind staying a bit longer. You're making such terrific progress."

"Let me try submersing one more time, and then we can wrap up. You've been so generous already. Perhaps I could trade you some advice on your writing for more lessons?"

"If we could make those arrangements, I would be delighted. First, let's try to go completely under. If you're feeling exceptionally brave, you can pick your feet up and see what it's like to float. When you're done, just stand up again."

Lucius was so thrilled with his progress that he followed the instructions without stopping to consider what he was doing. He plunged down beneath the waters. They closed above him, enveloping his body and dampening his senses. A momentary panic rose inside him, but he could still feel the bottom scraping against his toes. He could stand up if he wanted to, and he was determined to push himself. Eyes squeezed shut, he listened to the hollow rumble of breath bubbles rising to the surface and the distant swish of Eugene's body through the water. It felt like he was the only resident of a strange new world, floating serenely in the void.

He picked his feet up, the water buoying his body. The near weightlessness delighted him, and he would have laughed if he'd had the air. His fear had kept this from him, but it would do so no longer. There was nothing to worry about here. If calamity struck, he could just stand up.

Something wrapped around his jaw.

At first, he thought that Eugene was trying to pull him to the surface, worried perhaps that he'd run out of air or become disoriented. But this was no human hand. It was a fleshy tendril, a pseudopod, a tentacle-like thing that contoured itself to him with boneless dexterity. His hand groped at it before recoiling in horror. Had some sea creature gotten into the pool? His air escaped in a bark of horror that was immediately swallowed by the clenching water, resulting in nothing but a burst of bubbles.

He thrust himself toward the surface, but another fetid appendage wrapped itself around his shoulders, pinning him there. He thrashed. Suddenly, the pool seemed full of some slithering mass that bumped up against him, rubbing its squamous, scaly length against the skin bared by that ridiculous swim costume. Tentacles encircled his limbs. They wrapped around his neck and forehead. The tickling touch of them pushed at his eyes and mouth as if trying to work their way in. A sickening, slimy sensation spread through him as one worked its way into his right ear and another invaded his nostril.

They were trying to crawl inside him, to devour him from the inside out. The certainty ran through him, chilling him to his bones. As in the river, he fought with all his might, hoping for a rescue that might not come. Had these things also gotten

Eugene? Or was this like the last time, and it was all a figment of his imagination brought on by stress?

As much as he wanted to believe this was all a hallucination, it did not seem like one. He opened his eyes and saw nothing but a sea of slithering snake-things. What little water was left in the pool stung his eyeballs with a very real pain. He would have pinched himself, but he could not move. Could not breathe. Could do nothing but wait and see what they intended to do to him.

It's not real. It's not real. It can't be real.

The tentacles wrapped around his head, squeezing with such pressure that he thought it might squish like a grape. They twisted and tugged, manipulating him like a puppet, opening his jaw to let the water come rushing in. But somehow, strangely, it did not. He spoke instead in a language he did not understand, clotted consonants pushing their way out from some unknown place inside him, summoned by the boneless appendages that worked his jaw.

"*Ph'nglui mglw'nafh Cthulhu R'lyeh wgah'nagl fhtagn,*" he said.

He did not know what it meant. He did not recognize his own voice, nor know where it came from. His body was not his own. It was nothing but some cosmic marionette dangling on the strings of an incomprehensible entity, unknowable in its hunger. It would use him up, and then he would die.

The water rushed in, filling his lungs and making him cough explosively. He flailed, suddenly free from the pressure, his feet thrusting out to find the smooth floor of the pool. He stood, emerging into the open air, coughing out a great gout of water. Through his stinging eyes, he saw nothing but the pristine, clear water. There wasn't a tentacle in sight. Eugene clapped him on the back, nearly making him shriek.

"You were doing so well!" Eugene exclaimed. "But sadly, we don't have gills. Breathing the water never turns out well."

Lucius coughed again, weak and trembling. A small and shrinking part of him wanted to ask if Eugene had seen anything, but of course he hadn't. There had been nothing to see. Lucius had been hallucinating again. There was something truly wrong with him. His stomach lurched, unsettled by the lingering terror and the chemical coating the water had left in his throat.

"I think I might be sick," he blurted, rushing for the stairs.

After a shocked moment, Eugene said, "Let me help you," but Lucius was already half out of the water, driven by panic. He did not know if he would vomit or not, but either way, he wanted to be out of that pool and away from this place. If the water brought on these inexplicable mental attacks, he wanted nothing of it. He would leave swimming and boating to other folks and live out a nice, quiet, sane life on land.

He fled, dripping and wild-eyed, toward the building, bypassing the winding pathway and dashing across the grass and through the shrubbery. He emerged from behind a large hedge and ran smack into a young woman standing in the shadows of the trees, knocking her over. She stared up at him, eyes wide and startled, as he loomed over her, dripping. The sight of her frightened face enflamed his cheeks, shame mingling with his fear. He mumbled an apology before rushing away to retrieve his clothing.

It took hours before Lucius stopped shaking. He went back to his room, curled up on the armchair, and tried in vain to forget what had happened. Fear swirled in his stomach. His hallucinations had become too powerful to ignore. If anyone found out about them, he would likely get taken to an asylum. Who knew what would happen to him then?

But perhaps that would be for the best. He might pose some danger to people, not because he was a violent person, but because in one of his fits he might accidentally hurt someone. The young woman at the pool, for instance. Every time he recalled her shocked expression, he shuddered anew. He could not risk the safety of others simply because he was afraid to face what was happening to him. But he could not explain it no matter how hard he tried. How did one get from an intense fear of the water to visions of snake-things and frog-people? The logic didn't hold.

Perhaps he had some brain-fever? Illness could cause such hallucinations, and if that were true, maybe the water had changed something in his constitution that made the symptoms of the fever more pronounced. He hadn't felt sick before, but he certainly did now. In the morning, he would find a campus physician. Although it wouldn't be wise to confess that he was seeing things, he could describe the queasiness and the lack of sleep. That would be enough to warrant a full examination. If there was something wrong with him, surely it would show up then?

The plan should have settled his nerves somewhat, but he could not seem to let the problem go. He worried at it like a dog with a bone, skipping lunch and dinner in his unwillingness to leave the safety of his rooms. If he could get away with it, he would stay there permanently until the day came when he could go home to Rudi. If the problem hadn't been resolved by then, he would confess it all.

The sun slowly sank behind the trees and the light streaming through his windows grew watery and weak. His knees ached from spending too much time in one place, leaving him with no choice but to get up and stretch his limbs. He still had no appetite, and a deep, heavy weariness had settled into his bones. A good night's sleep might set him right. At the moment, he felt tired enough that he thought he could manage to get some rest.

He took himself down the hall to the communal bath to perform his nightly ablutions, brushing his teeth and washing his face as he did every night. Although he usually considered a nighttime bath to be an essential part of his routine, he could not bring himself to fill the tub. He had never had problems in the bath, but he couldn't risk it tonight. His heart couldn't take another episode so soon after the last one. Instead, he resigned himself to a quick wipe down with a hand towel; it would suffice until he worked up the nerve to bathe again. He tried not to think about how ridiculous it was to be afraid of the tub at his age. After all, berating himself wouldn't banish his fear. It would only make him feel worse, and he felt poor enough already. The optimistic Lucius of the early morning seemed so foreign to him now. That was a real pity, but there was nothing to be done about it.

He disrobed and set to cleaning himself methodically, rinsing the cloth out in the sink. The monotonous process soothed his jangled nerves. He scrubbed his tops and bottoms, backs and fronts, washing away the residue of the day's terrors. It did not return him to normalcy, but it helped.

Something on the back of his shoulder caught his eye, an oddly placed black marking of some sort. A bruise? The only thing he could remember that might have caused such damage was the collision with the woman outside the pool, but he couldn't see how he might have damaged the back of his shoulder. In fact, he had a small bruise on the front of his bicep which could probably be attributed to that unfortunate event. Over the years, he had come to notice that even the slightest impact could cause such a mark. Sometimes he underestimated how much age had made him delicate.

But he couldn't think of what else might have caused such a thing. He'd hit nothing else through the course of the day, and his probing fingers encountered no sore spots. He twisted before the mirror, trying to get a better look at the mark. It was difficult to see against the darkness of his skin, but as he shifted and hunched and craned his neck, he began to realize that it was no bruise. It looked like ink transferred onto his skin. He could make out a perfect, round circle, its edges blurred, and two intersecting lines. For a moment, he thought it looked like one of the letters from the original manuscript pages Helen had been translating, but that was ridiculous.

It's a glyph. A mark. Those things marked you.

His stomach flipped, ignoring his determination to set those irrational fears aside. He couldn't have been marked by the things in the pool, because none of it had been real. If it had, Eugene would have been screaming and fleeing alongside him. This was no glyph. No one had snuck up on him and drawn a letter from Helen's ancient Greek manuscript on his shoulder without his knowledge. It was probably some transfer of ink off some article of clothing. The bathing costume! Of course, that must be it. There had been some laundry marking on it or a shopkeeper's tag or something that he'd missed, and the pool water had transferred it onto his skin.

Now that explanation made sense. He could still be rational after all.

Even so, he could not deny the fact that the pressure on his chest loosened ever so slightly after he scrubbed it off. He did not need any more mysteries in his life. He had his hands full enough already.

He got dressed and returned to his room, where he went immediately to bed despite the early hour. He did not remember his dreams, but the man listening beneath the tree outside his window heard him exclaim a single word in the deep hours of the night.

"R'lyeh!"

CHAPTER FIFTEEN

Abdul Alhazred lifted his eyes from the manuscript pages, leaning back in Helen Galloway's desk chair and lacing his hands over his chest. Hazy memories floated at the edge of his consciousness, the metallic scented sands of an alien world, the slithering sibilants of its inhabitants. He was fairly sure he had studied with them for a while, although he could not recall their names. His search for answers – for power – had led him to the far reaches of reality, puncturing the veil between worlds that still remained otherwise undiscovered and unrecorded. A pity, that. If he'd remembered just a bit more, he might have been able to retrace his steps that allowed him to write the *Necronomicon* in the first place and avoided all of this tedious translating.

But the process was working. Despite his impatience, he could almost feel the cracks in his memory. A week ago, he could not recall those glinting metallic sands at all. But now, reading Galloway's analysis of his poetry, he had regained the barest glimpse of the place he'd been when he'd written those pages. He had originally thought to find the gate he'd hidden so well in his verses, but Galloway might serve as an even more valuable key if his work could unlock the knowledge hidden away in Alhazred's brain. Over the centuries, he had forgotten more than just the secrets sealed in this book; he was certain of that. The certainty nagged at him sometimes, hovering just out of his reach. Back then, he had lacked the mental fortitude to comprehend some of the things he'd learned. The beings he'd seen, some so immense and impossible that his mind had locked their existence away from his conscious mind as a protective measure.

He could remember a few of them: S'ngac, the violet gas being who had taught him the secret to eternal life in the vast nothing beyond the edge of the universe. Vorvadoss, the Lord of the Universal Spaces, whose flaming eyes still haunted Alhazred's dreams. Gloon, whose statues hold untold secrets for seekers wise enough to find them and withstand their pull. But for every piece of knowledge he retained, another hovered outside the limits of his recollections. What might he be able to achieve if his mind were to be fully restored? What power would he wield then?

Galloway somehow held the key. He had been touched by the hand of some powerful being, Alhazred had no doubt about that. The city of his dreams, described in laborious detail in his poetry, was not some allegory as most of the small-minded human critics claimed. In fact, Alhazred had begun to speculate that the poet was seeing the road to R'lyeh itself. He followed by instinct the path Alhazred had been trying to rediscover for centuries.

He flipped through the manuscript pages once again as the office door opened on silent hinges. The hallway lights had been extinguished for the night, and the two figures standing in the doorway were insufficiently lit, but he would have known their outlines anywhere even if he had not bothered to learn their names. One was a pilgrim in his flock and not worth the time or effort. He likely wouldn't survive long enough to justify either. The second was the acolyte who had followed him from Italy and selected Lucius Galloway. He was beginning to think that she deserved a name. If she managed to survive the trip through the gate, he would have to choose one for her so she could be reborn anew as he had been so many years ago when he had been renamed. With the name came the purpose.

The man came barging in without an invitation, the dim light shining off his bald pate. He was florid and flushed, puffed up with an overinflated sense of his own importance. But his local connections had been important in recruiting new pilgrims to Alhazred's cause. Little did he know that those connections had saved his life more than once.

"Master," he began, but the rest of his sentence was forestalled by Alhazred's lifted finger. *Wait.*

The pilgrim froze, rivulets of sweat trickling down his brow. Alhazred could not bear to look at him without wanting to snap his annoying neck. He focused instead on the acolyte, whose lips twisted in scorn as she stared holes in the pilgrim's back. But as soon as his gaze fell upon her, her eyes snapped to his, and her expression cleared. She bowed her head, waiting for admittance. The expression of respect blunted the edges of Alhazred's annoyance.

"You may enter," he said.

The pilgrim looked down at his feet and over his shoulder, nervous without quite understanding why. He was a new recruit, chosen only for his wide social network, and his acquaintances now filled out the ranks of the Pilgrims of the Drowned City here in Cambridge. But he had not seen firsthand what Abdul Alhazred was capable of. He sensed it on some deep and primordial level, and his fear sat at odds with his natural overbearing bluster. Perhaps today would be the day that it made him snap. Alhazred found himself rather looking forward to it. He could stand to burn off some of his agitation.

The pilgrim shook himself, cleared his throat, and stepped in front of the acolyte. Her fingers twitched, but she offered no protest.

"We've been following your boy Galloway," said the pilgrim. "Just like you ordered. I've got a full dossier of his movements, but honestly, there isn't much in it. Ever since that swim lesson, he's been working nonstop."

"And how would you characterize his mental state?" asked Alhazred.

An oily grin spread across the pilgrim's face.

"Oh, he's shaken for sure. The man barely eats, and he spends most of his nights wandering the campus or working. He's been drinking so much coffee that it's coming out his pores. I think he's afraid to sleep for some reason," he said. "I wonder why."

Alhazred took the dossier, flipped through it with desultory interest, and set it aside.

"Change out the watchers this week," he said. "It is exactly as I'd theorized: his mention of the holy city in his sleep suggests that his mind has been cracked open. I want him to have the vague sensation of being watched without being able to identify the source of his nervousness. Paranoia will only heighten his susceptibility."

"I can do that," said the pilgrim.

"Good. Dismissed."

The pilgrim blinked, the pleased expression draining from his face. He was not used to being dismissed by anyone, and on the contrary, he was usually the one doing the dismissing. He opened his mouth to make some protest before a flicker of fear crossed his face again. Grumbling in anger, he turned and shoved the acolyte out of the way before stomping out of the room. Alhazred and the acolyte watched him go with identical expressions of vague dislike.

By the time she turned back to face him, however, she'd schooled her expression back to its usual blank mask. Yes, this one had some potential indeed. He wondered how her mind would hold up if faced with some universal truth. Most people broke under the pressure. Would she? It was tempting to find out, if illogical. She would be no use to him if he reduced her to a crying, gibbering mess.

"Do you have any tasks for me, master?" she asked, bowing her head and keeping her eyes safely on her feet.

"Galloway's new chapter on architectural imagery. You have read it, yes?"

"Of course, master."

"Take note." He waited until she produced a pencil and pad from a pocket. "You will enter my rooms and fetch these tomes from my library."

She jolted. Alhazred never let his followers into his rooms, and the one time he'd allowed one of the pilgrims to glance at his books, the man had run shrieking from the house and thrown himself into the river fully clothed. He'd broken his neck in the tumble, and only the quick work of a group of rowers had saved him from certain death. Now he would spend the rest of his days in hospital, confined to a wheeled chair.

Alhazred continued without pause. She would catch up or she would fall behind. But aside from the momentary surprise, she seemed to be holding up well.

"You will retrieve the *Johansen Narrative*, the *Shrewsbury Investigation*... Hm. I suppose you could fetch Le Fe, but I don't think there's much there that will be useful. I think you'll be better off with Ibn Schacabac's *Nameless Manuscript*. I strongly suggest that you take extra care with my books and double check that you have selected the correct titles, acolyte. It would be such an inconvenience if something were to happen to you."

She gulped but nodded.

"Of course, master. I will treat your library with the respect it deserves. What would you like me to do with the books once I've retrieved them?"

"Read them. Cross reference the lines Galloway has found with descriptions of locations in those books. I need details, and the knowledge has faded from my memory over the passing of centuries. You will help me piece it together."

Her cheeks had gone pale, but she remained composed, her gray eyes lifting to meet his.

"Do I need to take any mental precautions?" she asked, her voice wavering so slightly that he would have missed it had he not been alert for any signs of fear. Good. She took the challenge seriously. "Or are these titles not... challenging in that way? I will read whatever I am told to read, master, but I will be of no use to you if I snap."

"You have been paying attention, I see." He leaned back in the desk chair, taking stock of her. She bore up under the scrutiny quite well. She showed no defiance and only a healthy amount of fear. "You should have no issues with these documents. They are merely records, with the exception of the *Nameless Manuscript*. I would stick with the first few chapters. The remainder of the book will be useless for our purposes, and you may find the content… challenging."

She was silent for a long moment, fiddling with a loose thread that hung from the hem of her sleeve. Normally, he had no patience for such delays, but he was curious to see what she would ask next. He had given her an opening. What she chose to do with it would serve as a gauge for her true potential. To his immense satisfaction, she did not disappoint.

"Master, may I ask a question?" she said.

He nodded, silent and waiting, his eyes boring holes in her. Such attention usually knocked people completely off kilter, but she offered no visible reaction save a slight paling of the cheeks. Her fingers ceased their restless motion, folding themselves before her. Only the whiteness of her knuckles betrayed her tension.

Impressive.

"How do I know if a tome is beyond my current capabilities? Is there some sign or benchmark that I can use, or is it too late as soon as I open the cover, and I must take extra care?" she asked.

"You are eager to study?" he asked.

"I want the sort of success you have had. I want to see the things you have seen. To wield the power you wield."

Her eyes glittered with a sort of manic determination, and she took a half step forward as if unable to restrain herself. He knew that hunger all too well. It had driven him through space and time, always pushing himself to the limits. It had kept him going even when his memory began to fragment and cracks appeared in his psyche. He had ventured well beyond the limits of human comprehension, opening his mind to the eldritch secrets that underpin our very existence. Nothing comes without a cost, and sometimes he staggered beneath the weight of what he had lost. But the sacrifice had been worth it. He alone had endured through the centuries, surviving on stolen knowledge and pilfered time. If given the opportunity to endure even further, he would leap on it without hesitation, no matter the price.

This acolyte shared his thirst for power. He could see it in her eyes. He could make use of that, if she had the mental fortitude to live with the knowledge of the things that hovered on the edges of human perception. Perhaps it was time to test her.

"There is no way to know until you are staring the truth in the face," he said. "Only then does the ultimate cost become clear. However, there are stages of esoteric inquiry. Some tomes are more dangerous than others due to the language of their text or the secrets contained within. A smart scholar takes small steps into the abyss to allow the brain time to rewire itself."

"How?" she demanded.

"There are catalogues," he explained. "Usually built by librarians and scholars. The books you find in them tend to be easier for beginners to swallow. The truly dangerous texts are the ones no one dares to write about. Their names are only whispered in the darkness."

She swallowed convulsively, as if the mere mention of such things made her ravenous. With every passing moment, he began to wonder if he'd finally found himself an apprentice worth teaching. He'd taken on students a few times throughout his long life, but they had inevitably proven to be disappointments, their names lost to time. In frustration, he had given up the search, but now, perhaps, the Outer Gods had delivered one to him. He mouthed a voiceless prayer of praise and gratitude, his throat convulsing as it twisted around syllables not meant to be uttered in human voice.

"So the *Necronomicon* is safe then? If Galloway is reading it, I certainly should be able to," she said.

He chuckled.

"Hardly. There are abridged versions out there that are perfectly safe, but the full manuscript contains passages that many translators choose to skip. Probably because their puny brains lock down the moment they approach the pages. They would tell you they've translated the entire thing, but they would be lying. Galloway has not received the full manuscript either. I've only donated specific pages to the collection and saved the more… complex ones for myself. But even though I have limited his exposure, he is beginning to struggle. The unseen world hovers much closer for him now, and he can feel its effects but not explain them. I predict he will continue to unravel until the project is completed. We must hold him together enough to complete the work but still allow him to taste the darkness; the touch of the otherworld will prove helpful so long as we don't tip him over in the process."

"I will continue to monitor him as best I can," she promised. "Right now, he seems stable enough, but if I notice anything concerning, I'll bring it to your attention immediately."

"Very good." He paused, cocking his head to consider her. "Would you like to see one of the forbidden pages? I brought a few of them out today in order to make some comparative analysis."

"Is it–?"

She cut herself off, leaving the rest of the question unvoiced, but he could fill in the blanks easily enough. She had intended to ask if it was safe but discarded the question as irrelevant. Yes, she was a woman after his own heart indeed.

He produced the parchment from the piles on his desk without needing to look. Power emanated from the pages, calling to him. Or perhaps he was tied to the manuscript forever as its maker. The *Necronomicon* had left its stamp on him, even if he could not recollect more than a fragment of its creation.

The brittle, yellowing pages had been rolled into a neat cylinder and tied with a fresh silk ribbon. He loosened the tie, releasing the curling parchment within. It sprang open, revealing symbols that curled and writhed on the page. This would not be the cautious exposure to forbidden knowledge that he had counseled earlier. It was much more like throwing a new swimmer deep into a stormy ocean and instructing them to swim to shore. But it would answer the question of her worthiness once and for all without wasting too much of his precious time.

She looked down at the inscription, eyes wide in her pale face. Her fingers twitched as a fragment of the prayer to Yog-Sothoth worked its way into her psyche, searing itself onto the very fabric of her soul. A new knowledge of the All-in-One and One-in-All kindled in her eyes. Tears streamed down her cheeks; a drop of blood worked its way out of one nostril. Her body seized, remaining upright only through sheer force of will. She took a single step back before her hands tensed to hold herself in place with white-knuckled determination. To Alhazred's surprise, she reached toward the sheaf of papers, intending to turn the page.

For a moment, he considered letting her do it just to see what would happen. But he had already risked too much. Her loss would hamper the project. He could afford to indulge his curiosity no longer. There was no sense in squandering such a valuable mind when he could find better use for it.

He reached out and stilled her hand. It was the first time he had touched her, and she froze at the contact, staring at him with mingled shock and concern. But he simply took the pages away, rolling them up again.

Her mouth worked, but no sound came out. The first time his master had shown him a glimpse of the greater mysteries, he'd taken to his bed in a delirium afterward. With a day or two, he had recovered, but he had never been exactly the same. These were more than mere words printed on a page. They were portals through which the Ancient Ones exerted their will. It took time to come to terms with that.

She rubbed at her nose, looking down in blank shock at the red blood that streaked her hand. It seemed to hold some fascination for her. She twisted and turned it, wiggling her fingers as if she'd never seen them before. Perhaps she never had, in this light.

"You may go," he said.

Like a puppet on a string, she turned obediently, staggering toward the door and seizing on the knob as if she needed its support. But she did not make a sound nor beg for assistance. Once again, Alhazred found himself impressed. There was still a chance she might disappear on him, fleeing in the night from a threat she didn't entirely understand. But he doubted that would happen. She would be a strong apprentice indeed.

Or perhaps… He leaned back in the office chair, twiddling his fingers thoughtfully. She was in the full bloom of her youth, a prime candidate to act as the next vessel for his soul. It would be a shame to sacrifice such a mind in service to maintaining his long life, but he would welcome a few years spent in a body with a strong will and such a natural aptitude for the arcane arts.

For now, he would leave his options open, but the more he thought about taking his first breath in the acolyte's healthy body, the more the idea appealed to him.

CHAPTER SIXTEEN

Faint rays of sunlight streamed through Lucius Galloway's window. He could not see the clock from his desk, so he pulled out his pocket watch and squinted at it, trying to force his weary eyes to focus. It was coming on six o'clock in the morning, a fact which shocked him deeply. It felt as if he'd just sat down with a cup of coffee, intending to write another page before trying to get some much-needed sleep. But here he was, almost eight hours later, and it felt as if no time had passed.

He had completed four pages, the margins full of notes and inquiries he would have to address in the next draft. His pride in the solid work quashed his vague sense of unease at his loss of time and injected a burst of energy into his tired bones. Joints popped as he stood up and stretched, moving his body after what seemed like ages. A great, cracking yawn distended his jaw, and the sight of his bed was very inviting indeed. But there was only one more page to go before he finished this section on funerary rites, and he wanted to get the ideas down before they disappeared on him entirely. Another cup of coffee would set him to rights long enough to finish what he'd started, and then he would take a day off to rest and recuperate. Helen and Dao wouldn't mind; they'd both been downed by a nasty summer cold for the past couple of days. Even if they were feeling better enough to return to work today, they'd need some time to catch up.

The muscles in his back twitched as he reached for his coffee cup. He groaned. In his younger years, he'd pulled plenty of all-nighters, writing feverishly into the wee hours of the morning before he had to hare off to one job or another. In his thirties, he'd joined a Harlem literary salon, sharing his work with fellow writers as the night hours ticked by, arguing gleefully about scansion and allegory and the value of satire until dawn. Back then, he'd flourished despite the lack of sleep, his passion for the work carrying him through the worst of the exhaustion only to do it all over again. But he'd been much younger then. When had he last pulled an all-nighter? He found that he couldn't remember, and that more than anything testified to his age.

But he wasn't dead yet, and something about this work electrified him once again. He felt the same old excitement burning in his veins. He was making something important here. Something that would change the world.

He finished his stretching and let himself out into the hallway. As soon as he emerged from his rooms, his eyes met the shocked gaze of Mr Badenhorst, who peered out at him from the cracked door on the other side of the hallway. Before he could say a word, the door slammed shut. Discomfited, Lucius locked his door just in case. The back of his neck crawled, his senses screaming that he was still being watched. Before he entered the lounge down the hall, he paused to glance casually over his shoulder, but Badenhorst's door remained shut. Frowning with a discomfort he could not shake, he hurriedly refilled his cup and returned to his room, re-locking the door behind him.

Badenhorst was beginning to feel like more than a garden variety racist, but Lucius knew from experience that there was nothing to be done about it. His work would be completed in a couple of weeks; he just had to remain safe until then.

Dwelling on the situation would accomplish nothing. He sat back down at the secretary desk and took a moment to rearrange the papers scattered over its surface, tucking them into the empty cubbies on top for easy access. The newly clean surface soothed him. He picked up his pen, marshalled his thoughts, and returned to his work.

Loud voices in the hallway brought Lucius back to full alertness with a jerk. He slammed his knee on the edge of the desk, sending a sharp pain through the joint. Grimacing, he clapped a hand to the offended limb. But the discomfort quickly lessened to less stomach-curdling levels. He would have a bruise later, but there was no one to thank for that but himself.

His head hurt as well. He pinched the bridge of his nose, considering the need for more coffee. Luckily, his cup was still half full, the contents warm. He downed it swiftly, hoping that the liquid would ease the pounding behind his eyes. The bed beckoned, but he resisted its tempting pull. That final page would not write itself, and he had already wasted enough time lost in daydreams. With a jolt, he realized that he had no idea what time it was. Once again, he consulted his trusty pocket watch, swiping a speck of dust off its shiny casing.

It had been six hours.

For a moment, he thought he must have forgotten to wind the timepiece, but the second hand ticked its merry way around the face. It was impossible that he had lost time again, especially after working all night. He'd only just sat down at the desk; his coffee was still warm. He stood up, his hips protesting. His overall stiffness suggested he had been sitting for a long time, but he still didn't see how that could be. The cup hadn't yet cooled, so it couldn't have been that long! How did that make any sense?

He went to the door of the sitting room to consult the clock hanging on the wall, half expecting that it would give him another time entirely. Perhaps there was something wrong with his watch. That would be a headache he'd be happy to endure if it meant finding a satisfying answer to this mystery. But the clock only confirmed that he'd somehow managed to lose a disturbingly significant amount of time.

His heart sped up as his brain threw out all sorts of awful theories. The list started with brain tumors and only got worse from there. Of course, the most logical explanation was his lack of sleep; he'd probably passed out on the desk, sleeping so lightly that he hadn't even realized he'd rested. The thought should have settled his nerves, but it didn't.

A sheaf of papers sat nearly in the center of the desk, their surface covered in a cramped and jagged hand. For a moment, Lucius wondered if he'd managed to snag someone else's work when he'd picked up the last set of manuscript pages from Dao. But – no. That was his writing. It was usually neater than this, but he had a distinct way of forming his capital letters, adding extra flourishes that he'd never been able to shake despite the fact that the habit slowed his writing speed significantly. He could see them on the page quite clearly: the extra tail on the S, the curlicue on the L. He had written these pages, and he had no memory of it whatsoever.

There were five new pages in total. The ink on the topmost one glistened wetly, so he set it aside to dry while he read through the others. The work was undoubtedly his, even if the altered handwriting disturbed him. Aside from a few adjustments to paragraph structure and some additions of details that came to mind as he was reading, the material had turned out quite good. But he still could not reconcile the fact of its existence at all. He had sat here for hours working on these pages. At some point during the process, he must have refilled his cup. Why didn't he remember?

That line of thought took him in uncomfortable directions. Had he forgotten anything else? What else could he have done during one of these spells? This one had been harmless enough, but who was to say that he hadn't been roaming the paths of Harvard at night like some tragic embodiment of Mr Hyde himself? He pushed away the growing panic with firmness. That line of thought made no sense; he had clearly pushed his body too far and paid the price. He had been awake for how long? Thirty-five or thirty-six hours? The fact that basic math currently escaped him said something. No one could soldier on indefinitely under such circumstances. If he would only quit being so stubborn and take himself off to bed, the problem would fix itself.

Feeling somewhat ridiculous, he shucked off his suit and put on his nightshirt, pulled the curtains against the bright light streaming through the windows, and tucked himself in. Fatigue pulled at him up until the very moment his head hit the pillow, and then he was incontrovertibly awake. He attempted every trick he knew to welcome slumber, counting sheep and slowing his breath, tossing the covers off to allow the heavy air to circulate. None of them did any good whatsoever. Whether he liked it or not, he was awake now.

Perhaps sleep would come if he tired himself out physically. He'd spent all night sitting in that chair writing, followed by an entire morning of the same. He couldn't recall the last time he'd eaten anything. Had he remembered to get dinner yesterday? The days all blended together, and he couldn't be absolutely certain. He was fairly sure he'd eaten lunch. A sandwich of some sort, not notable enough to be memorable. It would be wise to get something more substantial into his belly. All of that coffee on an empty stomach couldn't be good for him. The last thing he needed was an ulcer.

He rose and dressed again in fresh clothing, trying to ignore the throbbing in his head. When he cautiously let himself back out into the hallway, no one peeked out at him or slammed doors in his face. He left the building without incident, squinting against the bright daylight. A brisk walk across the sunny campus took him to a family diner where he sat at the counter and enjoyed a nice bowl of soup, making small talk with the waiter about innocuous things like the weather. He hadn't realized how hungry he was until the food hit him. When the counterman offered pie, he couldn't find it within him to refuse.

By the time he paid his check, he was yawning, his eyes watering with fatigue. The combination of a full belly and fresh air had worked their magic. He wanted nothing more than to go back to his rooms and take a nice nap. Hopefully that would be the first step in fixing his sideways sleep schedule once and for all.

As he strolled back across campus, he found himself passing the faculty mail room, and he realized with a pang that he hadn't picked up his packages lately. In his haze, he'd lost track of time entirely. When had his last letter from Rudi been, and more importantly, had he responded to it? He must have done so, but his tired brain failed to provide any details. Dashing inside to pick it all up would only take a minute, and then at least he would know for certain. Otherwise, he might lie awake worrying about it, and that would be a step decidedly in the wrong direction.

The efficient clerk handed him a small stack of envelopes with a polite smile. Clumsy with fatigue, Lucius managed to drop his correspondence on the floor, but a nice young woman in spectacles helped him pick it all up. He murmured embarrassed apologies before making his exit, his cheeks flaming. He felt like an old man today, feeble and empty-headed, and he did not like it one bit.

There were three letters from Rudi. Perhaps one of them had crossed paths with his last missive, and Rudi was neither irate nor worried. He tried to believe in that pleasant fiction with all his might, but it was a struggle. He was of half a mind to open the letters now and settle the question once and for all, but he didn't trust in his dexterity enough to do so. He'd already dropped the lot of it once.

He began to walk, distracted by his efforts to recall what he'd put in his last letter. He'd written since the incident with the boat; he knew that for certain because he'd spent so much time agonizing over whether or not he ought to mention it. But after that, had he written at all? It had been weeks, but the time all blended together in his memory with the exception of the day he went to the pool. That, he tried not to think of at all.

The effort of piecing together his recent schedule was so engrossing that he nearly missed the turn into the quadrangle that led to his building. He made a sharp veer through the grass, trying to shake the cobwebs from his brain. His eyes snagged on a figure standing beneath the shade of a weeping willow at the corner of the building. The young woman standing there looked familiar for some reason. Their eyes locked, and she looked horrified about it.

She was blonde and pretty, dressed in a smart black suit complete with trousers. She must have been one of those New Women who insisted on it. The sight still shocked him, but why shouldn't ladies be allowed freedom of movement? All the uproar over it was ridiculous, if you asked him. Still, the wardrobe made her memorable. Where had he seen her before?

With a jolt, the dots connected. He'd knocked her over in his panicked flight from the pool on the day of his first and only swimming lesson. No wonder she was pretending not to have seen him. He'd barged into her and had then been rather a cad about it. At the very least, he owed her an apology for his rude behavior that day.

He swerved again, setting off across the grass before he could second guess his own intentions. A loud exclamation suggested that this had been a poor decision moments before someone slammed into his back with a not-insignificant amount of force. His letters went flying, and he was nearly flung to the ground himself. A hand gripped his arm with no uncertain strength, steadying him. Then, just as abruptly as it had grabbed onto him, it was gone. A sweaty young man dodged around him, tipping his hat in apology.

"So sorry, captain!" he said. "Didn't mean to barge into you, but I'm late for work again!"

With those brief words, he turned and sprinted across the courtyard. Lucius envied his quick recovery. He stretched, his back twinging from the combination of the impact and the hours spent hunched over his desk. He needed a hot soak tonight. He'd put it off long enough, and after all it was only a tub.

The breeze caught one of his letters, pushing it a few inches down the path. He gathered the spilled envelopes before they could make a break for it in earnest, ignoring the protests of his spine. He definitely needed a rest now, although the excitement of the encounter had once again blunted his fatigue. Hopefully he'd feel tired again once his head hit the pillow. He was so scattered that he kept forgetting things…

The girl! He tensed and immediately regretted it as his back yowled in protest. But there was nothing to be done about it unless he wanted to see a physician – which he didn't. Besides, the pain wasn't bad enough that it should stop him from making his apologies. He didn't want to be known as the lout who went around knocking down young ladies and then was rude about it later. After all, as his mother had always said, reputation is everything.

But the young woman had vanished in the tumult. He scanned the quad, hoping that she'd headed off toward one of the buildings, leaving him the opportunity to catch her, but she had disappeared into thin air as if by magic. Had he truly been distracted for that long, or had she run off with that young chap? Perhaps they'd both been late for work, or intended to catch a few kisses in the hallway outside on the way in.

Now he was just letting his imagination run away with him. Wasn't that the first sign of senility? He took himself home, trying to pretend he didn't feel positively ancient.

CHAPTER SEVENTEEN

After a fitful and aborted attempt at a nap, Lucius decided he might as well get some more work done. A few ideas for the big chapter on architectural structures had begun to coalesce in his mind, and he might as well get them down on paper before they flitted away entirely. Besides, the room was too bright and the sun too hot to make sleep a reality no matter how exhausted he might be. He'd dozed off for a few minutes, and the brief rest seemed to have done the trick. He felt positively refreshed and ready to give the manuscript another go.

As he slid back into his clothes, a nagging voice reminded him that he'd vowed to take the rest of the day off, but he shunted it aside. It would be one thing if he didn't want to work, but he truly did. Besides, what else did he have to do? Helen was his only true friend here, and she was incapacitated by that cold at the moment. He might sit down and read for a while, but then he'd just be staring at more words on the page. If he was going to do that, he might as well just write.

He sat back down at the desk, the leather chair creaking under his weight. His back protested again, sending twinges down his spine which he stubbornly ignored. A good night's sleep would set him back to rights. If he could only keep himself occupied for the next ten hours or so, he could head off to slumberland at the appropriate hour. Certainly, he would be able to sleep then.

He picked up his pen and pulled out a new sheet of paper. The emptiness beckoned him, demanding to be filled. He closed his eyes and tilted his head back, words from the ancient manuscript flitting through his mind, blending with lines from his own work until he could not tell which was which. The impossible outlines of cyclopean buildings rose in his mind's eye, their non-Euclidean angles defying all logic. Chunks of the manuscript created a word map of sorts, but sadly the material was incomplete. If only the missing pages had survived, he could complete the whole picture, but the scattered pieces would have to suffice.

Some small part of him whispered that he could finish that map himself, that he had walked those same streets described by some unknown long-ago scribe in his dreams, but of course that was a load of rubbish. The fact that his own poetry complemented the work in this manuscript could be nothing but a coincidence only bolstered by his preconceived notions. He pictured the city in the Berringer manuscript the same way he saw the city of his dreams because he'd been primed to. There was no strange mystery to that, but he would have to be careful to comb out any references to his own work lest they creep into these pages and take them over.

His thoughts marshaled, he put his pen to paper and began to sketch out the basic structure of the chapter. His elbow caught

on some stray paper, sending it skittering across the floor, but
he paid it no mind. The muse had grabbed him, and once again,
he lost himself in his work.

Shadows clung to the corners of the room when he came up
for air again. His neck screamed at him, the muscles tense and
aching. He stretched cramping fingers marked with divots from
gripping the pen for so long. Manuscript pages had been flung
all over the desk and onto the floor, full of that jagged, half-
familiar writing that he now recognized as the product of one
of his fugues. But the concerns about that behavior felt far away
and less important than the sense of excitement that thrilled
his veins the way it always did after he'd written something
special. Something true. The fact that he couldn't recall exactly
what that was failed to dull his sense of triumph.

He would have to put the work into order before he could
read it, and he supposed he ought to get something to eat
before the hour grew too late. Had he missed dinner again? He
gazed blindly around the room and realized with dismay that
the sun had almost fully set. Perhaps if he hurried, he might
grab something from the dining room before it closed up for
the evening. The porters were usually sympathetic to a polite
request for a sandwich made from whatever had been left over.
But he would have to leave right away to catch them.

For some reason, he didn't do that. He fully intended to get
up, stretch his aching legs, and take himself off to fetch some
well-earned victuals. But instead, he picked up the manuscript
pages from the floor. None of them had been numbered, and
he'd written almost twenty. It would take some work to order
them. The first page was obvious; he'd indented a short way
down the page, and he could remember the first sentence. At

the very least, he should be able to puzzle together the rest based on the devolution of his writing as he worked.

He flipped through the pages, murmuring to himself. That must be the second page… yes, it continued that sentence on the differences between traditional Greek architecture and the physics-defying buildings described in the verses. But he didn't see a potential third page anywhere…

The wheels on his desk chair squealed as he rolled backward to get a better look at the floor. Paper crunched beneath them, suggesting that his search had concluded before it even began. But to his dismay, he found that he hadn't rolled over the missing page at all. It was just an envelope, and he would have tossed it to the side if only the familiar handwriting hadn't caught his eye.

Rudi's letters! He'd forgotten all about them! He ought to be ashamed of himself for getting so distracted again. Hadn't he sworn that he wasn't going to repeat yesterday's pattern of overworking himself? But he hadn't kept that promise, and as a result, he'd lost another day entirely. He looked out the window and sighed. It was too late now to get that sandwich, but at least he might read his letters, and then he would take himself off to bed, and that was final.

He collected the sheaf of manuscript papers and shoved them into the secretary desk before closing the lid on them. Keeping them out of sight should help him avoid getting sucked back in again, and if he averted his eyes from the work while he stowed it away, that was no superstition at work. He simply knew himself better than to tempt fate. One glance at an interesting phrase, and he'd be a goner. He got like this when the muse struck him. It was nothing special.

There had been three letters, and he only held one. It took a bit of searching to find the other two. One had slid most of the way beneath the door to the closet. The other wedged itself into the seams between the armchair seat cushion and back. He couldn't even begin to imagine how that had happened. Had he been so engrossed in his work that he'd been flinging random papers everywhere? Although it was rather out of character, the evidence suggested so. He tried to view it as an amusing anecdote, squashing down the vague unease at this tangible proof of his unrecalled activities.

Still, his hands tremored ever so slightly as he tore open the envelope and pulled out the single sheet of paper inside. That didn't bode well. Rudi tended to be a longwinded correspondent, his letters full of aimless anecdotes and whatever nonsense happened to be currently on his mind. Early on in their relationship, he'd written Lucius a five-page letter that was almost entirely about penguins. He'd kept it with his other precious mementos in a box tucked beneath his bed, and to this day, the mere mention of a penguin made him smile.

From the looks of it, this would be no happy letter full of random musings. Rudi only got terse when he was angry, and Lucius couldn't blame him. He would have panicked if Rudi had suddenly gone silent. They'd always written steadily every time they'd been separated for more than a day or so. Although Lucius knew that he hadn't ignored this task, guilt still curdled his stomach. He had some groveling to do.

He steeled himself before opening the letter. The first word was in all capital letters, the entirety of the short message written in hurried, emotional strokes. It read:

> *Lu,*
> *WEDNESDAY! I am arriving at the train station on*
> *Wednesday, and you still haven't responded to any of my*

*letters. Have you been cocooned in layers of manuscript
like a mummy? Did you run off with a strapping young
undergraduate with nice shoulders? Have you decided to
leave it all behind and run off with the circus? I jest, but
let me be clear – you're frightening me. I fully expect you
to meet me at the station at noon, where I will hit you and
cry, and you're not allowed to chastise me for making a
public scene.*

*Please be there? I need to see with my own eyes that
you're well.*

Rudi

Lucius slumped on the armchair, his guts roiling. He could
no longer deny that his obsessive tendencies toward his work
had gotten him into a pickle. This had happened before, but
never quite as bad as this. Usually, Rudi was around to pull him
out of his distracted daze, to force him to eat and socialize and
sleep. But without those constant reminders, he'd fallen back
into those old habits, and he could admit that now. He wasn't
exactly sure how many days he'd lost. Was it his imagination,
or did his trousers fit a little loose around the hips? He'd never
been a sturdy man and didn't have extra pounds to lose.

He was fairly sure that tomorrow was Wednesday. He
definitely hadn't missed it, or Rudi would have come stomping
in here to shake him to his senses. But he found himself
dreading the reunion. He had bags under his eyes the size of
suitcases and a well-tailored suit that sagged off his frame. One
look at his unkempt appearance and Rudi would give him a
tongue lashing. The worst part about it all is that he would
be justified. Lucius knew it, but he still had no desire to be
lectured.

Maybe there was enough time for him to put a good face on things. He could clean up his messy rooms, have a full meal and a long overdue bath, get a good night's sleep, and show up at the train station tomorrow with a smile on his face. Perhaps he could claim to have caught Helen's illness. That would explain the weight loss and any lingering signs of fatigue. Was it harmful to tell a white lie and save Rudi the worry given that he'd already learned his lesson? True, he wanted to save himself the humiliation of being lectured about his mistake, but he had well and truly realized his error. In that light, he would be doing them both a favor by glossing it over, providing that he didn't repeat the behavior again, and he had no intention of that. He had never liked losing control of himself, and he had never let it get this bad. But he'd allowed his worries to overmaster him, and he would not make the same mistake again. That was enough. It would have to be.

CHAPTER EIGHTEEN

The morning before Rudi's arrival, Lucius woke up feeling delightfully refreshed. He had eaten and slept like a normal person. The lid to the secretary desk had remained closed, its contents hidden from view despite his late-night urge to open it and have just a little scribble to help settle him before bed. But he'd recognized that potential pitfall before it had ensnared him, and he'd taken himself out for a stroll before getting into an uneventful bath for the first time in longer than he'd care to admit. The warm water had washed away his lingering fears along with the accumulated grime, and he'd taken himself off for a night of well-earned sleep.

It was ridiculous to take pride in successfully performing basic tasks, but that fact did little to dull his satisfaction. As he finished readying himself for the day, he examined his reflection in the small looking glass hung over the dresser. He looked like a man who had been through a rough patch but was well on the way to recovery, and if he was a little vague about the exact nature of said rough patch, there was no harm in that.

After breakfast, he took out his manuscript pages and sat down in the armchair to try and order them properly, keeping a close eye on the clock. Rudi would likely be hungry when he arrived, so he could hold off on lunch, but he wanted to give himself plenty of time to stroll to the train station. The fresh air would do him good, and he was determined not to hole himself up in his rooms working and then waste money on a taxi.

He worked up until he needed to leave and then set the papers aside with what he considered a somewhat ridiculous sense of accomplishment. But perhaps he'd had the wake-up call he'd needed and could avoid such foolish behavior in the future. The more he thought of how he'd conducted himself, the more embarrassed he became. His choices would have been justifiable for a young undergraduate on his own for the first time, but he was tromping toward old age. He ought to have known better. He would take his licks and not speak a word about it to anyone.

His mind made up, he put his hat on and opened the door to reveal Helen standing out in the hallway, her fist raised mid-knock. They both jolted, wearing twin expressions of surprise.

"Helen!" Lucius exclaimed once he'd recovered. "You nearly gave me a fit!"

"I could say the same to you, you rascal. Have you been sitting in there all this time, waiting for me to show up?"

"I've certainly missed you," he said smoothly. He pulled the door shut behind him, locked it, and then tested the knob twice. One couldn't be too careful. "I trust you're feeling better?"

"The cough still comes and goes, but I'm much improved. For a while there, you would have thought that I spoke with the voice of Satan himself. I've never heard a more awful croak in my life."

She was a bit pale and fatigued looking, but as far as he could tell, she spoke the truth. It was a relief. He'd hate it if something happened to her.

"I'm glad," he said and meant it. "And Dao?"

"The poor girl had it worse than me, so she's still on the mend. Hopefully she'll be back tomorrow, but I wouldn't hold my breath. I thought I'd check in and see how the work was going. Have you gotten anything done, or did you take advantage of my absence and spend the week lollygagging about?" she asked with a teasing smirk.

He gestured for her to precede him down the hallway, and the two of them ambled away. The tense sensation in his chest eased as they began to descend the staircase.

"I've churned out pages faster than ever, to be honest. I really hit my stride this week."

"Probably much easier when you're not interrupted every five minutes by my impertinent questions, eh?"

"I wouldn't call them all impertinent," he mock protested.

"I may have been sick, but I can still kick you in the shins, my lad."

The two of them grinned at each other as they emerged out into the quad. Bright light warmed Lucius' face, making his eyes water. He tilted his head, blocking the sun with the brim of his hat. Helen had no such protection; she tended to go around without a hat a shocking amount of time, leaving her with no choice but to tent a hand over her eyes and squint. He shifted, blocking the light with the bulk of his body.

"Thank you," she said. "Maybe I won't kick you after all."

"I'm much obliged, ma'am."

"So when can I see your newest work of literary genius? And where are you off to? I suppose I should have asked that before, but I got distracted by your smart mouth."

He chuckled.

"I'd be happy to drop off the new pages later, but at the moment I'm on the way to the train station. Rudi is coming into town for a visit," he explained.

"He is?" She smiled, her delight apparent. "Well then, I'll just have to tag along and say hello. I promise I won't be a permanent hanger-on. I'll just stay long enough to make you wish I'd leave, and then I'll disappear in a puff of magic like Houdini."

"I'm sure he'll be delighted to see you," he said, gallantly offering his arm.

She rolled her eyes a little but slipped her hand into the crook of his elbow.

"Such a gentleman," she said. "I bet you're quite popular with the ladies."

He cleared his throat. Such inquiries always made him uncomfortable, especially given that they were often followed by offers to set him up with eligible young ladies, all of whom were most certainly wonderful creatures. He hated having to disappoint them.

"I am less successful on that account than you might think, Helen," he said. "I'm not all that interested in marriage. Never have been."

"No, I don't suppose you would be," she replied inexplicably.

He didn't know how to reply to that, and any inquiry would only prolong this difficult line of conversation. Had she guessed the truth of his relationship with Rudi? There was no way to inquire without potentially causing trouble. Instead, he made an observation about a shop across the street, and with a sharp glance in his direction, Helen allowed him to steer the conversation elsewhere.

• • •

The train chugged into the station, belching out immense billows of black smoke. Lucius could barely see through the haze for a moment, but the stiff breeze soon cleared it all away to reveal the giant, gleaming machine as it rolled to a stop. He found that he disliked the sight of the train much less than he had when they'd first arrived in town. Perhaps that was because he didn't need to board it, or perhaps it was because he'd discovered boats to be much more disagreeable. In that light, he'd welcome a nice long train ride, although he would have to be careful about saying that in front of Rudi, or he'd return home to plans for an entire year's worth of excruciating travel. After this project was complete, he fully intended to enjoy the comforts of home for a long, long time before setting out again.

The train lurched and hissed before settling into place. Almost immediately, the doors slid open with a haste that suggested the occupants were desperate to make their escape. Lucius could understand the feeling very well. A harried conductor stepped out first, studiously ignoring the small crowd clustered on the platform as he took his station next to the door. People began to trickle out in twos and threes, rushing toward friends and family with open arms or clutching briefcases as they set off on whatever business had brought them here.

Rudi made his appearance on the stairs, striking a dramatic pose which the conductor studiously ignored. He looked good, from the tips of his shiny wingtips to the smoothly sculpted arc of his jet black hair. Lucius' heart skipped in his chest as he took in the view. He'd always scoffed at romance tales that said such things, but that was in the dark years before Rudi. Every time they reunited, he was struck anew by the depth of his feelings. No matter what was going on in their lives, they had each other, and that would be enough.

At this point, Rudi popped Lucius' lovesick bubble by marching over and smacking him lightly on the side of the head. The shorter man glared up at his partner with all the fierceness of a scrappy little dog facing down a giant breed.

"You had better have a good excuse for scaring the bejeezus out of me, Lucius James Galloway, or I swear I'll punch you right in the face," he declared.

He was even angrier than Lucius had expected. He'd invoked the full name, which meant business. The last thing Lucius wanted was to make a scene right out on the platform, and in front of Helen no less. She was chuckling now, thinking it all a joke, and it would be better for all involved if it stayed that way.

"I'm sorry, Ru," said Lucius, his voice low and soothing. "I caught a summer bug, and it laid me up for longer than I'd hoped. I didn't make it to the postmaster's to pick up your letters until a couple days ago. By that time, it was too late to write you a response. I didn't mean to frighten you."

Rudi's eyes flickered over to Helen and then back again, searching his face. The hot anger began to leak out of his shoulders, replaced with a weary relief.

"A summer cold?" he asked. "Couldn't you have dashed off a note at least? I was dreaming up all kinds of trouble. I've barely slept."

Belatedly, Lucius realized that Helen could upend this entire little white lie of his by speaking the truth. Or she might look down on him for trying to pull the wool over Rudi's eyes. He should have explained it to her in advance or better yet, thought to send her away. But he hadn't been thinking at all, and now the whole house of cards might just come tumbling down around him. Rudi would be hurt. He wouldn't understand that Lucius was just trying to spare them all the drama.

But Helen said, "It wasn't your average summer cold. Dao and I both got it too, and I lost Lord knows how many days from it. I went to bed on Monday, and next thing I knew, it was Friday. At least I think it was; I'm honestly not quite sure what day it is now, but don't tell anyone that or they'll think I'm going senile."

The last vestiges of temper vanished from Rudi's expression, and he relaxed into a smile.

"Well, I'm glad you're both okay," he said. "I wish I had known, because I could have come earlier to play nursemaid. I make a mean chicken soup, you know."

"It's true," Lucius confirmed. "And now I'm hungry. Shall we head to the diner? Their soup isn't as good as his, but it'll have to do."

"Yes, please. I'm famished. You're joining us, aren't you, Helen?" said Rudi, offering his arm.

"I don't mind if I do," she responded.

The three of them began to stroll in that direction, taking their time. Lucius tugged Rudi's suitcase out of his free hand, intending to carry it for a while. After all, he wouldn't have come all the way here if Lucius had only written him back. As happy as he was to be reunited for a short while, his guilt still persisted. He would not absolve himself so easily.

The suitcase was heavier than he'd expected, even for Rudi. It felt as if he'd packed for any and everything. If Lucius told him at this very moment that they were going to a fancy dress masquerade, Rudi would somehow make it work with whatever he'd stuffed into that case.

Rudi smiled at Lucius over his shoulder.

"Are you sure you want to take that?" he asked. "It's not light."

"Funny, I was just thinking to myself that you'd probably brought the contents of our entire apartment just to be safe.

How long do you plan on staying, exactly? Forever?" teased Lucius.

"Well, only a couple of nights, but then I'm on to Arkham, so…" Rudi shrugged. "I don't think I went that far overboard."

"On to Arkham?" asked Lucius blankly. "What do you mean?"

"You don't think I was going to go all the way back to my sister's, did you? I like train travel and all, but that's just *ridicule*."

"Well… I just…" Lucius trailed off, at a loss for words.

Rudi stopped on the street outside the diner, bringing Helen to a gentle halt and swinging her around to face him. He wore an amused expression, and he patted Helen's hand as it rested in the crook of his elbow.

"Helen?" asked Rudi. "What are the chances that Lucius didn't actually read all those letters I sent?"

Her eyebrows went up.

"I don't see why he'd do such a thing," she admitted. "I don't know him as well as you do, but he's no fool."

"Mon beau?" asked Rudi, his eyes twinkling.

The fond nickname combined with the impish expression on Rudi's face nearly outdid Lucius entirely. He wanted very much to wrap Rudi in a hug and apologize for everything, even if he wasn't necessarily ready to admit exactly what he needed to atone for. But he couldn't do that, not out here in public. So he clung to the suitcase and hung his head.

"I'm sorry," he said. "I opened the last one first, and I knew I'd upset you, and my place was a mess, and I panicked more than I might like to admit. I think the other two are stuffed unopened in my desk with about a week's worth of work."

At least that was the truth. That had to count for something, didn't it?

Rudi threw back his head and laughed, and at that moment, all was right with the world. Lucius' lingering worries and concerns loosened their hold on his shoulders, and he lifted his head. Helen looked between the two of them, clucking her tongue.

"I can't take you two anywhere," she said fondly. "Let's go eat before we make more of a scene."

CHAPTER NINETEEN

Lazy coils of smoke curled up from a raucous table of gentlemen in the corner of the patio, but otherwise Rudi and Lucius had the place to themselves for a nice romantic dinner. They'd dined on pasta and fresh baked bread – or rather, Rudi had. Lucius couldn't seem to drum up much of an appetite, but the conversation more than made up for that. They'd caught up fully now, although perhaps Lucius had glossed over the events with the boat and the swimming lesson in an effort to avoid ruining the evening. Now they sat back in their chairs, arms folded over stomachs, enjoying the starry night.

Rudi's sister Caroline was a maid who worked in a ritzy part of town, and she always had atrocious stories about the antics of her employers, and Rudi faithfully passed every single one of them on to everyone he talked to.

"So, by this time, Caro is pretty sure the lady of the house is skating around on her husband, but she keeps her head down because according to her it's none of her beeswax. But when the old man comes home early from his business trip, she knows the whole thing's about to blow," said Rudi, gesticulating as he told the latest and greatest of his sister's tales. "So she takes the wash out to hang it up, figuring that'll give her the best vantage point to see what's what, and wouldn't you know it, that cat runs off, wrapped up in one of the clean sheets. She doesn't even know how he got there. She was going to offer him a pair of drawers, but he didn't stop long enough to listen…"

The rustling of the ornamental bushes behind Rudi caught Lucius' eye, distracting him from the story still in progress. His tired mind turned them into something monstrous. They wavered and waved. At any moment, they would spit out something unthinkable, something with tentacles instead of bony limbs and too many eyes, something that would slither and slide its way toward them, mouth gaping with hunger. He closed his eyes as if that would help shut out the imagined threat. It wasn't real. None of it was real, and he knew that, so why couldn't he stop?

Rudi stared at him expectantly. He was supposed to say something, but he hadn't been listening. He fumbled for some innocuous comment to thrust into the silence.

"You got to give it to the fellow; it sounds like he's got stamina," he said.

Rudi snorted. "Something like that. Caro was worried someone was going to give her grief about the missing sheet, but I suggested a quiet word to the lady of the house, and that seemed to work quite nicely. The dame didn't want word to get out, after all."

The movement of the bushes intensified. Lucius felt his pulse thundering in his temples, his heart fluttering in his chest as his anxiety intensified. The wind had picked up; the movement of those plants made perfect sense. He hated how irrational he was being; perhaps he needed some kind of calming tonic? Those advertisements had always struck him as faff and nonsense – after all, he'd written a few himself back in the day, crafting empty promises of things like "increased nerve power," whatever that was – but at this point, he was willing to try anything.

Rudi stroked his mustache thoughtfully as he gave Lucius a thorough once-over. Something had tipped him off, even though Lucius knew he'd kept his fears off his face. He'd had years of practice in hiding his true feelings for safety's sake, and he was damned good at it. But Rudi knew him too well. Their connection went down to the bone, and most of the time, Lucius was thankful for it.

But this was not most of the time.

"What's going on, Lu?" he asked.

Lucius tore his eyes away from the bushes and resisted the urge to wipe his sweaty hands on his trousers. He took a deep breath and let it out. There was nothing to fear. He was just sleep-deprived, and most people would be jumpy under such conditions. If he could understand it, he could deal with it. He'd always been that way.

"Like I said, I've been sick," responded Lucius. "I'm not at my best yet."

"Right," answered Rudi, in a tone that made his lack of belief quite clear.

"But enough about me. Did I hear you correctly that you're headed to Arkham after this? I've been wanting to ask, but I was too embarrassed over…" Lucius waved a hand, unwilling to say the words out loud. "… you know."

"Not reading those letters that I slaved and slaved over?" asked Rudi, his concern forgotten in the wake of his amusement. "Honestly, I expect you to be able to quote them verbatim next time I see you. I want a full dramatic reading."

"I feel like such a cad."

"Good. You should spoil me rotten to make up for it, too." Rudi grinned to soften the blow. "I may also be persuaded to accept some groveling."

"I'll make note of that."

The easy banter eased some of the weight that tugged at Lucius' heart. No matter what had happened or what would come, they would always have each other. Over the years, they'd weathered arguments and danger and prejudice. They'd flourished despite it all. That counted for something. He wanted to say, "I love you," but of course such a thing couldn't be done in public. But their eyes met, and the message passed wordlessly between them anyway.

After the moment had passed, Rudi said, "When I leave here, I'll head to Arkham. I thought I'd stay there until you're ready to head home. Then I'll come back through town and snag you up on the way."

"Are you taking a room by yourself?"

"No, there's no need to worry about that. I've written to Harvey, and *he* actually reads my letters, unlike *some* people I know. He has a spare room I can stay in. From what I understand, he's quite busy at the moment with some historical provenance something-something. I honestly didn't follow half of it, but he's assured me that if he's called out of town, I'm welcome to stay on at the house."

"And have you told him about … ?" Lucius trailed off, uncertain.

"Yes. I'm still dreaming every night," responded Rudi, his humor fading. "I had to tell him. Harvey's a solid chap. He took it all in stride."

Lucius felt his shoulders release as the relief took hold. There would be someone to keep Rudi safe in his absence. Now if he could only set himself to rights, everything would be fine. He glanced back at the bushes, still rustling in the wind. At that moment, he could not understand what had made him so frightened. They were just bushes.

He looked down at the mountain of noodles still clustered on his plate. Perhaps he could eat after all. He took an experimental bite. The food had long grown cold, but the sauce nipped at him, awakening his hunger. Finally! He twirled his fork, readying another bite.

"What do you plan to do while you're there?" he asked.

"I've got some meetings," said Rudi, and then he clamped his mouth shut.

That made Lucius go on high alert. A quiet Rudi was a guilty Rudi. He arched a brow, waiting. Silence was Rudi's ultimate weakness and always had been. It took less than a minute before it broke him.

"Spiritualists," said Rudi, the word exploding out of him as if by force. "I'm going to meet with a spiritualist group. They're experts on dreams, Lu. I met a fellow at Caro's who had a cousin who used to have terrible nightmares every night, and she went to see this Arkham group, and they cured her. No more dreams. *Accompli.*"

"How did they do it?" Lucius asked, trying to keep the skepticism out of his voice. He owed it to Rudi to hear him out at the very least. After all, he could understand the desperation to do something. Anything.

"Hypnosis, maybe? I'm not entirely sure. August wasn't clear on it himself, and his cousin died in some freak accident of some sort that I didn't want to pry into too deeply, so we couldn't ask her for more information. But she was dream-free up until then. Imagine how lovely that would be. No more nighttime fistfights. We'd just go to bed at night and wake up in the morning, refreshed, like normal people. I'm just glad you're here so you can actually catch up a little. I hate the fact that I keep you up on the regular."

"You know I don't mind."

"Well, I mind enough for the both of us."

"Look, that's all well and good, but you're–"

Lucius cut himself off before he could finish the sentence. He wanted nothing more than to shake some sense into Rudi. These so-called spiritualists would squeeze him for every dime he'd ever made, feeding off his desperation and fear and filling him with empty promises, and then they'd scatter to the four corners, never to be heard from again. Rudi ought to know better than to believe in such superstitious claptrap. In fact, he probably did, deep down. All he needed was for someone to shake some sense into him.

All of this was true, but something stopped Lucius from being that person. While he considered it a moral duty to protect his loved ones from exploitation, he hated the fact that he would have to kill Rudi's hope in order to do so. There had to be a better way. He was a wordsmith deep down to his core; he ought to be able to strike the impeccable balance between the two.

So he cut himself off abruptly and stared into the distance, lost in thought. He had no idea how long it lasted, but when he came back to himself, he found Rudi staring at him with a bemused expression.

"Welcome back," said Rudi.

Lucius flushed. "Sorry. I was thinking."

"Oh, I know." Rudi gestured with a cigarette he hadn't been smoking before. But somewhere in those lost minutes, he'd finished half of it. "You get fidgety when you're brainstorming. For a minute there, I thought you were going to make an origami bird out of that napkin."

Lucius looked down at the wrinkled fabric clutched in his hands and sheepishly set it back on his lap.

"Yes, well…" he said. "Sorry again. That was rude."

"I'm used to it." Rudi smiled to take the sting out of the comment. "But please go on? I think you were about to chastise me for my idiocy."

The comment was delivered in light tones, but they'd been together for too long for Lucius not to see the true hurt that hid underneath. Rudi's smile strained at the edges, and he clutched at his own napkin like he might undertake the bird folding endeavor himself.

"I was," said Lucius, "but that would be wrong of me. I know how much this wears on you. You're desperate for it to end and afraid of what will happen if it doesn't. I'd be lying if I said the same worries didn't keep me up at night."

Rudi nodded, his lips clamped shut. The twinkling lights strung across the patio glinted on the wetness in his eyes, but the tears didn't spill over. Instead, he hurriedly wiped them away.

"Yes, well," he said. "Thank you for that. And I'll have you know that you've entirely brainwashed me. The whole time I was making the arrangements, I tried my best to channel your skepticism. I tried my utmost to come up with every argument you'd make and then asked about it myself."

Lucius didn't know why this admission touched him so much, but he chuckled to cover it up.

"I'd best be careful, or you'll make me obsolete!" he said.

"*Impossible.* You could never be replaced so easily."

Their eyes met, and Lucius found himself unable to breathe. Funny how after all these years, sometimes it still felt like the early days when they'd been so consumed by each other. It hit him every once in a while out of nowhere, and he wouldn't have traded it for anything.

"Ahem." He cleared his throat, and the moment passed. The two of them relaxed imperceptibly, exchanging secret smiles. "So, what did you find out?"

"I'm not to pay a cent until after the treatment is complete and I'm fully satisfied that I'm cured. All donations are entirely voluntary."

"Huh. I wonder how they stay afloat. Is this just some hobbyist group?"

"Not from the sounds of it. They're researchers. They'll be recording all of our sessions and using whatever they learn for their scientific papers. I've run it by Harvey, and he's skeptical about the validity of the research, but even he admits that it does seem legit."

The presence of another skeptic made Lucius feel a bit better about the situation. Perhaps he would reach out to Harvey himself. Not that he didn't trust Rudi, but to settle his own nerves. It sounded like Rudi had been exercising uncharacteristic caution, but he'd always been overprotective, and the circumstances were tailor-made to stimulate those instincts.

"That's somewhat reassuring," he forced himself to say. "Although I'd get it all in writing before you begin, if you haven't done so already."

Rudi beamed.

"One step ahead of you. I insisted on a contract, and they're aware that I won't do a single session before it's signed. Harvey knows a fellow there in Arkham who will review it for me. Barnaby, I think his name was? Anyway, he'll make sure that all the I's are dotted and the T's crossed. I've also asked to be referred to by a pseudonym to avoid spreading my personal business around anymore than I need to. It sounds like most of their patients or clients or whatever we are do that. I'm thinking Valentino. Don't you think I have a movie star vibe?"

Rudi struck a dramatic pose, and Lucius couldn't help but laugh.

"It sounds like you have it all under control," he said.

"From you, that's high praise. Thank you."

"I don't know why you're thanking me. I nearly jumped down your throat. I feel like a lout."

"Rightly so. Sometimes I think I rely on you too much. You're so responsible that I just let you handle things as a default. I tell myself that I'm carrying my weight, and I do in some ways. When you're deep into one of your writing jags, I make sure you eat and stand up every so often. But you're my safety net. I know I can pitch a fit whenever something bothers me, because you'll be right there to interject some rational thought. That's not fair to either of us. I'm working on it, and that's all anybody can ask, isn't it?"

"Quite so," said Lucius, his voice gruff.

Rudi stubbed out the forgotten cigarette and looked down at the neglected pasta congealing on Lucius' plate.

"You're really not hungry?" he asked.

"Afraid not. My schedule's gotten abysmal in your absence, if we're being honest about responsibility."

Rudi flashed a grin. "How about we get a paper pail and take it back to the hotel? My room is big enough for us both, you know. Perhaps you'll be hungry later."

"That sounds like a swell plan to me," replied Lucius, holding up his finger for the check.

CHAPTER TWENTY

Lucius walked impossibly winding streets that launched themselves into the air, twisting and turning in a manner that defied gravity and confused the eye. He found himself hanging upside down from his feet, strolling along without a care in the world. Inexplicably, he wore his nightshirt, but the hem didn't flip over his head. It stayed at his knees, undulating in the gentle breeze. He touched it in wonder, looking around to see if anyone else was there to take in this extraordinary sight, but he saw no one.

For a short while, he amused himself by walking back and forth through the loop-de-loops, trying to sense any difference between being upside-down and right-side-up, but both felt the same. The world around him made just as much sense when he hung by his feet as it did when he stood on the ground. He sensed no vertigo nor unease in either position.

A rhythmic throbbing drew his attention to the left, where a group of buildings clustered in the distance. It was as if some great band played there, drawing all and sundry to a fete for the ages. Lucius had never been much for parties, and there wasn't a single other being in sight, but he found himself heading in that direction regardless, strolling down the impossible road toward the distant metropolis. He might never get there, but the journey would be of interest all on its own.

The sound grew, slow and steady, until it pulsed at his temples and pulled at his feet. He could feel it in his chest. The ground beneath him began to vibrate. He clapped his hands to his ears by instinct, but there was no need. Despite the overwhelming volume, his ears didn't hurt at all. Overcome with wonder, he lowered his arms, wishing once again for some companion that he could look to and say, "Can you believe this? It's amazing!"

Familiar words untwisted themselves from the tumult. It was impossible for him to make them out this far away, but he knew this rhythm like he knew the backs of his own hands. It pulsed through his body like lifeblood.

"Ph'nglui mglw'nafh Cthulhu R'lyeh wgah'nagl fhtagn."

Every inexplicable syllable was accompanied by a great thump that rattled the world. His teeth shook in their sockets. Rock creaked and cracked, great fissures opening in the desolate landscape. The impossible road shimmied in the air. He watched all of this with a sense of detached amusement. Somehow, he knew that he of all people had nothing to fear here. He belonged in this place. That was why the song didn't hurt him. It recognized him as a part of itself.

The stone nudged at his feet, driving him forward. He stumbled, taken aback, but quickly regained his balance. He was walking now. No, he was *running*. The road rippled beneath him, propelling him toward the distant city, and he scrambled to keep up, but there was no need for that either. He sprinted with ease as a great wave of earth pushed him from behind. How good it felt! A laugh of pure delight escaped his lips. He hadn't run like this since he was a boy, eager to get home from school as fast as possible to join his friends in a game of marbles or kick the can. Faster, faster. The world blurred. The wind rushed by him with a roar so great that it blocked out the thunderous chant for a moment.

It all stopped. The ground eased its forward push, his feet stopped on a dime. He didn't so much as stumble. No sweat clung to his brow. His breath was as even as if he'd just taken a casual stroll. The city swallowed all of his discomforts and fatigue, leaving him in a state of perfect homeostasis. He had never in his entire life felt so good.

He stood in an enormous circular chamber that opened to the eerie orange tint of the sky. Although he could not see beyond the walls, he had the sense of great height. Perhaps it was the thinness of the air or that mysterious link he had with his surroundings, but he knew he stood atop some massive structure. The building vibrated with the noise he'd heard out on the plain, the constant rhythm of the continued chant sinking into the very stone. Dust and debris rained off the smooth twists of the walls, off arches that looked as if they'd been sculpted by hand out of liquid stone. Tube-like crenellations emerged from the structure at random intervals, and the flickering light glinted off the occasional movement from somewhere deep inside. It was impossible for him to hear over the thunderous noise, but somehow, he could make out the faint mews of something inexplicable being birthed within those cylindrical depths.

Tiered floors ran around the exterior of the structure. He stood at the very edge of the topmost floor, alone and undisturbed. The inner circles descended into the darkness, each one deeper than the last, and all of them full to the brim with chanting, undulating creatures. They had squat, beetle-like bodies covered in mottled, green-tinged skin. Their faces were a mass of tentacles that emerged from where their mouths should have been. Perhaps there was some maw hidden deep within the slithering masses, but he could not see them.

The sight of the tentacles hit Lucius with a pang that jolted him out of his delighted reverie. Panic overtook him, along with the faint memory of tentacles in the deep and the burn of lungs desperate for air. Something had happened to him; something bad. But it hovered outside the edges of his memory, the detritus of another time and place he no longer needed. He reached for it desperately, but the continued thump of the chant soon pulled him back under again. It didn't matter. Soon enough, nothing would.

He shifted closer to the edge of the floor, looking down at the teeming, chanting masses. They were packed in so tightly that every few seconds, one of the creatures would plummet off the edge onto the floor below. Somehow, the upper floors never seemed to grow any less crowded despite this constant depletion. It was as if the denizens multiplied to overfill any available space.

Lucius looked toward the center, down and down into the deep where the light could not penetrate. He could not make anything out, although he presumed there would be more floors descending into eternity. Although the more he thought about it, that couldn't be right. Every circle has its center. At some point, those endless floors had to wind up somewhere. He squinted, trying to get a glimpse of whatever it might be.

Something enormous in the depths shifted, as if a being the size of a building rolled over in its sleep, searching for comfort.

The chant grew faster, tugging at the edges of his consciousness and threatening to sweep him away entirely. He didn't even know what it meant, but the words dragged at him until he joined in, the unfamiliar sounds flowing off his tongue as if he'd been born to speak the language.

"Ph'nglui mglw'nafh Cthulhu R'lyeh wgah'nagl fhtagn. Ph'nglui mglw'nafh Cthulhu R'lyeh wgah'nagl fhtagn," he chanted.

The very walls answered him. He had called their name. R'lyeh. The place he had been dreaming of all this time. It was called R'lyeh, and it was his home. He had never felt so relieved. Here was a place where he would be welcomed, just as he was. There would be no bigotry. No sideways glances. No unfair treatment. No need to hide who he was or who he loved. He could just be. He shouted his joy, the words coming faster now, raising his arms up in celebration. The walls shook as if they shared in his delight at coming home.

"Lucius!"

Someone grabbed him, and he flailed, alone in the sudden darkness. The cathedral-like room, all of the chanters, and the slumberer in the depths all disappeared, to be replaced by nothing but inky black. He did not know where he was, and he flapped in desperate fear, his heart thundering in his chest.

"Lucius, stop!"

This time, the voice was familiar. Hands came out of the darkness, wrapping around his shoulders. He would have recognized their gentle touch anywhere. Rudi hugged him close, springs creaking as he settled on the unfamiliar bed. That was right. He had stayed the night in Rudi's hotel room. He tried to get a hold of himself, tried to tell himself that everything was fine and he was safe, but he did not feel anything like it. All of the certainties of the dreamworld fractured in the waking one. He had not been safe in the dream city, not at all.

He had been trapped.

The knowledge chilled him to the bone. To his immense shame, he clung to Rudi, and he wept.

A while later, Rudi brought him a glass of water. The lamps had been turned on, bathing the room in a warm glow. Lucius took the glass with shaking hands, slopping a little over the edges. Rudi watched him, keen eyes not missing a thing.

"You had best tell me what's going on," he said.

Lucius took a drink and found that he was intensely thirsty. He drained the whole thing before setting the glass down on the bedside table. Now he was feeling more like himself.

"There," he said. "That's better."

"Well?" Rudi persisted.

"It was just a dream. I'm sorry I woke you."

"Just a dream? You were shouting."

"Was I?"

A chill ran through Lucius' entire body. Normal dreams faded as soon as he woke, but he could still hear that chant. It echoed through his mind in an incessant loop he couldn't seem to shake. Had he spoken it aloud? He didn't want to ask, and honestly, he was fairly certain he already knew the answer. The dream hovered right at the edge of his consciousness, threatening to overtake him if he so much as relaxed his guard. If he closed his eyes, he would be shunted once again into that incomprehensible chamber. It reminded him of some eldritch cathedral, its worshippers kneeling at the feet of an unknowable, implacable cosmic god.

Some instinctive part of him worried that if he found himself there again, he would never get out.

Rudi was frowning. Had he spoken, and Lucius had missed it? Lucius couldn't bear talking about it, not now. Saying it aloud would make it more real than he wanted it to be.

"I'm sorry," he said. "Can we talk about this tomorrow? We both need our sleep."

After a moment's hesitation, Rudi nodded. "Sure. Okay."

The two of them settled into their twin beds, separated by only a few feet. Lucius lay on his back, hands folded across his chest. He did not dare close his eyes, not until the last vestiges of the dream faded away. He would not allow himself to contemplate the possibility that this might never come to pass. Dreams faded. This one would do so too, with enough time.

The faint light that filtered through the hotel curtains glittered off Rudi's eyes. He had turned onto his side to stare at Lucius, exhibiting no signs of fatigue. It would be better not to engage. Lucius had no desire to spend the entire night arguing over dreams and phantoms. To do so would give them more power than they already had, and they already held too much sway over them both. So he feigned a yawn and rolled over as if settling down for good. As soon as he could do so without attracting attention, he opened his eyes again. He had never felt less tired, but he would stay here until Rudi fell asleep. There was no sense in the both of them spending a restless night.

But Rudi's breathing never changed. Over the years, he'd developed a slight snore which Lucius had to admit was rather adorable. It had never gotten loud enough to disrupt his rest; it was more like the purr of a satisfied cat, and its rhythmic rumble had soothed many a restless night over the years. He could have used it tonight, but it never came. The two of them sat awake until the light of the rising sun seeped through the curtains to creep over the ceiling. Lucius dozed on and off, but when true morning came, he could not honestly say whether or not he'd slept.

And neither of them said a word.

The next two days were uncharacteristically strained. Over the years, Lucius and Rudi had had their arguments, especially in the early days when they were trying to navigate the realities of developing a relationship that had to be kept secret. It had taken time and patience for them to feel secure with each other regardless of what the world threw at them. But they'd settled nicely. Sure, they had their tiffs, but that was to be expected in a relationship between a hot-headed extrovert and a logic-minded introvert. Their little arguments had always passed quickly because neither of them was willing to prioritize winning over each other. As a result, they rarely had to endure long stretches in which they weren't in perfect sync. Not until now.

Rudi very badly wanted to discuss what he considered their dreaming problems. He was convinced that there was some connection between their respective nighttime struggles. Lucius didn't know what he thought was happening, but he wanted to believe that stress and suggestiveness played a part. Once he got back home, the dreams would ease. He wanted to believe that. No – he *had* to. Sure, he'd been dreaming before this, but those nighttime jaunts had been harmless. If anything, they'd fueled his writing. He'd only become nervous about them because of Rudi's sleepwalking problems.

Now he was stuck in a difficult situation where he had no desire to discuss the phenomenon, whereas the dreams were all

Rudi wanted to talk about. After an entire day of being pelted with questions he had no desire to answer, he had ended up snapping.

"Dreams aren't contagious," he said. "Everyone knows that."

After that, Rudi had fallen into a sullen silence which had lasted through dinner. Thankfully, he was supposed to leave early the next day. Lucius wanted nothing more than to get back to work. He would put himself on a firm schedule and arrange periodic meetings with Helen to make sure he stuck to it. When he left the room for dinner, he would lock up the secretary desk with his work inside and not unlock it until the morning. Now that he'd had some time to think it over, he knew his overworking tendencies must have contributed to his problems – the paranoia, the hallucinations, the interchangeable bouts of insomnia and vivid dreams. So he would finish this project up as soon as he possibly could, snatch Rudi from the clutches of the spiritualists, and take them both home where they would live happily ever after, or at least until Rudi started to ask him to go on a boating trip again.

After a tense breakfast, they set out for the train station. Lucius carried Rudi's heavy bag for him, but the two spoke barely a word as they walked side by side. The day was overcast, with low clouds that threatened rain. Lucius pointed that out, and Rudi agreed that it might indeed sprinkle, and that was the end of their conversation.

The last thing Lucius wanted was to leave things on such a sour note between them. He wanted to protect and cherish Rudi, not make him miserable. But he didn't know how to do that without opening the door to more frustrating conversation. It irked him that he didn't know what to say despite a lifetime of making a living off his ability with words.

They stopped on the platform, the silence stretching out between them. Lucius wracked his brain for the right words to express his feelings but came up empty. As he stared thoughtfully off into the distance, a figure standing far at the end of the platform caught his attention. Bright blonde hair glinted in the watery sunlight, and with a pang, he realized that he knew this young woman. What were the chances that he'd keep seeing her over and over again after knocking into her at the pool? The more anxious part of his brain whispered that it might not be a coincidence, but he would not give into that. At the very least, he had learned the error of his ways.

"What are you looking at?" asked Rudi, frowning.

Lucius pointed down the platform, but the young woman wasn't there, and a quick scan of the people on the platform failed to turn her up.

"I thought I saw someone I know," he said. "Well, not exactly. I knocked the poor girl off her feet once when I wasn't paying attention, and I never did get to apologize. I keep seeing her around campus, but I've never had the opportunity to talk to her."

A flicker of a smile crossed Rudi's face.

"She's probably soft on you. You're quite a dashing figure, you know. If she heard you sing, she'd be a goner," he said.

"Don't be ridiculous. And listen, Rudi, I–"

But Lucius never got to finish his sentence. Rudi jerked in surprise, his eyes locked somewhere in the distance behind Lucius. He smiled again, more fully this time. It was the first time he'd done so in far too long.

"Helen!" exclaimed Rudi. "Over here!"

Lucius turned to see Helen, beaming as she pushed her way through the growing crowd. She edged past a rather astonished looking gentleman, sweating in a business suit and overcoat, and came to a stop before them with an impish salute.

"Hallelujah. I made it in time and in one piece! Some yahoos around these parts don't know how to drive. I'll have you know that I nearly died three times on my way here," she replied. "Hope you don't mind that I came to see you off."

"Not in the least." Rudi took her by the shoulders, leaning down to press his lips to her wrinkled cheek. "I would have come by the office, but I didn't want to disturb genius at work."

She snorted. "Flatterer."

Lucius let his mind wander as they bantered. He couldn't resist the urge to scan the platform for another glimpse of blonde hair. Where had the young lady gone? No train had arrived during those short moments between her appearance and disappearance. If she'd headed for the exit, she would have been visible. The only explanation he could think of was that she'd hidden behind the pillars at the far end of the platform, but he'd kicked his paranoia and would no longer indulge those kinds of thoughts. Perhaps she was waiting for a young man and didn't want to be spotted. Perhaps she'd wanted to get out of the sun. There were a million potential explanations.

Still, it was quite a coincidence that he kept spotting her. She must work in a nearby department on campus, and they kept similar hours. It wasn't completely out of the question.

He shook off the lingering disquiet left by that train of thought only to realize that both Rudi and Helen were staring at him. Had he missed some inquiry? His cheeks flushed.

"I'm sorry," he said. "I was woolgathering. Again. I'm a cad."

"You are," Rudi agreed, but there was no heat in it. "Do you see what I mean, Helen?"

"I suppose I do," she allowed.

"Why do I get the feeling that I've missed something?" asked Lucius, looking from one innocent expression to the other.

"Because you have, my boy," said Helen, grinning. "But don't fuss yourself about it. It wasn't all bad."

"I feel very ganged up on," Lucius complained.

To be honest, he rather liked it. Much better to be teased by a grinning Rudi than to sit in uncomfortable silence. Besides, he could admit that he deserved it. He'd been very distractible lately, and no amount of denial would change that.

The train chugged into the station, with a billow of smoke and a hiss of the enormous engine. He'd spent so much time at the station that the sight no longer held the interest it once had. If anything, this trip had almost made him blasé at the thought of train travel. That was growth, wasn't it?

"They're singing my song," said Rudi. "Guess I'd better shove off."

The two men stared at each other for a long moment. With a pang, Lucius realized he'd forgotten to bestow a goodbye kiss in the hotel room where it was safe to do so. Now he'd lost his chance, and he could have punched himself for it. Rudi's pinched mouth suggested that he shared the same regret, but they could neither speak nor act upon it. All they could do was meet each other's gaze, back in perfect concert again.

"Have a safe trip," said Lucius.

"You take care of yourself, you idiot," replied Rudi roughly.

They clasped arms. Rudi's hands clenched Lucius' forearms with a desperate strength, clearly not wanting to let go. Lucius felt the same, but there was no time. Rudi was right; he was an idiot. The argument had been ridiculous, and he wanted nothing more than to take it all back so they could have enjoyed their short time together. He tried with all his might to communicate that with his eyes. Rudi's softened, picking up on his wordless plea, and the world was right again. They released each other in unison, rubbing at eyes that were suddenly a bit damp.

"Damned smoke," Rudi muttered before raising his voice again. "Helen, it's been a pleasure. You'll have to come up to the city sometime. Let us show you all the places worth seeing."

"I'd be delighted."

"Right. Cheerio, then! I'll see you in a few weeks, Lu. Do write this time, would you?"

"I promise to bury you in letters," replied Lucius. "Be safe."

Rudi forced a smile, tipped his hat, and made his way onto the train. Lucius stood there with his heart in his throat until the great locomotive made its way out of the station once again. To her credit, Helen waited patiently with him, not saying so much as a peep. But as the train pulled out, she laced her hand through his elbow.

"Shall we?" she asked.

"Pardon?" asked Lucius, startled. "Oh, yes, of course. Where are you headed? I'll walk you."

"Back to my office, I think. If you have the time, we can review that last set of pages. I think we're rather close to the finish line, but I'd feel much better about that statement if you looked over everything with me. I've stared at that blasted manuscript for so long the words have started to blur."

"I've been there. When I was writing *The Drowned City*, I remember one night when I swear to the heavens that the words danced off the page and circled my head. Of course, I'd been writing for about three days straight at the time and was probably half batty from lack of rest."

"You don't say…"

Helen pursed her lips thoughtfully but made no other comment as they strolled out onto the street. Lucius had a sneaking suspicion that he knew what she was thinking. He guided her past a street vendor hawking newspapers and great big baskets of fruit before deciding that it would be best to face the question head on. He didn't want her to worry about his ability to finish their work. Not now, when they were so close to completion.

"What did Rudi tell you?" he asked.

She flinched, momentary guilt flickering over her face.

"Not sure what you mean, champ," she said.

"My dear, it's a good thing you don't gamble." Lucius chuckled. "You'd be awful at it."

She snorted. "Well, you can't blame the man for being concerned. You've had your head in the clouds for the past few weeks now. Even I can see it, and when it comes to people, I have the insight of a myopic goose. I had a fiancé once make that very same observation. I told him that was the stupidest saying I'd ever heard and he should shove that myopic goose up his – *ahem*. Well, you know."

"Yes, I believe I do. But don't you change the subject on me. What did he say?"

"He wants me to keep an eye on you. Make sure you're sleeping and eating. The man's no idiot; he didn't buy your story about being sick, and before you ask, yes, I know you lied, and no, I didn't say a word."

"I wouldn't have blamed you if you did, Helen. I had no intention of putting you in the middle. I just didn't want to make a big thing out of it. He worries, you know. Case in point."

She waved a hand.

"You don't have to justify yourself to me. People are odd ducks, and who knows why anyone does anything?" she said. "And trust me, I don't want drama any more than you do. Just don't die on me. If you do that, I'll find some way to resurrect you just so I can scold you for it."

"I wasn't planning on dying, Helen. But I'm going to endeavor to be a bit better about maintaining a reasonable schedule, or I really will get ill and the whole thing will come to a screeching halt. Perhaps we could have the occasional lunch or dinner together? I don't want to make you sick of my face, but having somewhere to be will help tear me away from my desk, and as the past few weeks have shown, I need that motivation without Rudi to keep me on the straight and narrow. Otherwise, I'll turn into a hermit who only emerges on alternate Tuesdays with my fingertips stained black with ink, blinking owlishly at the light and telling anyone who will listen that it's too bright out."

She snickered. "Honestly, I'm so sick of the tumult at the boarding house that I'll come for supper every night if you'll have me. The sewers have been touch and go, and Mrs Pitts has the habit of boiling everything into mush. It's the one thing here that reminds me of my mam in a bad way. That woman's cooking could have degreased an engine."

Lucius laughed. "Then please, by all means, come to dinner tonight. We can even go down to the dining hall like proper academics."

"Why, are you asking me on a date, Mr Galloway?" she asked, fluttering her eyelashes. Lucius gaped, horror suffusing his limbs, up until the moment when she roared with laughter. "I do wish I owned one of those cameras, because your face is just priceless. I'm kidding, you idiot. That's what friends do, you know."

He cleared his throat, blushing to the tips of his ears.

"Right," he said. "I'm going to change the subject now, lest I die from embarrassment and you and Rudi hold a séance to yell at me."

They paused at a street corner to wait for the light to change, and she beamed up at him.

"Well, look at you," she said. "Maybe you're not such an idiot after all."

CHAPTER TWENTY-ONE

The next week turned out to be much more pleasant than the preceding ones. Lucius stuck to his word. He worked normal hours, cutting off at lunch for a meal and a brief stroll around campus with Helen. Then they worked until early evening and broke off for dinner. They finished two chapters in a matter of days. Dao had recruited a friend to help her catch up with all the typing but still hadn't quite gotten her feet under her after her long illness. Lucius hadn't even seen her, although the pages kept arriving with her neat notes in the margins.

His sleep pattern had somewhat improved. No one in the building had complained that he'd been shouting in the wee hours of the morning, anyway, and he hadn't woken up anyplace he didn't remember falling asleep. Although he still dreamed every night, he'd come to terms with that. Dreaming was a normal experience, and he'd only become so worked up about it because of Rudi's problems. He considered his nighttime excursions a signal that his subconscious was working overtime. Besides, he was safe in the city of his dreams. Was it such a bad thing to long for a place he could truly belong? He didn't think so.

Things were good. But all good things come to an end.

Late morning on the Thursday, he arrived at Helen's office, sweaty and bothered. She took one look at his expression and groaned.

"Oh no," she said. "No luck?"

He blinked at her for a moment, failing to connect the dots in her statement, but then the words all slid into place. He'd spent the past couple of hours in the library, trying to figure out where a missing page of the manuscript had ended up. They'd spent the better part of the evening before tearing apart Helen's office and Lucius' desk in a desperate effort to find the paper in question, but to no avail. It would be a significant problem – not to mention an even more significant expense – if they were to lose track of such a priceless object.

"No, that's all taken care of. It ended up getting filed in completely the wrong chapter and stuck to the back of another page. I had a word with the library assistant about it, and we reviewed the whole thing together. It looks like someone got some sort of glue on it." He took in her expression of horror and held up a hand, urging calm. "It's clear that it wasn't us, and the library fellow is quite confident that their people will be able to restore the pages to their original state. We've also discussed alternative methods of storage. I was finally able to get the man to admit that some cardboard and string weren't acceptable even as a stopgap measure for a document of such historical value."

Helen rolled her eyes.

"Honestly," she said, "it's a wonder anything gets done without us."

"Right."

"You look rattled, though. I take it he was rude about it?"

"No, no, it's not that." Lucius took a deep breath. "Would you give me your objective opinion about something? I know I'm being irrational, but I can't seem to set it aside."

"How very mysterious." She took off her reading glasses and leaned back in her chair, folding her hands. "Please, sit down. I am all ears."

He took a seat in the extra chair, the leather creaking. His knees knocked against the outside of the desk again, but there was nothing to be done about that so he simply ignored it. Instead, he took a deep breath and began his tale.

"After that swim lesson, I was… panicked. I can't remember if I told you about it or not, but I ran from the pool in what I can only describe as a hysterical fit, and I knocked over some poor young woman."

"I heard about it from Eugene," replied Helen. "I know I said it already, but I'm so sorry about that. I thought I was helping."

"I know you did, and it was worth a try. I just have to come to terms with the fact that swimming isn't for me. It's quite fine. But ever since then, I keep seeing that same girl. She's outside my building when I leave for lunch or in the mail room when I stop by to pick up my letters. I saw her at the train station. I've run into her when I walk late at night. Yesterday, she was in the dining hall at the same time we were, and she spent the entire time staring at us."

"Is that why you got up so fast? I thought you'd seen a mouse, and you didn't want to say so out loud and cause a panic."

He allowed himself a small smile, but now that he had finally found someone to confide in, he could admit how shaken he was by all of it. It felt good to be honest with himself about that sort of thing. Denial had only gotten him into trouble in the past, but he wasn't yet too old to learn better. Besides, Helen had listened to his troubles before without judgement. Frankly, he wasn't sure why he hadn't talked to her before. His damn fool reluctance to rely on anyone hadn't been doing him any favors.

"At first, I just wanted to apologize to her. I wasn't in my right mind when we collided, and I'm honestly not sure if I said anything or not. I'm a bit mortified about it. But every time I try to approach her, she vanishes into thin air. I know there's a rational explanation. The campus isn't particularly busy right now, so it's logical that I keep seeing the same people over and over again. She stands out because we have that humiliating history, and she wears trousers to boot. She's probably just living her life, or perhaps she's avoiding me because she thinks I'm rude as well as clumsy and she's afraid I'll barge into her again. That all makes perfect sense, but at some point, is it rational to feel like someone is following you? Because I see her more than I think is reasonable. She dogged my steps on the way here, and I ended up stepping off the path into the bushes to lie in wait for her like some common criminal. I feel like I may have lost my perspective."

Helen sat in silence for a long moment, her brow arched, as she thought it over.

"I don't suppose I could blame you for a little healthy suspicion," she said. "It's not like you're jumping to conclusions. Have you considered the possibility that she might be… infatuated? I've known a few young women who were… shall we say overeager in their pursuit of a man they'd set their cap on?"

"At my age?" He chuckled. "The young lady in question is objectively attractive. I don't see that she'd need to stoop so low."

"It's still a possibility." Helen leaned back, tenting her hands over her chest as she contemplated. "Maybe she's a ghost."

"Not you, too! I thought we'd agreed no spiritualism. If you go back on your word, I'll hit you over the head with this dictionary." Lucius hefted a sizable volume and stared her down with an expression of mock sternness. "Don't think I won't."

"And I'd thank you for it, trust me. All teasing aside, I suppose I understand why the situation would nag at you. It's the kind of thing that you can't stop noticing once it's caught your attention."

"Exactly. Every time I walk outside, I find myself looking for her. That sort of obsession can't be healthy."

"Are you sure it's the same young lady every time? You've been distracted and more than a little sleep deprived. If you're just seeing this person in passing and at a distance, you might be misidentifying her. I intend no insult to your vision, by the by; I honestly think I'd have the same problem. I'm distracted enough that I barely recognize Dao when I see her across the quad, and she stands out."

"No insult taken, but I highly doubt it. The trousers, remember? She stands out also."

Helen jerked upright, her eyes widening.

"Wait a tick," she said. "Does your mysterious young woman have blonde hair? Rather on the long side?"

"She does! Do you know her after all?"

"The only New Woman I know who's on campus with any regularity is Ari Quinn. I'm not going to lie; she's a nasty piece of work, that one." Helen frowned, her shoulders tense.

Strangely, Lucius found himself more reassured than anything about this new information. At the very least, his instincts hadn't steered him wrong. He hadn't been hallucinating. These seemed like very small things to be celebrating, but now that he knew she was a shady figure of some sort, he didn't have to worry that he was backsliding.

"Do you think she might be up to something nefarious? I'm trying to determine whether or not I ought to be concerned," he said. "Is she the sort of person to hide 'round a corner with a cosh or something?"

"You've been reading too many adventure books," she teased. "No, it's not that at all. Quinn is a history lecturer, and not a very good one in my opinion. I've heard so many stories about her; female academics gossip like undergraduates if you pour a little sherry down their throats, and almost everyone I know has a story about Quinn. I'm honestly not sure which one to tell you. We could be here all day."

With every passing moment, Lucius felt the tension drain from his shoulders. This was exactly the sort of drama that rolled right off him like water off a duck's back. In fact, he found it rather comforting.

"I'm intrigued," he said. "But I suppose we have work to do. I take it to mean that I have nothing to worry about, though?"

"No," she said slowly. "I'm not sure it's that at all."

He arched an inquiring brow. Helen considered for a long moment, stroking her chin in thought, before replying.

"If you look her up, you'll see that she's very successful. She's a specialist in ancient civilizations. Already building a strong reputation for academic writing, that sort of thing. The problem is that I'm fairly sure it's all rubbish. At the posting I had last summer, I had an excellent young research assistant. So good, in fact, that I tried to get her to join our project team here, but she was already committed elsewhere."

"Sounds like a talented young lady."

"Indeed. She roomed with Quinn when they were students. When it came time to turn in their final Master's projects, she discovered that Quinn had copied her work and passed it off as her own. She'd even gone to meet with some of the professors over the past few weeks to establish her ownership of it. My assistant could find no way to prove what had happened, so she ended up pleading illness and starting the entire thing over in order to avoid any accusation of academic misconduct. Quinn had done such a good job of covering her tracks that she worried she'd be the one thrown out if she made a stink about it."

"That's positively awful!"

"The rumor mill says this isn't the only time she's done it, but no one has ever been able to pin her down for it. So we endure her until the moment when someone finally manages to expose her for a fraud. When it happens, I expect there will be quite a party."

"It sounds like I had best steer away, then. Although I do wonder if she's up to something fishy again. When I ran into her that first time, she was lurking about in the trees. She does that quite a bit, in fact. Could she be spying on someone, do you think? Like… us?"

"I wouldn't put it past her in general, but I think we ought to be relatively safe. I'll put the word out at Radcliffe, although I expect the other ladies in residence already know she's been sniffing around. Just keep your distance. She wouldn't be able to pass off our work as her own; she couldn't read ancient Greek to save her life, and she doesn't have access to our manuscript anyway. But I wouldn't chance it. Whatever she's up to, I wouldn't put it past her to pin the whole thing on anyone who let their guard down. It's best to keep a wide berth, if you know what I mean."

"Yes, certainly. I'm glad I brought it up, because I was starting to feel a bit foolish for fretting over it. I'll take extra care with our pages just to be safe. I feel quite bad for your research assistant, though. It seems unfair that this Miss Quinn is already a lecturer while her former roommate is still toiling away in an assistant position."

"Well, they do say that crime doesn't pay, but if this is any indication, they're aggravatingly wrong about it." Helen pursed her lips. "But that's enough of that nasty business. I'll sit here chattering like an old biddy all day long if I don't exercise some restraint. Shall we get back to it?"

Lucius snickered. "Definitely. Let's run through those corrections on chapter seven, and then we can take a break for lunch. I promise to leave the biddy chatter until then."

"You, my friend, are a scoundrel, and I mean that as a compliment."

He doffed an imaginary hat to her.

"I aim to please," he said.

CHAPTER TWENTY-TWO

At the beginning of the second week of August, Lucius wrote the final sentence of his conclusion. The chapter on stellar imagery had given him some difficulty – there were repeated references to the stars scattered throughout the manuscript as well as multiple illustrations thereof, each with subtle differences. It had taken quite a time to unravel them all, but he felt confident that he'd found the thread of meaning between them, using the poetical scansion and word choice to support the connections he made between the scattered lines to create a full and compelling argument for the ancient Greek understanding of the heavens and their use in navigation. He'd even uncovered some discrepancies between the stars as recorded in this manuscript and ancient Greek star maps found in Widener Library.

He'd have to make sure to keep these pages out of the hands of that Miss Quinn. Although he was no historian, he felt confident in saying that he and Helen had created something special here. Maybe even something worth stealing. He had no desire to chance it, and when he'd seen her around campus, he'd made sure to steer clear. He had no patience for plagiarists.

He compiled the pages into a neat pile and tucked them into a folder, beaming all the while. It had been quite a summer, full of unexpected highs and lows. Now he could look back and honestly say that he was proud. This book might open new doors for him to engage in more scholarly work, and after some rest, he just might accept an offer if the right one were to come to him. Although he would insist on bringing Rudi next time. He needed that strong anchor to keep him steady.

Speaking of Rudi, Lucius needed to stop by the mail room to see if he'd received a response to his latest letter. They'd been writing faithfully ever since that uncertain visit, and he didn't want any silence on his part to reignite the tension between them. Perhaps he could swing by on the way to Helen's office to drop off the final pages, and then they could plan a nice celebratory dinner to commemorate the completion of the first draft. Of course, they still had a number of revisions and proofreading to do, and then there was the reference list, which he'd tried his best to keep up to date with. But he wasn't too confident about his recordkeeping during those weeks where he'd barely slept a wink, and he really ought to go through the whole thing to be certain he hadn't missed something.

But this milestone still deserved celebration. He had spent a summer at Harvard, walking the same halls as so many great minds before him, and he had co-written a scholarly work he could be proud of. If only his mother could see him now. He paused for a moment to soak in the accomplishment, and then he put on his hat.

When he stepped out the front door of his building, he saw Ari Quinn standing beneath the trees again. Although she was on the other end of the quad, their eyes met and held for a long moment. Then Lucius turned away firmly. He'd never had his words stolen before, and he intended to keep it that way.

He took his time strolling to the mail room, where he found to his delight that Rudi had written him a note. The envelope felt thinner than usual. But even a short letter was better than none at all, so long as it didn't indicate anger. As much as he wanted to tear into it immediately, he had things to do, and sometimes those letters contained personal sentiments best not shared in public. They had always been careful about what they put in writing, but sometimes even the cleverest of masks slips off. It was better not to risk it. So he tucked the letter into his pocket and continued on his way, intending to read it in the privacy of his rooms later.

When he arrived at the office, he found Helen grumbling amidst a mess of papers. Manuscript pages had been piled on every available surface including the floor. Lucius could see no rhyme or reason to any of it, and he hovered by the open door, too afraid to step inside lest he disturbed the piles and upset… whatever she was trying to do here. He honestly didn't know.

"Should I come back later?" he asked, rapping on the door.

Helen jerked, her spectacles sliding down her nose, and dropped a single sheet of paper. She let out a very unladylike oath, snatched it back up again, and placed it with finality onto the pile sitting directly in front of her.

"Sorry," she said. "Dao's made some intelligent observations about the order of the chapters, and the sections within the chapters, and… well, as you can see, I've torn the whole thing apart and am trying to piece it back together again like Frankenstein's monster. All we need is a bit of lightning, and it'll be all fine and dandy."

He chuckled, still hovering at the door.

"I'd offer to climb up on the roof with a rod, but I don't see any signs of a storm. Do you need a hand in a more helpful capacity?" he inquired.

"I'd take you up on it, but I'm honestly not sure that I can explain what's where with anything approaching coherence. At this point, I'm not quite sure myself. I've woven this tangled web, so it's up to me to find my way out." She pushed her glasses back up on her nose and peered at him. "Is it lunchtime? Do you have more pages for me? If so, bring them back later, I beg of you. I'm up to my nose already!"

"Well," he said, drawling with mock nonchalance, "if you insist, I suppose I could bring you the final pages later."

"That would be very – wait a tick. Did you say 'final'? Is it done?" she demanded, standing up.

He held up the folder and nodded, beaming. Although finishing a manuscript wasn't the flashiest of accomplishments, it still represented the culmination of hours upon hours of hard work. Non-writers never quite seemed to understand how much of a relief it was to get to the end, even if that finish line only led to round upon round of editorial changes. Even Rudi had been inclined to shrug off the accomplishment of completing a first draft, although he more than made up for it with his extravagant release day celebrations.

This time, things were different. Not only was Helen a fellow writer, but they shared this accomplishment. Spread across this room at this very moment were thousands upon thousands of words written by the two of them in tandem, creating what would eventually become a compelling story about life and poetry in ancient Greece. They had accomplished something that most people only dreamed of.

She whooped aloud, throwing her hands up and dancing a little jig right there at her desk. From somewhere down the hall, an exasperated woman yelled, "Would you keep it down? Some of us are trying to work!" Helen made a rude gesture toward the door but quieted anyway, picking her way across the floor to grab Lucius by the shoulders and kiss him soundly on the cheek.

"We did it, Galloway," she said, grinning. "And they said a project of this magnitude couldn't be finished in a summer. But we showed them, didn't we?"

"They did?" asked Lucius, brows raised. "Who exactly said that?"

"Oh, everyone. I'm sure you thought the same thing yourself at one point or another. Writing a full historical and poetical analysis in three months? To even contemplate such a thing is pure insanity," she said, waving a hand. "But enough of that. Come on, hand them over!"

He offered the folder to Helen. She snatched it from him and immediately opened it, scanning the pages with excitement.

"Did you end up writing about those star maps?" she asked. "The printer was asking for an estimated number of figures, and I wasn't sure whether they'd be necessary to include or not."

"Actually, that's the best part. You'll see my explication starting on page five. Those maps have extra celestial bodies that don't appear on other maps. I theorize that they've included the planets, although there's a possibility that these

are stars that no longer exist. It's an interesting conundrum –
but I'll let you read it rather than rattling off the whole thing
here."

Helen grinned at him, her cheeks flushed with excitement.

"I cannot wait to dig in, my boy. But first, an accomplishment
of this magnitude requires celebration! I've planned for this.
Step inside so I can close the door, and we'll have a bit of a
tipple."

"It isn't even luncheon yet," protested Lucius, closing
the door before someone could see the illicit hooch. Helen
planted him in a bare spot in the corner before picking her
way over to the desk and producing a flask from one of the
drawers.

"I don't have glasses, but you can go first," she said. "A good
liquor will kill off just about anything anyway."

"I suppose I shouldn't be surprised that you've got a stash in
your desk," he teased.

"I'm Irish. If you cut me, I bleed whiskey." She thrust the
flask at him. "I know it's early, but it's tradition. Just a sip for
luck."

He saw no harm in it, so he took a nip. The liquor burned its
way down his throat, setting his stomach aflame. He coughed
with the intensity of it. Had liquor always been this heady? It
had been a long time since he'd had a good quality drink, so
he must have lost his tolerance for the stuff. He returned the
flask, and she tilted it toward him before drinking and stowing
it away again.

"See, that wasn't so tough, was it?" She clapped her hands,
rubbing them together with relish. "Now what? I think we
should take the rest of the day off and plan our acceptance
speeches for the awards they'll undoubtedly heap on us."

Lucius thought back to his acceptance speech for the Howard Award and wrinkled his nose.

"That isn't the motivation you think it is," he said. "I hate speeches."

"Well, then, I'll plan to speak for the both of us! I have things to say, you know. But I'm serious about playing hooky for the day. We've earned it."

"I was thinking the same, although I'm not sure what we could do. I'll have you know that if you even mention the word 'boat,' I will run willy-nilly through these piles and scatter them all. Don't think I won't," he teased.

She held her hands up in mock alarm.

"No, no, I promise not to say that word I'm not permitted to say!" She paused, her grin fading as she thought. "I know! I'll take you to the Sussex for lunch. It's my favorite restaurant. Do you like seafood?"

"You know I do. I have the fish almost every night at dinner."

"Oh, right. I guess you do." She grinned. "Well then, let's go there. We'll need to borrow Dao's car, but that's alright."

"If you say so," he said uncertainly.

"I've got to put this mess to rights before we go. With my luck, one of the cleaning ladies will come in and rearrange all my piles, and then where will we be? Would you mind fetching the keys and walking to the boarding house to pick up the car? I should be ready to go by the time you get back."

He hesitated.

"You do know how to drive, don't you?" she asked.

"I'm not that ancient, Helen. Yes, I can drive."

"I wasn't making a jab at your age, Galloway. I've had a few friends from the Big Apple, and quite a few of them couldn't drive."

"Ah. Well, I can. It's just … are you sure she won't mind?"

"I'm sure. Invite her to come along if you like. I'm not sure she has the time, but maybe we can bring her back some grub."

"Can do."

After a brief search, Lucius finally located the tiny room where Dao and her friend sat, clattering away on their typewriters. As Helen had suggested, she didn't even blink at the request to borrow the car, and she politely refused his offer to accompany them, pointing out the piles of pages still left to type. When Lucius mentioned Helen's reorganization efforts, both young women groaned aloud.

"Are you sure there isn't anything I can do for you?" he asked. "Could we bring you something?"

"Where are you going again?" asked Dao.

"I think Helen called it the Sussex. The seafood joint?"

Dao brightened.

"In that case, yes, please!" she said. "I will gladly trade you the use of my jalopy for crab legs with loads of butter. Oh, a girl could just die thinking about it."

"I'm so hungry," echoed her friend.

"Crab legs for two, then?" he asked.

"Please," she said, standing up on her tiptoes to kiss him on the cheek. "You're a good egg, Mr Galloway."

"Yes, well…" He trailed off, flushing. "It's only polite."

"Let me fetch the keys from my bag," she murmured.

It took a moment to locate them in the crowded depths of her purse, but finally she held out a set of jingling keys.

"Here you go," she said. "It should be the only one parked at the boarding house. Mrs Pitts also has a car, but she has bridge today."

244   *Arkham Horror – The Drowned City*

"Thank you kindly," he said, taking the keys with a mixture of nerves and excitement. Under normal circumstances, he never would have agreed to such a thing. But they deserved a celebration, and he couldn't let his worries derail it.

"You betcha," replied Dao.

It took some time to walk all the way across the Radcliffe campus to the boarding house, but Lucius didn't mind. The weather was lovely, the breeze refreshing, and it felt as if a weight had been lifted from his shoulders. There was nothing like the high of finishing a project. It felt like his feet barely touched the ground, and he couldn't keep from whistling as he strolled along.

The boarding house was quiet, its curtains closed, as he approached. A lone car sat in the driveway. Although Dao had called it a jalopy, it looked brand new. He found himself a little nervous as he approached it. Black men had been arrested – or worse – for much less. He glanced up at the building again, wishing that some of the folks he'd met at the mahjong party so long ago were sitting out on the porch, ready to confirm that he was indeed a friend. At that moment, he would have even welcomed Marco's appearance. One of the curtains on the third floor twitched as he stared up at it, and for a moment he thought maybe his wishes had been answered, but there was no sight of anyone. It must have just been the breeze through the cracked window.

He looked up and down the street, heart thumping with agitation, but it was just as still as the boarding house. No blaring radios or housewives out hanging up the laundry. It was as if the entire neighborhood had just up and left for the day. Odd, but he wasn't about to complain if it meant he could retrieve the car without being disturbed.

He did just that. The automobile started up with a purr, and he eased it out into the road without incident. It was a pleasure to drive, and once he got over his nervousness, he began to enjoy himself immensely. The motor responded to his slightest touch with a power he'd never felt before, and he wondered how fast it would go on the open road. Although he wouldn't dream of driving it out of town without permission, he did end up taking the long way back onto campus, telling himself that Helen might need the extra time to sort through that mess on the floor. He would refill the gasoline before returning the car, so he needn't feel guilty about the waste.

He circled around the campus from the north, intending to turn back onto the main street in just a few blocks. As he slowed in anticipation of the turn, the car jolted hard. Something behind him crunched. He was thrown forward, his head slamming into the glass and the steering wheel jabbing into his gut. A horn blared, and for one dizzy moment, he wondered what had happened. Then his head cleared, and with a sinking in his stomach, he realized he'd been hit. There would be police. Dao would be so upset. His heart hammered with adrenaline, mortification, and a growing fear.

He twisted around in his seat to get a better look at what had hit him. It was a large truck, the broken grate on the front letting out wisps of smoke. As he watched, it began to back up, metal squealing against metal. Then it shoved forward a second time, ramming into him with what could have only been deliberation.

It made no sense, but Lucius had learned that in a dangerous situation, it was always better to move first and reason later. He pressed the accelerator pedal to the floor, speeding away. After a second's hesitation, the truck zoomed up close behind him, its horn blaring. He could see the outlines of two occupants in the front seat, but the glare prohibited him from making out any details. Were they convinced that he was at fault for the accident? Were they racists? It didn't really matter anyway. Clearly, they weren't in the mood to talk. The truck swung wildly back and forth behind him, honking incessantly. Pedestrians stopped to gawk as he sped past, the car rattling, with the smoking truck hot on his heels.

He drove without quite knowing where he intended to go, only that he had to get away. He had to get somewhere safe. In Brooklyn, he would have known exactly where that was – which neighborhoods would welcome and protect him, and where he should avoid. But here? He just wasn't sure, so he drove blindly and hoped against hope. Perhaps he should return to the Harvard campus. The security guards might help him if they knew he was a visiting scholar. Even if that position didn't hold the water he hoped, they wouldn't sit by while some enraged driver bashed into things, would they? It wouldn't exactly fit with the image of genteel academia the university tried to project, so it seemed like a gamble worth making.

He was coming up on an intersection, and the truck loomed behind him, scraping against the back of the damaged car. If he slowed down to make the turn, he couldn't be certain that the other driver would brake. He could end up getting pushed down the street – or worse, crushed beneath the larger vehicle. So he gritted his teeth, clenched the wheel a bit tighter in his sweaty hands, and turned at the absolute last minute, the wheels screeching on the pavement. He risked a glance over his shoulder as the truck receded from view, whooping in relief and triumph.

His heart beat so hard that he could feel it in his throat. Sweat dripped down his forehead. He turned back forward just in time to see a car stopped at a red light in front of him, the bumper looming too close for comfort. He slammed on the brakes, panic choking him. The car screeched to a stop just in time.

But there was no time to celebrate the near miss. The truck came barreling down the street behind him, billows of smoke emerging from beneath the crumpled hood. The driver must have turned around. Their persistence chilled him to the bone. The only way to escape this would be to flee. Otherwise, the driver of this truck might resort to the sort of unspeakable violence that left someone dead in the end.

This realization frightened him, but it also threw things into perspective. He needed to get away. Nothing else mattered at this moment.

The car in front of him still sat at the stop sign, the driver chatting with a young lady who leaned coquettishly into the passenger window, although at the moment she'd stopped her flirting to gape at the oncoming truck. Lucius swerved around the stopped car and ran the intersection, slamming the accelerator down to the floor. Now where was he? He'd gotten turned around in all the chaos, and he didn't recognize these houses at all. As he whipped by the street signs, he squinted at them in the hopes of seeing something he recognized, but to no avail.

The truck surged toward him once again, and he braced himself for another impact, hoping that the car would hold on long enough to get him away safely. From the sounds of it, some broken bit of metal hung off the back, clattering against the pavement. But the truck swerved at the last minute, pulling up alongside him to race down the street.

"Leave me alone!" he yelled through the open side window. "Or you'll kill someone with this nonsense!"

There was no answer. He dared a glance in the direction of the truck. It was much taller than Dao's little car, but he could see the head of the person who sat in the passenger seat. Unfortunately, they wore a black hood which had been pulled up to obscure their face. He glanced back and forth between the road and the person in the truck in the hopes that he'd be able to describe at least one of his assailants later when he spoke to the police.

"Hey!" he yelled to get their attention. "I'm talking to you!"

The passenger turned toward him. The sun should have shone right on their face, illuminating their features. Bright rays streaked the side of the truck, lit up the side of the dark hood, and then inexplicably skipped over the features of the person inside. The phrase "cloaked in shadow" came to mind. It was the sort of phrase he used when telling ghost stories to Rudi's nieces and nephews during their rare visits, but he had never believed it could actually happen. There was something unnatural about how the darkness clung to this person. A shiver ran down his spine as his senses screamed that he was in the presence of something malevolent. This was no ordinary road quarrel. The thing in this truck wanted him dead.

It kept staring at him, and somehow, he knew that deep within the hood, it was grinning.

There was another turn up ahead, near the sign for the marina, and he had no idea how he'd managed to get all the way across town, but that didn't matter. He took the turn so fast that he felt the wheels come up off the ground. The truck squealed as the driver slammed on the brakes, but it would take them a moment to recover.

This was his chance! He took a quick left, hoping to find somewhere he could pull off the road and hide until his pursuers decided to give up or their vehicle gave out. They might try to hunt him on foot, but he wasn't fool enough to leave the safety of the car until he knew they were far, far away. He tried to swallow against a throat that only managed to produce a dry click. It felt like there was no moisture left in him despite the fact that sweat poured down his face, stinging his eyes.

The truck wasn't behind him. He didn't see it. He took another turn onto a gravel road, hoping that he might find a hiding place somewhere off the beaten path. Another vehicle approached the intersection; he could see just the bumper before he turned again, hoping to evade notice. He twisted in his seat, trying to see if that had been the truck, convinced that at any moment it would once again appear behind him.

The road to the rear was empty save for plumes of dust kicked up by his car. Adrenaline made his hands shake uncontrollably as he turned back forward just in time to see the wide expanse of the river before him. Shock and horror warred for dominance within him. The path he was on ended abruptly right before the water, and he slammed on his brakes, but the wheels slid on the gravel. The car went rocketing over the side. It hovered in midair for what felt like an eternity, and Lucius glanced out his window to see the steaming truck and two figures cloaked in black standing outside it, parked right next to the marina. One of them raised a hand as if waving to a friend as he plummeted toward the water.

The car hit the surface. Lucius was thrown about the passenger compartment, his head banging painfully on the window, the door, something else? He was too disoriented to tell; his head swam, although somewhere deep inside a voice was screaming at him to get out, get out now, before it was too late! But the fogginess of his mind made such action impossible. Water was running somewhere, and it made him think of his dreams, of the city where the water always flowed and stairways climbed at impossible angles. His body was immersed in it now. It felt like home.

Everything went black.

CHAPTER TWENTY-THREE

Abdul Alhazred stood on the Plateau of Leng, beneath a glittering expanse of stars that appeared on no earthly map, and celebrated. In his hand, he clutched a single piece of paper, which he carefully tucked into his belt. That page was more precious than gold, more valuable than a million jewels. His long centuries of searching had come to an end. He had found the door to R'lyeh, and tonight, he would lead his cultists through it.

But he did not move yet. Relief weighed down his limbs, and he allowed himself a moment to sit there and soak in his triumph. Although he would never have admitted it aloud, he had sometimes worried that his quest might not succeed. It tugged at him whenever he closed his eyes to sleep, his lost memories surfacing in his dreams, only to slip through his fingers once again when he awoke. He had meditated and raged and studied, but to no avail. All he knew was that the ultimate reward awaited him there. If the world must end – which it would eventually – he would be standing at the pinnacle during those last moments. He alone would endure. It had been promised to him, although he could not remember the details.

Now, those days were finally here. The end days. The culmination of all that he had worked toward in his long life. If only his old master could see him now. The old goat wouldn't believe that his student had succeeded where he and all who had come before him had failed. Alhazred flashed his teeth in a rare smile at the thought of it.

A skittering noise caught his attention, and he turned to see the purple bulk of a Leng spider as it climbed up over the edge of the plateau. It was a sizable specimen of the breed, about the size of a small elephant, its glowing body large enough to crush him beneath its bulk. The creature reared, forelegs clawing at the air, its thousand eyes glittering as they locked on him. Its body pulsed with hunger.

Alhazred chuckled to himself.

The enormous creature continued its dramatic display, which was meant to distract him from the quiet approach of its brethren behind him. Alhazred did not need to turn his head to follow their approach. He had felt their attention the moment they'd scented him, and he welcomed them closer.

"Come into my parlor, said the spider to the fly," he murmured.

He tugged off the soft kid gloves that covered his hands, revealing the arcane symbols inked over every inch of skin. It was a shock to see his own flesh again. He had become so accustomed to hopping from body to body that he sometimes struggled to remember his own features. But his astral projection still retained the form of his original birth, and so he could walk the roads of the Dreamlands as himself. It was rather refreshing not to have to pretend anymore. When he finally reached R'lyeh, he would be reborn again in an eternal body all of his own. It would be much more preferable than all this playacting.

One of the spiders behind him charged, its awful feet clattering across the stone, poisonous spittle dripping from pincers the size of his head. The rest of them followed suit, letting out awful screeches of hunger and fury. They were known to tear each other apart in their haste to get to the choicest prey, and apparently he'd been deemed worthy.

He smiled again, holding out a hand, his fingers opening to reveal the symbol etched into his skin, and spoke a single forbidden word. The etching flared into an awful light of all colors and none, a light that swallowed everything in its path. It howled as if it was alive, a deep sound that penetrated him down to the marrow. It was as if a black hole had opened in the center of his palm, devouring everything before it, pulling in the spiders as well as bits of the plain beneath them. They vanished into nothingness.

He closed his palm, powdered ink sloughing off his skin and sifting through his fingers like sand, its arcane power depleted. But the single remaining spider did not know that. When he turned to face it, he found it frozen in terrified confusion, its mandibles testing the air for any sign of its clustermates. He took one single step toward it before it bolted, shrieking in fear. He let it go undisturbed. Although he possessed lesser sigils that would take care of a single beast such as this one, it would be foolish to waste them. He did not know when he would have time to re-ink them, and he did not know exactly what would await them on the road to R'lyeh. It would be wise to preserve his power in case the road was not a welcoming one.

So he let the beast go, trusting that it had learned its lesson. He took one last glance at the sky to confirm his calculations, pulling out the piece of parchment once again. Based on the star map and the directions Galloway had pulled out of the *Necronomicon*, thinking they were so much poetical imagery, he recalculated the location of the hidden doorway once again and came to the same conclusion. There, to the south. Now that he knew its location, he could almost feel its pull. Luckily, he only had to resist it a while longer.

Practically vibrating with triumph, he reached up a hand and rubbed the symbol from his forehead that had brought his astral body to this juncture of time and space. A strong wave of motion overtook him as his soul traversed the pathways between the Dreamlands and the waking world and plunked back into his borrowed body. He sighed and stretched his neck as the old pains settled back into aged bones. At least he would only need to endure this for a few hours longer. He was ready to be rid of mortal frailty once and for all, without the need to constantly find new vessels to inhabit. He could devote himself to other pursuits in the new world. It would be full of new places to explore and new peoples to serve him.

He couldn't wait.

When he opened his eyes, he found his acolyte staring down at him, her hands folded into the voluminous sleeves of her ceremonial robes. Before he had left, she'd been wearing her usual smart suit, but she must have gotten cold. A rime of ice clung to the heavy fabric and spread across the surface of the desk before him. Sometimes opening the gates between the worlds came with unexpected side effects. His borrowed body shivered uncontrollably, but he did not allow its discomfort to register. Now that they were so close, he had much more important things to do. Besides, the frost had already begun to soften, melting in the hot summer night.

His acolyte didn't comment on it either. She waited for him to speak, lips parted with barely contained excitement.

"Did it work?" she asked, her voice a breathless gasp.

"I have found the location of the door," he replied, baring his teeth in a feral grin. "Tell your fellow Pilgrims that finally they will see the Drowned City our fellowship is named for."

"When?" she breathed.

"Tonight. Have them pack up with the utmost haste. I have already waited long enough. Anyone who is not ready to leave at eleven tonight will be left behind. The door opens at midnight, and I will not miss it."

"What about Galloway? Do you have any instructions?"

Alhazred pursed his lips, considering. Should he order the man's termination on principle alone? Galloway was no slouch; he'd been walking the Dreamlands for months. The fact that he'd survived was a testament to his raw arcane skill, even if he lacked the training to fully utilize it or even understand what he was doing. With time, perhaps Alhazred could have made something of the man, but there was no use now. When the world ended, it would sweep them all along with it. Galloway, his acolyte, all of them. But if anything did go wrong, it would be wise to keep Galloway in his back pocket. If necessary, he could drag the poet into the Dreamlands to unravel any unexpected mysteries.

"Leave him be for now," he said. "He may serve as a resource for later."

She nodded, her lips quirking.

"Very well," she said. "I don't think he suspects anything anyway. I wonder what he would say if he knew what he has done."

"What *I* have done," he corrected.

Her amusement vanished from her face as if it had been wiped out of existence. She nodded, eager to demonstrate her agreement.

"Yes, of course, master," she said. "In the days to come, everyone will know the name of Abdul Alhazred, finder of the lost door to R'lyeh."

"Do not say that name aloud," he hissed, folding his arms. "I will not risk the possibility that some late-night cleaning lady might overhear you. You ought to know better."

"Yes, master," said the acolyte, putting her hands into her sleeves again and bowing.

Abdul Alhazred stood, stretching Helen's body and getting used to all its contours once again. She was not the oldest vessel he'd ever commanded – he'd spent a few years hopping from world to world, inhabiting the bodies of ancient librarians to gain access to forbidden tomes – and he'd rather enjoyed his time in her skin. She was a woman of formidable will, that Helen. Somewhere in the depths of her mind, her spirit still struggled to free itself after months of imprisonment. They usually stopped after the first few weeks, driven mad by their inability to control the actions of their own body. But not Helen Berringer. She would have made an excellent sorcerer, if she'd ever had a chance. Too bad she would die with all the rest of them.

Alhazred shrugged, ignoring Helen's furious howls as they echoed through the chambers of his mind. She would be quiet soon enough.

CHAPTER TWENTY-FOUR

Lucius awoke sitting on the hallway floor outside his rooms, his suit coat thrown open and his vest gaping wide. He came to only to see the disapproving expression of Mr Badenhorst as he leaned down to smell Lucius' breath. After a long sniff, he stood back up, huffing in disapproval.

"I told the trustees that they were making a mistake with you," he grumbled, "and it's clear that I was right to do so. You don't have the composure to be a Harvard man. What's wrong with you, coming home intoxicated before luncheon is even over? Have you no sense of propriety? What would the students think if they saw you in such a state?"

Lucius gaped at him, unable to form words. He didn't even know how he'd gotten here. Last thing he remembered, he was drowning...?

"Pull yourself together, or at least have the decency to go into your room and debauch yourself in private! The trustees will be hearing about this abominable display of poor behavior, I'll tell you that!"

Gesticulating widely, Mr Badenhorst went stomping away, every footfall sending daggers of pain into Lucius' temples. He pushed himself up to a standing position, groaning as his head pounded. What on earth had happened? The last thing he remembered, he'd driven off the road into the water, but his clothes weren't even damp. He reached up and gingerly touched his forehead. Although he vividly remembered hitting it on the glass, he found no wound. Had he dreamed the entire thing? If so, how had he gotten out here in the hallway? Why did his head hurt and his throat burn so badly? If he didn't know better, he'd say he was hungover, but he'd only had a sip of that rotgut brew Helen had offered him. But if he'd dreamed the whole thing, then he hadn't had that drink, so how did he still feel its effects? None of this made any sense, and it unsettled him even further.

With shaking hands, he unlocked the door to his rooms. Inside, nothing was amiss. The bed had been made, the curtains thrown back. His slippers sat neatly beside the bed where he'd put them that morning. He sat down on the bed next to them and tried to pull himself together. There had to be some clue to what had befallen him, if only he could just think! He checked his pockets and found nothing out of place. His eyes fell on the secretary desk, and he launched to his feet in excited agitation. Of course! If the manuscript pages were still here, he would have proof that none of it had been real. He'd been sleepwalking. Honestly, at this point, it would almost be a relief.

He rolled the desk open to reveal an empty workspace. The folder should have been right here on the blotter. So he had gone to Helen's at the very least. Did he still have the keys to the car? He checked his pockets only to find them empty. None of this made sense. Perhaps Helen would be able to shed some

light on this mystery. At this moment, he very badly needed to
see a friendly face. He could not suppress the queasy feeling
deep within him that something was very, very wrong, but
Helen's good sense and acerbic wit would help set him to rights.

His mind made up, he closed the desk and headed for the
rack to fetch his hat, but the peg where it usually hung was
empty. It was his favorite hat; he never went anywhere without
it. But a quick search failed to turn it up. The longer he looked,
the more unsettled he felt, and his attempts to talk himself off
the edge of panic weren't as successful as he might have liked.
Perhaps he'd left it at Helen's office. It seemed that all roads led
him there.

When he emerged out the front door, he found that it had
begun to rain. Under normal circumstances, he would have
gone back for his umbrella, but he couldn't stand the delay.
His skin crawled with the sense that someone was watching
him – perhaps that Quinn woman. Could she have been one
of those hooded figures that had run him off the road? But they
weren't real, were they? He didn't know what to think; he only
knew that his senses screamed at him to run now, before it was
too late. But he didn't know where to run to, or what he was
running from, exactly.

He dashed across the quad, dodging shocked pedestrians
with umbrellas and rain slickers. Up ahead, the bright glint of
blonde hair caught his attention. Although he could only see
her from behind, it had to be Quinn. As Helen had said, there
was only one trouser-wearing New Woman on campus. He
didn't know what he was going to say, but he desperately needed
answers, and he could afford to leave no stone unturned.

His mind made up, he strode up to her, grabbed her by the
shoulder, and turned her around. The shocked and frightened

face that spun to face him was not the mysterious Ari Quinn after all. This woman was much younger, much more timid looking. She shrank before him, letting out a whimper, and he realized belatedly that his lips had pulled back from his teeth into an unbecoming snarl. His fear had made him near feral. What was he thinking, putting his hands on a random white woman? Did he want to get himself killed? A familiar fear pushed aside his strange new worries, and somehow, that settled him.

"I'm so sorry," he said, pulling back and holding up his hands to show how harmless he was. "I thought you were someone else. Please forgive me."

"It's okay…" she whispered, still shrinking away from him.

He stood back, making a point of allowing her to scurry away, ignoring the disapproving looks from other pedestrians nearby. The rain dripped down his face. He continued on to Helen's office, keeping an iron hold on his emotions. To let them go in such a careless manner was dangerous, and he would not make the same mistake again.

As he approached Helen's door, she came out into the hall with a large cardboard box. When he charged up toward her, she jumped, nearly dropping it. Something inside clattered.

"Oh, good Lord in heaven," she said. "You nearly scared me to death!"

"I'm so sorry. Let me take that off your hands," he replied with automatic politeness.

"I've got it."

"Please. I insist."

He took the box from her over her protests. It wasn't all that heavy, but Helen was so bird-boned and tiny that it would be more of a struggle for her. Besides, exercising this simple politeness made him feel more in control of himself. Everything was normal again, and in a normal world, trucks didn't slam into people at random.

"Did you see me this morning?" he blurted. "It is still Monday, isn't it?"

"Ye-es," she said cautiously. "You dropped off those pages, remember? I've got them in that box with a few other things from my desk. I thought that since Dao is so busy with the typing, I'd take care of putting the place back together so the woman who owns it can return to her usual pigsty." She gave him a closer look. "You have that lost-at-the-end-of-a-project look about you. Don't worry, my boy. You'll have plenty of edits soon enough."

"That's not it…" He scrambled for words. "I was supposed to get Dao's car. For lunch. Remember?"

Her brows rose, and she snickered.

"Dao doesn't own a car, silly. You must have gone back to your rooms and fallen right asleep. Sounds like you had one hell of a dream too." She patted him on the arm. "There's nothing to worry about, Galloway. The manuscript is done. Everything is fine. Did you want lunch? Give me a minute to drop off my stuff, and I'll take you to my favorite place. We ought to celebrate, and it sounds like you could use a meal and a night off."

"The Sussex?" he asked.

"Pardon?"

"Your favorite restaurant. Is it the Sussex?"

"I've mentioned it before, have I? Let me take that from you."

She took the box from him while he tried to get his legs back underneath him. Had Helen mentioned that restaurant before this morning? He didn't remember it, but she must have, and his subconscious had tossed out the factoid in his dream. A bit dazed, he held the box out to her. As he did, it rattled again, drawing his attention. The metal flask they'd drunk from clinked again, the chain that connected the lid to the mouth of the bottle swinging to and fro. Once again, he wondered if he'd gotten drunk. After all, that liquor had burned more than he'd expected. Perhaps it had been stronger than he was used to?

"Lucius?" Helen asked, holding out her arms.

Had she said his name a few times already? He didn't know.

"Sorry," he said, only half paying attention. He could not shake the nagging feeling that something had gone dreadfully wrong. No matter how hard he tried, he couldn't make the pieces fit back together again. The flask beckoned him, and he wondered if he picked it up, would the liquor burn like it had before? Or would it just be normal rotgut whiskey in that flask? Would it really matter?

"You look positively peaked," she said, clucking her tongue. "When was the last time you ate?"

"I'm honestly not quite sure," he replied. After all, could he be certain that any of this was real?

"Sit down," she said firmly, pushing him toward the desk chair. "Give me the box. I'll be back before you know it."

He allowed himself to be seated and finally relinquished his hold on the box. His head spun unpleasantly, whirling with impossibilities. Someone would have seen the car chase. He wasn't injured. It couldn't have happened. If only he could stop obsessing, everything would be fine. But he kept worrying at it, like an injury he couldn't help but toy with even though every touch made it hurt anew.

Helen let herself out, closing the office door. A nice, soothing gloom settled over the cluttered space. She had already begun to move some of the previous owner's piles back in. A tower of books sat on the guest chair, a few loose pages fluttering in the breeze from the open window. The room was quiet and still relatively cool. He closed his eyes in exhaustion, hoping that the peace would soothe his headache and allow him to think clearly once again.

The doorknob rattled, startling him out of a doze. He jerked awake, rubbing at his face and realizing to his utter embarrassment that he'd been drooling. His hand rasped against his unshaven cheek. He had been falling apart in slow stages and hadn't even realized it. Hopefully Helen wouldn't notice.

But the woman who stood silhouetted in the open doorway was much too tall to be Helen. Ari Quinn stood there, the hallway lights glinting off her bright blonde hair. She startled when she saw him, her hand dipping into her pocketbook and not coming out again. Likely gripping some sort of weapon. He straightened and plastered on a polite smile out of sheer force of habit, driven by a lifetime of training to appear docile and unthreatening. But that was backward. He was supposed to be here, and she was not. He straightened, the smile slipping from his face.

"Helen is not here," he said. "Did you need something?"

"Where did she go?" she demanded.

"I don't see how that's any of your business, Miss Quinn."

She cocked an eyebrow, frowning thoughtfully at him. A long, tense silence drew out between them.

"Is it done?" she finally asked.

"Is what done?"

"Your translation. The Berringer manuscript. Is it done?"

"Why do you want to know?" he demanded. "Your reputation doesn't make me inclined to answer your inquiries. And I'll have you know that your behavior is damned suspicious."

"And Helen's isn't?"

He opened his mouth and closed it again a few times, but no words came out.

"Exactly," she continued. "Are you sure you can believe whatever line she fed you?"

He slumped in his chair, his head pounding once again.

"I don't know what to believe," he muttered, rubbing his face. "Nothing makes sense anymore."

"I've been there, Mr Galloway," she said sympathetically. "Let's start over. What did she tell you to warn you off me? Perhaps I can refute it to your satisfaction so we can be honest with each other."

"Alright." He hesitated. "Although I suppose I ought to warn you that Helen should be coming back any minute now. She just went upstairs to drop a box off to our research assistant."

"Helen and Dao left the building an hour ago," she said.

The office clock had stopped long ago, its hands frozen at precisely twelve o'clock. He pulled out his pocket watch and flipped it open, frowning. Miss Quinn spoke the truth; he'd been sleeping longer than he'd thought.

"We were supposed to go to lunch..." he said. "But I knew something wasn't right."

"Oh?"

Her eyes lit up with curiosity. Ari Quinn was a pretty young woman with the kind of open face that made her seem quite trustworthy, but Lucius wasn't in a trusting mood. He shook his head firmly.

"Not yet. First, you tell me what you're doing here. Are you trying to steal our work and publish it yourself?" he asked.

"Is that what she said?" Miss Quinn recoiled. "Why, that backstabbing, two-faced..."

"She said you're known for it. You stole the work of her research assistant and made her have to repeat her final project."

"Mr Galloway, *I* was her research assistant. I have a photograph of us together, the day I got my PhD. Let me show you."

She set her pocketbook on the corner of the desk and began pulling things out of it. The first object was a wicked looking black pistol, which she carefully turned away from him before setting it on the desk. Their eyes met, but neither of them commented as she pulled out a set of jingling keys, a small compact, a leather wallet, and finally a small commonplace book similar to his own. She flipped it open, revealing pages full of neat, spare print. A black and white photograph marked the final page, and she held it out to him.

"See for yourself," she said.

He took the picture, holding it up to the light to see it better. It was just as she said – a young Ari Quinn, resplendent in a scholar's cap and gown, with braided cords draped over her neck, stood with her arm around Helen Berringer's shoulder. Helen looked very much the same, tiny and impish, although perhaps a little less wrinkled. But she had her arm around Miss Quinn's waist, and the two of them were grinning as they displayed what looked like Quinn's diploma, although the print was too small to make out anything but her name, in ornate letters.

Ariana Quinn, PhD.

They appeared quite friendly. More to the point, they certainly looked like they knew each other much better than Helen had indicated. If this photograph had been taken at the completion of Miss Quinn's PhD, it would have occurred after the supposed Master's project theft. He had a hard time believing that Helen would get such a major detail wrong, but did he believe that she'd lied to him outright? He wasn't sure yet.

He handed the photo back, and Miss Quinn safely stowed it away.

"Let's say I believe you," he began. "You have to admit that your behavior has been a bit suspicious. Every time I've seen you, you've been lurking in the verge like a character in a spy caper. If you weren't trying to steal our work, what were you doing? Why are you here if you know that Helen has left?"

"Reasonable questions. This is a long story, and my feet are killing me. Just a moment." She picked the tottering pile of books up off the chair and set them on the floor next to it, sitting down with a sigh of relief and pulling her feet out of her shoes. "I hope you don't mind. 'Lurking in the verge,' as you put it, does a number on a person. I think my blisters have blisters."

He didn't know what to say to this. Was she trying to charm him in the way that pretty girls often did? It certainly wasn't going to work on him, so he just waited.

After a moment of massaging her stockinged feet one after the other, she said, "Sorry, you're waiting for the answer to your question, aren't you? Like I said, it's a long story, but let me attempt to sum it up. I belong to an organization with many unusual duties, one of which is to investigate cult-like activities. We determine if there is a threat and report the organizations involved to proper authorities."

"Cults?" Lucius arched a brow. "Like Point Loma? My friend Rudi has a distant cousin who got sucked into that ridiculousness. He stole a bunch of money from the family and invested it in silkworms for reasons I never entirely understood."

"I haven't worked with that group in particular, but it's my understanding that they were relatively benign in the larger scheme of things. The Point Loma folks were simple swindlers, as your friend's uncle found out. Other groups are much more dangerous than that, I'm afraid."

"So you're investigating a cult? I'm not entirely sure what to think about that. How on earth does a person get into that line of work?" he asked, curious despite himself. Perhaps if he stalled long enough, Helen would return and everything would sort itself out. He could only hope.

"It's an unusual job for sure." She flashed him a smile. "My degree is in archaeology, and I specialize in ancient civilizations. The structure of their cities can tell you a great deal about its people. But I'll stop there, because once I get going, it's near impossible to stop me. I was on a dig in Africa when I ran across my first cult. They wanted an artifact, and they weren't afraid to kill to get it." His eyes widened in alarm, and she nodded. "Exactly. Someone must stop them, and my academic background makes me a good candidate. You'd be amazed at how many of these groups have penetrated academia. Their leader decides that some newly discovered ancient artifact is an item of unknowable power, and they have to have it. You can imagine what's next."

"Fascinating…" Lucius pondered this explanation for a moment. It was so outlandish that he was inclined to believe it, too ludicrous to be a lie. But that still didn't explain her presence here. "You don't think Helen Berringer is a cultist, do you? That's laughable."

"I would have said the same up to six months ago. She's such a sweet lady. I never heard her say a bad word about anyone in all the years I knew her. When my house burned down, she let me stay at her place for a full month. Refused to take a penny in return, either. I kept trying to give her money, and she'd sneak it back into my pocketbook when I wasn't looking."

"Helen, sweet? She's got the most acerbic tongue I know. She'd give you the shirt off her back, but she'd make fun of you while she did it."

Their eyes met. Lucius wanted to call her out on the error – maybe she didn't know Helen as well as she claimed. But the clear worry etched into the corners of her mouth made him hold his tongue.

"I don't like that at all," she said. "They reprogram you, those cults. If she's not acting like herself, she may be in deeper than I thought."

"Look, Miss Quinn, I'm not calling you a liar, but if you're telling the truth, it sounds like you weren't a very good friend. If someone special to me were to get mixed up with a cult, and a cult I presumably knew a great deal about, no less, I'd show up on their doorstep and talk some sense into them. Why didn't you say something?"

"Trust me, I've tried. I tracked the Pilgrims of the Drowned City to a tiny monastery in Italy, and from there, they just vanished. The monastery burned to the ground, and at first we thought maybe they'd all died inside, but we only found one skeleton when we excavated the remains. It's still unidentified as far as I know. We were watching the nearby ports in the hopes of catching them there, but they must have chartered a boat. Or one of their members owns one. The group goes through members at a frightening pace, so it's difficult to keep up with them. Anyway, by the time I tracked them here, Helen was already in deep. I tried to warn her. At the time, I thought you were in on it too, so I sent her some letters."

She paused, sighing heavily.

"I take it that didn't go well?" he asked.

"The first one was torn to shreds and stuffed back into the envelope. I found the second stuck to my door with a carving knife. I decided to stop sending them and focus on my investigation. Maybe if I had evidence, she'd listen to me."

"And what did you find?" he asked, somewhat breathless with anticipation. Could he believe this seemingly tall tale? To do so was preposterous, but the whole situation was preposterous on its own, wasn't it? He could do nothing for now but listen and try desperately to get his feet under him in these strange, unknown waters.

"Nothing substantial, I'm afraid. I know you're working on a manuscript that was donated anonymously to the university. I know that your project with Helen is important to the cult because I've overheard them talking about it, but I'm not sure why. I tried a few times to get access to the manuscript in the hopes that I might be able to identify it, but I'm not on the list, and my attempt to break into Widener nearly resulted in my getting arrested. I haven't managed to work up the guts to try again."

"I'm on the list," said Lucius.

"You are," she allowed. "Would you take me to look at it? It could provide some answers."

He gave the request careful consideration before he answered. He couldn't deny that odd things had been happening ever since he'd arrived here, and although he wasn't yet certain that he could trust Miss Quinn, he had to admit that her story might explain some of his strange experiences. Perhaps the cult had been playing mind games on him. Or drugging him, even. They did that sort of thing in adventure tales, but he wasn't sure how much of that was fact and how much fiction made up by a bunch of over-imaginative writers. If he wanted answers, he would have to play along, at least for the moment. Reviewing the manuscript seemed like a reasonable next step. After all, those pages couldn't be removed from the library, so they would be safe regardless of Miss Quinn's true intentions.

"Let's go there now," he suggested. "I'm eager to get to the bottom of this."

CHAPTER TWENTY-FIVE

Miss Quinn waited in the Ladies' Reading Room while Lucius headed to the circulation desk to request the first few pages of the Berringer manuscript. The line for assistance was longer than usual, and he couldn't help but shift with impatience as he waited for the gentleman before him to work his way through a prodigious list of requests which simply had to be filled right now, despite the fact that some of the volumes had been checked out by other patrons. He could do nothing but wait while the man ranted and raved, although he might have liked to say something. Some folks didn't welcome his intervention. He'd had enough bad luck recently; there was no sense in courting any more.

Finally, the angry gentleman huffed away, clutching a stack of books and grumbling under his breath. Lucius fixed the harried desk attendant with a smile as he stepped forward. The fellow must have been new – Lucius hadn't seen him before – and not having the best of days.

"Some people," he said, shaking his head.

"You're telling me," the young man replied, rolling his eyes. "How can I help you today? If you're looking for books on European economic history, I can tell you with certainty that we're plumb out."

Lucius chuckled. "No, no. I was hoping you'd fetch a few pages of the Berringer manuscript for me. I'm on the list. Lucius Galloway?"

"Sorry, the what manuscript?"

"Berringer. It's a part of the Widener collection."

"Right-o. Not familiar with that one; give me just a minute."

The young man turned to the shelves beside him and pulled out a ledger book, flipping the pages and scanning their contents. Lucius waited patiently, unwilling to make a spectacle of himself the way the last man had. But the longer he waited, the more agitated he got. He was caught in a web of inexplicable situations with no idea who to trust. Ari Quinn seemed to be telling the truth, but Helen was his friend. To believe one was to call the other false, and he struggled to believe that the past few months had been built on lies.

"Berringer with a B?" asked the attendant, flipping another page and frowning.

Lucius spelled it out for him.

"I'm sorry, sir, but I don't see any record of the manuscript here. Are you sure it's part of the Widener collection?" said the young man.

"Quite sure," replied Lucius. "I've spent the whole summer writing about it. It's a recent donation; perhaps it's not in that ledger yet?"

"It ought to be. Mr Dexter is strict about that sort of thing. Otherwise valuable bequests go missing, and that sort of thing doesn't exactly encourage donations. It's a full manuscript, you say? Bound?"

"No, it's a collection of unbound pages in a folder wrapped with twine. We had a situation where one of them went missing, and I complained about it. I couldn't believe that such a valuable donation would be treated in such a callous manner."

The young man folded his arms, obviously uncertain.

"I confess that I'm not quite sure if you're pulling my leg," he said. "I am busy, so if–"

"I can understand why you'd think so, but I assure you, I'm perfectly serious. Perhaps we might ask the young man who usually helps me. I must admit I don't recall him looking in the ledger at all, now that I think about it. He always just seemed to know what I was after."

"O-okay. What's his name? Or what does he look like? I know the whole crew here pretty well."

"He's…" Lucius trailed off with growing unease. He'd spoken to the fellow multiple times a week over the past couple of months, but he'd never heard the man's name and couldn't provide a single distinguishing characteristic about him. He was the sort of bland, unmemorable chap that vanished from your memory when you weren't looking straight at him. "Well, white. Kind of sandy hair. Average height and build. I know that's not very helpful. Oh, I know! Often when I come in, he's got his jacket off and his shirtsleeves rolled up. It's deuced uncommon, so it always stuck out to me."

"Mr Dexter would tan us if we weren't dressed properly for our work," replied the young man. "I can't see any of the fellows doing such a thing, but give me a minute. I'll ask around."

The young man went down to a neighboring desk and began a short conversation with the fellow stationed there. His heart thumping, Lucius took the opportunity to sneak a peek at the still-open ledger before him, scanning the list of documents and resources, each written in a neat hand with a date of acquisition followed by a row of letters and numbers to designate its location. The attendant had left the ledger open to the B's, and he did not see the Berringer donation listed anywhere within the past year.

Perhaps it was listed under another name. After all, Helen called it the Berringer manuscript, but it had come from some anonymous donor without any name at all. As soon as he thought of it, he felt incredibly stupid. Relief suffused his limbs. He approached the still-conversing gentlemen and cleared his throat apologetically.

"Yes?" asked the attendant.

"I think I've been rather foolish," said Lucius. "My project group refers to it under that name, but it probably isn't listed that way in your records. It came from an anonymous donor. How would one look that up? I always just said the Berringer name to the early morning chap, and he knew what I was asking for."

"The early morning attendant is a red-headed Scotsman named MacTavish," replied the attendant. "So I don't know who you were talking to. But I'll give it one more look, and then I've got to help other patrons. I've got quite a line."

He gestured to the queue of academics waiting for assistance, and Lucius ducked his head to avoid their glares for a moment. Then he remembered – he belonged here. He'd proved that. Regardless of what anyone else thought, he would always have that to hold onto. He straightened once again.

"Of course," he said. "I appreciate your assistance. I'm sorry to be so difficult."

"Yes, well…" The young man closed and re-shelved the first ledger and pulled out a second one. "Okay, tell me what you can about the manuscript. Language? Number of pages? Estimated date of donation?"

"Ancient Greek, exactly seventy-nine pages, donated earlier this year. Spring, I believe they said," replied Lucius.

"Sir, next time, lead with that," said the attendant, shaking his head in exasperation. "Let's see… I don't see anything in April… March… here we go! End of February. Seventy-nine pages in ancient Greek, including astronomical illustrations."

"That's it!" exclaimed Lucius. "Hallelujah. I'm going to be honest; I was beginning to doubt my own memory for a minute."

The young man smiled briefly.

"I'm glad we found it for you." He squinted at the register. "Although I'm afraid you're out of luck. That document was unlisted yesterday and pulled from circulation."

"Unlisted?" Lucius went cold. "What does that mean?"

"Usually, it means it's been donated or sold elsewhere, but I don't see a final destination recorded here just yet. The paperwork is probably sitting on someone's desk at this very moment."

"No one mentioned that to us. My writing partner was working on a project specified in the bequest, and it's not completed yet."

"That is odd." The young man sighed. "But I'm afraid that's all I can tell you. Perhaps you should come in tomorrow morning and find your mysterious gent in the shirtsleeves, since he seems to know everything. I'm afraid I've got to help the next person. Good day, sir."

Lucius wanted to make some protest, but what exactly could he say? He had the sinking suspicion he knew what had happened: the cult had managed to abscond with both manuscripts. Helen had taken the translation with her, and now they'd somehow absconded with the original. There would be no getting them back.

He returned to the Women's Reading Room empty-handed, gesturing for Miss Quinn to follow him out. As they left the building, he explained everything that had happened. As he finished, she let out a very unladylike swear that reminded him of Helen with a pang of regret. Had he ever really known her at all? They'd been friends. He'd trusted her, and he didn't do that easily. How could he have been so wrong?

He refused to believe it had all been a lie. Their mutual trust couldn't have been faked. Helen must have been manipulated – somehow – by that cult. It was the only possible explanation.

"The cult probably took it," said Miss Quinn. "You realize that, right?"

He nodded.

"They took them both," he said. "The bastards. Helen had our completed manuscript in a box last time I saw her. For all I know, she had the Berringer manuscript in there as well. I had it right in my hands and never knew it. I'm of half a mind to march down to her boarding house and see if anyone there knows where she is."

"That's the last thing I'd do," replied Miss Quinn evenly. "Everyone at that boarding house is a member of the Pilgrims of the Drowned City. I'd stay as far away from that place as possible. I'm not sure it's safe."

Now it was Lucius' turn to swear.

"Well, then, what do we do?" he asked. "Helen is my friend, and she was there for me when I had a rough time. I'm not just going to abandon her."

Miss Quinn considered for a moment, tapping her fingers thoughtfully on her folded arms. Twice, she seemed about to say something before thinking better of it. Finally, she sighed.

"Are you sure you don't have any of the pages? I'd feel much better about this decision if we had some idea of what they're up to," she said.

"I'm sorry, I don't. I gave all of my finished chapters to Helen or Dao. Blast it all, Dao must be in on it as well. I suppose we could check the typing room, but I'm assuming they cleared that all out, too."

"Any notes?" she asked. "I know you keep a book; I've seen you writing in it."

He pulled it from his pocket, rubbing his hand over its cover.

"There are a few references to the work, but I don't think they'll do us much good. I mostly jotted down reminders to myself." He flipped the book open, scanning its final pages. "Here's one that says, 'Consult star maps at library,' but that's all, and I could have told you about that. I don't have any..." He trailed off as she gazed hopefully at him. "Actually, maybe I do have a few pages in my rooms. I went through a phase where I wasn't sleeping, and the longer I went without sleep, the worse my handwriting got. I recopied those pages before I turned them in, and I save all my scrap paper for jotting down ideas. I'm sure I've thrown away some of it, but there should be a few left. Will that be enough, do you think?"

"It's worth a try. They're in your rooms, you say?" she replied, leaping to her feet.

"Yes. If you like, I can bring them back to you?"

"Why waste the time?"

"Oh, I just thought..." He trailed off awkwardly, trying to find some polite way to explain it. "I was trying to be gentlemanly."

"Ah. That. I'll have you know that I have no interest in pursuing a romantic entanglement with anyone. Romance is such a fuss and bother, and why anyone would want to go through that is beyond me. The only thing I'm after is answers, Mr Galloway," she replied, matter of fact.

"Same, Miss Quinn. If you're sure you feel safe, we can fetch them immediately."

She grinned, the expression lighting up her face.

"I'm wearing practical shoes, and I carry a pistol in my handbag. Lead on," she said.

A short while later, they stood before Lucius' secretary desk as he rummaged through the papers stuffed in the cubbies. He'd amassed a remarkable amount of material in the months of his residence – receipts from the laundry, mail stubs, letters from Rudi – which reminded him that he still had a missive left to read when he found a spare moment to do it. He shot Miss Quinn an apologetic look as he pulled out a new stack to look through.

"Beg pardon," he said. "I ought to have tidied up, but I was desperate to finish the first draft."

"My desk isn't much better, but time's a-wasting. Do you mind if I help?"

"Not at all. Pick one and start looking. The writing is a rather distinct heavy scrawl quite unlike my normal hand. It should be easy enough to spot."

She did so, and for a moment, there was no sound except the shuffling of pages. Then:

"You say you were having trouble sleeping? Did you notice anything else strange while you were working on this project?" she asked.

The Forbidden Visions of Lucius Galloway

He stiffened, and the two of them locked eyes. Hers were calm and open, and for a moment, he considered confessing all of it – the strange dreams, the dangerous situations that could not have been real. The tentacles in the pool. The car crash that hadn't happened. He had the strange feeling that she would take it all in stride. But that was ridiculous; admitting it all out loud was a surefire way to find himself whiling away the last of his days in a nice sanitarium by the water.

These days, he wanted to be as far from the water as possible.

"Not at all," he lied weakly.

He half expected her to call him out on the obvious falsehood, but instead she let out a surprised "Hey!" before holding up a sheet of paper.

"Is this it?" she asked, flipping it over to face him.

The paper was covered with the jagged scratchings of his nighttime work. He nodded, his throat suddenly tight.

"Yes, that's one of them," he forced out. "Can you read it?"

"Of course I can. My handwriting is rather worse than this, if I'm going to be honest. There are a few more pages here – can you help me figure out the order?"

They spread the papers out on the desktop and made quick work of putting them in order. Miss Quinn then retired to the armchair to read them while Lucius searched for any stragglers. There were only two cubbies left, so he had the feeling they'd found all they would. Hopefully those five pages would be enough to help them understand what poor Helen had gotten herself into.

He was just flipping through the final stack of pages when Miss Quinn let out a startled bleat. He rushed toward the room, his heart thumping madly, unsure of what he would find. His mind whirled with possibilities that most people would have considered madness if he'd dared to speak them aloud. But when he reached the open door, there was nothing to see other than Ari Quinn sitting bolt upright in the armchair, her face drained of all color.

"What is it?" he demanded, looking around. "What's wrong?"

"I recognize this book," she said, turning wide and frightened eyes on him. "It's worse than I thought."

CHAPTER TWENTY-SIX

"These pages are from the *Necronomicon*," said Miss Quinn, her voice shaking.

"I'm not certain which worries me more, the name itself or the fact that you look like the world is ending," Lucius replied, crossing the sitting room to settle in the spare armchair next to her. "Are you sure?"

"I've never seen the full manuscript before, but there are a few lines that are rather famous in certain circles. You've got one here." She tapped her finger to point it out.

"'That is not dead which can eternal lie,
And with strange aeons, even death may die.'"

Lucius read the lines aloud and a chill ran up his spine. Somehow, they seemed much more nefarious now than when he'd written those pages. Then again, he didn't remember writing them, which was nefarious enough on its own.

"So what does this mean?" he asked, licking suddenly dry lips.

"I've only read abridged versions of the book, so some of this is hypothesis, but bear with me. You can think of it as a grimoire – the writings of an immensely powerful sorcerer by the name of Abdul Alhazred, hundreds of years ago."

"A sorcerer?"

He wanted to roll his eyes, because after all, he did not believe in such things. But he found to his surprise that he could not. So much had happened that he could not explain. Perhaps Helen had been right after all, and so-called magic was, in fact, real. But it wasn't simple wish-fulfillment; it came with natural rules and limitations just like everything else. It could be recorded, and perhaps later generations would find ways to codify it into a science. The fact that it hadn't been done yet did not automatically mean it was imaginary.

"A sorcerer," she said firmly. "I heard about a man who supposedly discovered a version of the full manuscript hidden in the mountains of Hindu Kush."

"And what did he say about it?"

"Nothing. He sprinted full speed off a cliff immediately thereafter. The other members of his party were so frightened by what had happened that they burned the pages. A few years later, I was on a dig with one of his research assistants, and he told me about it one night when we'd been drinking. I don't think he would have spoken of it sober, and when I tried to bring it up again later, he pretended not to know what I was talking about."

"That's rather chilling."

"Exactly. The abridged version is disturbing, but there's nothing in it to evoke that kind of response."

"What are its contents exactly then? The pages I read were a bunch of disjointed poetry about all kinds of things. Stars and buildings and prayers to unnamed gods, and that sort of thing."

"That sounds about right. You can think of it like an arcane encyclopedia, but with a very poor sense of organization. I had the sense that Alhazred was taking notes on whatever he learned, perhaps with the intention of returning later to make some sense out of it. And before you protest, I know how it sounds. An arcane encyclopedia in verse sounds like the punchline to a joke. But how do you hide information in plain sight? You—"

"Hide it in verse," interrupted Lucius, gripping the arms of his chair hard in excitement. "It does make sense."

"Exactly. But here's where it gets dicey. The full version of the *Necronomicon* is said to contain a bunch of forbidden knowledge. Incantations and magic sigils and whatnot. But remember what I said about cults – they're searching for power or money, and this book suggests the pilgrims are after the former. The *Necronomicon* is said to contain instructions on how to get to a city called R'lyeh."

"Never heard of it."

"You know Atlantis? It's kind of the same story. After some unspecific cataclysm, the city sank beneath the waves. But it's said to be the hiding place of some incredibly powerful artifact."

"Like a magic scepter or something?" Lucius asked, the corner of his lip twitching.

"Joke all you want, but I'm serious. Remember that couplet? 'Even death may die,' Mr Galloway. What if this thing can reanimate the dead? I know it sounds like a pulp story, but what if it really were possible?"

"Look, Miss Quinn, I won't try to tell you that the story

isn't compelling. But if this really is the *Necronomicon*, it didn't make me run off a cliff, and I'm finding it difficult to believe that Helen is wrapped up in a plot to raise an army of the dead. I'm afraid the whole thing is a bit too farfetched for my taste."

"Is it?" she asked, fixing him with a steady stare. "Tell me you haven't had any unusual experiences while working on it. You were less than convincing about that."

His momentary good humor vanished without a trace. A new wave of terror made his palms go wet, but he could not give in to those feelings again. Not when he was so close to answers.

"Is it written on my face?" he asked quietly.

"Those of us who have touched the inexplicable have a certain look about the eyes. You'll grow to recognize it in time," she replied, not unkindly. "Tell me."

He hesitated.

"I once watched a young woman leap into a shadowy corner and vanish. I searched that room myself, Mr Galloway. There was no secret staircase, no hidden egress. The shadows swallowed her up and spit her back out again. The next day, I saw her in a crowd. She winked at me before disappearing again."

"Did you follow her?"

"I tried, but I lost her in the chaos. Everyone was running from–" She broke off, the color draining from her face. "I don't think I can explain what we were running from. No words could capture how awful they were, and I'm no poet."

"I am, and I still lack the ability to fully describe what I've seen," he said, still reluctant despite his relief at being believed. Finally, he could unburden himself. Whatever happened now, he would not face it alone.

"Tell me," she repeated, her eyes intense.

Lucius unloaded it all. At first, he told his tale hesitantly, half expecting her to laugh in his face, but she remained unflappable. He told the story in spare terminology, trying to stick to the facts of what he remembered. His voice remained steady through the narration of it all, although he could feel his body shaking. As he spoke, Quinn's expression grew darker and darker.

"We need to get that manuscript," she said when he finished.

"You believe me? It's rather an outlandish tale," he asked, torn between wanting her to confirm that he wasn't losing touch with reality and wanting her to laugh it all off as a joke.

"I believe you." She stood up. "I'm going to the boarding house. Hopefully they haven't left yet."

"Left … ?" he asked, confused.

"The cult was behind all of this from the beginning, and every move they made has had its purpose. Why did they hire you?" she asked. "Haven't you put it together yet?"

He swallowed the annoyance that rose within him at the impertinent question and considered. The cult had a copy of the *Necronomicon*. If they wanted to get at that powerful artifact, they would have to get to R'lyeh, the instructions to which were hidden in the verse. Helen had translated it, but they still couldn't figure it out, so they'd brought him in to analyze the poetry. That last chapter must have provided the final piece, perhaps in the star map. After all, sailors used them for navigation all the time. What better way to find a sunken city? Anyone could read it, but he'd pulled out the instructions on how to use it from the rest of the manuscript. He'd thought it was a thematic element, but he'd been wrong. Those instructions had been hidden deliberately, and he'd put them right into the cult's hands. He couldn't even begin to untangle the tumult of emotions that realization engendered in him. How dare they? But there would be time for self-introspection and blame later.

He sprang to his feet.

"I'm going with you," he said.

"Look, Mr Galloway, I appreciate the sentiment, but this is likely to be a dangerous and disturbing experience. Count yourself lucky to have survived it with your mind intact and go home."

"No. I won't sit by while my work is used for evil. We can either waste more precious time arguing about it, or we can go. It's your choice."

His voice was steadier than it ought to have been. Now that he had allowed himself to fully believe in what was happening here, he understood the risk he was taking. But wasn't there already a risk? They could come for him – for Rudi – at any time to erase any knowledge of what they'd done. He had no idea who these cultists were; he would not recognize the threat until it was too late. Besides, he could not back down and live with himself later. He had always undertaken to make the world a little brighter with his writing, and he would not give up on that goal now that he had realized said world was more complicated than he'd known. If anything, it was more important than ever.

She locked eyes with him for a moment before nodding in acceptance of whatever strength or determination she saw there.

"Very well," she said. "If we're going to be partners, call me Quinn. Everyone does."

"Lucius." He offered his hand, and they shook. "Let's go before I lose my nerve."

"Story of my life, Lucius," she replied, and they headed to the door together.

CHAPTER TWENTY-SEVEN

As soon as Lucius and Quinn turned the corner onto the street near the boarding house, the air changed. The temperature dropped suddenly, offering what should have been a relief from the summer heat, but the unnatural cold reached into him like a questing tentacle. It wrapped around his spine, filling him with a dread that made him shake.

Next to him, Quinn gritted her teeth and carried on with what looked like sheer determination despite the fact that her lips were tinted blue.

"Was it like this before?" she asked.

"Cold? No. But I've never seen anyone else around. Strange, isn't it?"

He gestured to the rows of silent houses that led up to the cult's headquarters at the corner. This time, it was clear that the structures had been abandoned. Tall weeds cluttered the front lawns and climbed up the porch pillars. His neck prickled as if the buildings themselves watched him. It felt like a ghost town, haunted by the memories of the people who had once lived here. For the first time, he wondered where they had gone.

The door to the boarding house hung halfway open, creaking slightly in the breeze. As they climbed cautiously up to the porch, Lucius scanned the place for any signs of occupancy, but nothing moved save the door and the fluttering curtains. He turned to look at Quinn, who pulled the wicked looking pistol out of her pocket. Lucius had never so much as handled a firearm in his long life and had no real urge to do so any time soon, but the sight of the weapon was a welcome one. Whatever happened here, they would not be defenseless.

"Should I say something?" he mouthed, indicating the door.

After a moment's thought, she nodded, shifting to stand next to the jamb, the gun held down by her side where the voluminous legs of her trousers would hide it from view.

"Anybody home?" he called out. "Helen?"

There was no answer. The door creaked again. The deep and somehow unnatural silence played havoc with Lucius' nerves. His heartbeat sped up like a drum at a jazz club. He could hear his pulse thundering in his ears. But there was nothing to do but move through it.

He pushed the door open, and after a breathless moment, he stuck his head in.

"Hello?" he said.

The overcrowded sitting room sat in a jumbled mess. The sofa had been upended and jagged rips ran the length of the lining underneath, like some massive, clawed thing had escaped from within. Debris had been heaped everywhere, doilies and dolls and pillows torn to shreds or dirtied and discarded. The rug was stained with fluids he did not want to examine more closely. They glistened in a most disturbing manner beneath the beams of light that filtered in through the open doorway. Large chunks of wood suggested a large furniture piece had been somehow obliterated, and for one dazed moment, Lucius tried to figure out what it might have been. Had there been a coffee table when he'd come to visit? He couldn't recall, and ultimately, it did not matter.

Quinn's eyes rounded in shock as she took it all in. If she hadn't been there, he would have thought he was dreaming again, but this was real. It had all been real. He knew it in his bones.

Lucius had never been a fool. He was not the sort of person to court danger, as his very existence was dangerous enough as it was. He had survived – and even thrived – by avoiding trouble, and his instincts screamed at him to leave. Run now. Don't look back. But Helen was his friend, and she had been caught up in this mess. He could not abandon her, nor Quinn. He had a duty to see this through, so he took a deep and fortifying breath and stepped inside. Quinn dogged his steps.

Halfway through the room, the musk hit him again, the stench of something rotten and foul that made his gorge rise. He swallowed hard against the spray of acid in his mouth, covering his nose and mouth with one hand in a futile attempt to block out the smell. Wordlessly, Quinn handed him a stick of chewing gum, popping a second one in her mouth. It helped, but only a little. The scent was too strong.

It grew stronger near the stairway to the second floor. Lucius did not want to investigate this any further. For the first time, he wondered if the smell might indicate a dead body that had been hidden in some out-of-the-way closet and left to rot in the summer heat. If so, it had been there a while. That ill-fated mahjong night had been over a month ago, and he did not want to see what a body would look like after all that time. But they could afford to leave no stone unturned in their search for Helen and the *Necronomicon*.

The stairway was cloaked in darkness, and anything could be lurking in those deep shadows. If only he had brought a flashlight. An old-fashioned lamp hung on an ornate wooden holder at the foot of the stairs, miraculously undamaged. Oil sloshed in the base when he hefted it, and a tin of matches nestled in a little slot against the wall. Within moments, he had it lit, banishing the shadows to reveal a new set of dark stains on the stairs.

Quinn took the lead this time, holding the gun in both hands and pointing it at the floor in front of her feet. She climbed with slow deliberation, placing each foot carefully to avoid making any noise. He tried to mimic the movement, but it turned out to be more difficult than it looked. If the occasional shuffle of his footsteps bothered her, she gave no indication.

At the top of the staircase, a long hallway stretched out before them. There were three doors on either side, all open, their interiors dark and silent. At the end of the hall sat a single closed door. The two investigators froze for a moment, watching and listening in the fitful pool of light cast by the lamp. From beyond the threshold, Lucius could hear the faintest of thumps as the shadows beneath the door shifted. Someone was inside, and they were trying to avoid detection.

Quinn met his eyes; she'd heard it too. In unison, they crept down the hallway, pausing at each pair of doors lest some *thing* come dashing out at them. The bedrooms had been similarly destroyed, the furniture tossed or obliterated entirely. Heavy drapes had been pulled over the windows, miraculously untouched. At one room, a black and oozing handprint clung to the frame, viscous fluid still dripping onto the floor.

Plink.

Plink.

His breath ragged with fear, Lucius continued toward the closed door. He did not want to open it, but there was no choice. He was committed now, and he would see this through.

Quinn paused a few steps away, lifting her gun to what Lucius thought of as half-staff – not pointed at anything, but not right at her feet either. She twitched her chin toward the door, the meaning clear. She wanted him to open it. If something came flying out at them, she would shoot.

Lucius reached toward the doorknob with sweat-slippery hands, careful to stay out of the line of fire. He twisted the knob and threw the door open in one smooth movement.

A flood of bodies came pouring out the open doorway. For a moment, Lucius struggled to believe what he was seeing. He knew these things: the scaly bodies and misshapen froglike mouths haunted his dreams. They had pulled him beneath the water and nearly drowned him. Now they attacked, gibbering and croaking, webbed feet slapping wetly against the floor.

They were real.

Quinn's gun went off, the sharp retort echoing in the hallway. Lucius reeled, stunned by the ringing in his ears, and one of the hideous creatures leaped on him, slamming him into the wall. The impact made him bite his tongue hard. Wet copper filled his mouth, and the pain jolted him back to reality.

The thing had its hands around his neck now, shaking him back and forth. This creature's visage was slightly more human than the ones he'd seen in the water, but it still possessed the same unnatural strength. He struggled for air, fingers scrabbling at its slippery skin as he tried to wrench free.

"Lucius!" Quinn yelled, retreating back down the hallway as the pistol discharged again, overwhelming his senses.

The creature's grip loosened with a surprising abruptness. He sucked in a great gulp of air, chest heaving, shrinking before it. Oxygen flooded his starving cells as confusion gripped his mind. Why had it released him? Should he take this opportunity to make a break for it?

"Lucius?" it said, the word garbled by its distorted mouth. "I told you before, a man shouldn't have to deal with such frippery. It's unseemly."

The words made no sense, but they echoed in his mind, somehow familiar. A face swam to the surface of his memory. Marco had said that to him at the mahjong game. But...

He looked closer at the creature before him, wondering at how human it looked despite the mottled skin and the animalistic features. The mouth had been stretched, but it hovered somewhere between human and amphibian proportions. The wide-set eyes bulged, but they didn't glow a sickly green like the creatures in the water. Why, above the wide mouth was a thin pencil mustache. You couldn't get more human than that.

Then he realized it with dawning horror – Marco had that same mustache. He had the same brown eyes, the same voice as this thing. There was only one conclusion, and it made his blood run cold. Somehow, they had made him one of them.

"Join us, Lucius," the Marco-thing said, its mouth stretching even further into a smile of disturbing width. "We'll play mahjong."

"Lucius, get out of there!" yelled Quinn from the far end of the hallway. "There are too many of them!"

The Marco-thing tugged Lucius toward the room at the end of the hall. Although Lucius couldn't see inside the room from this angle, a faint greenish glow spilled out the open doorway. The last thing he wanted was to go in there. If Marco had been transformed into one of these creatures, they could do the same to him. Perhaps that's what the things in the water had been trying to do when they put him on the altar. If Helen hadn't pulled him out, this could have been him, and she was no longer here to protect him. He had finished the manuscript and been discarded. He could see that clearly now.

He struggled against the Marco-thing's implacable grip, but the abominable creature was too strong. It dragged him across the floor as he scrambled to get away. Its grip was like iron. He hit its arm and only managed to hurt his fist. He would not overpower this creature physically. His only hope for survival was to use his wits.

What would hurt a water creature?

He needed fire.

The lamp had fallen from his grip during the chaos, but luckily, it hadn't broken. It sat cockeyed against the wall surrounded by a small puddle of lamp oil, the flame guttering. He had to get to it before it ran out, but if he stooped down to pick it up, he would lose what little leverage he had. The creature would drag him into the glowing green room, and he would not come back out again as the same person, if at all.

There was no time to think. He had to risk it. He reached down and ripped his suit coat open, buttons pinging onto the floor. Then he dropped to his knees.

The sudden movement loosened the creature's unnatural grip, and he managed to slip one arm out of the jacket. Fabric tore, the sound unnaturally loud. He sucked in air in big panicked whoops as he groped for the lamp, the Marco-thing tugging him backward. His fingers grazed the hot glass, nearly toppling it over. A muscle in his neck spasmed, and he let out a pained yelp, propelling himself forward with a convulsive thrust of his legs. The remaining sleeve of his jacket came most of the way off, and he snagged the lamp by its base, ignoring the burning pain as his fingers closed around it.

He swung around hard, slamming the globe against the wall and shattering the glass to reveal the flame inside. Now that it was upright, it burned tall and strong. Hopefully it would be enough.

The Marco-thing let out a laugh that was half croak.

"Planning to stab me?" it asked gleefully. "It won't do you any good."

"No, I thought I'd douse you in oil and see how long you burn."

Lucius spoke in a flat tone to show he meant business. The Marco-thing released him quickly, backing up a step in obvious fear, but that soon faded. Its eyes glittered as it reached for him again.

"You don't have the nerve," it said.

He thrust the lamp forward, the flame licking at the Marco-thing's arm. It gave a whistling shriek and retreated, hissing and snarling. He had to make his escape before it marshaled the nerve for another attack. He stumbled to his feet, the torn jacket flapping, and nearly tripped over the prone body of one of the other ichthyic man-things. Its dead eyes stared into his. Then he was up again, and there were three of them crowded before him.

Blam!

The gun went off again, but he did not see where the bullet went in the dim light, and none of the creatures fell. They hesitated though, eyes locked on the lamp still clutched in his hand.

"I'll burn you all!" he said, charging at them in a reckless, desperate assault. He could not afford to give them time to realize they outnumbered him, or they would rally. Instead, they scattered before him, and he slammed into Quinn just as he had the first time they met, nearly knocking her down the stairs.

"Look out!" she said, firing off another shot over his shoulder.

He didn't need to look behind him to know they were hot on his heels. The obvious fear etched on Quinn's face told him everything he needed to know. He reached back and slammed the lamp onto the ground.

Flaming lamp oil splattered everywhere. The creatures howled as the floor was instantly set aflame, the hungry fire leaping as it found new fuel to burn. Lucius stumbled backward again. Burning motes peppered his face, stinging his skin. The loose sleeve of his jacket caught, and he tore it the rest of the way free, dropping it into the fire.

"Go, go!" he shouted.

The hallway was already filling with an acrid smelling smoke. He could see the shadowy figures of the piscine creatures on the other side of the conflagration, but none of them seemed eager to make the leap. They needed to make their escape while they could.

The two of them thundered down the stairs, heading for the open front door. But as they crossed through the ruined remains of the living room, there was a deafening clap of something like thunder coming from somewhere down beneath them. Lucius' ears popped. His head throbbed. Wetness trickled down his upper lip; his nose had begun to spontaneously bleed.

"What the heck was that?" he asked, his voice high and frightened.

Quinn's face had gone paler than ever, but she swallowed hard and squared her shoulders.

"No clue," she said, "but it's my job to find out."

"You've got to be kidding me," he said.

"Someone has to," she replied simply. "You coming?"

She was right. If they didn't do something, who knew what these things would do? Innocent people would likely suffer. Besides, he still hadn't found Helen. He hoped she hadn't become one of those things, or that she wasn't working with them voluntarily. But if he didn't find out for certain, it would haunt him forever.

"I'm coming," he said. "But I think that sound came from the basement. We could get trapped down there if the fire spreads."

She took in a raggedy breath, steeling herself.

"I know," she said simply. "Let's go."

CHAPTER TWENTY-EIGHT

A massive spiderweb of cracks jutted a good three feet from the basement door in the kitchen. Chunks of plaster from the damaged walls and ceiling dotted the floor, and the broken tiles crackled underfoot as Lucius and Quinn made their careful way across it. The damage had twisted the jamb, sticking the door in place, and he had to yank on it hard to pull it free. He did not want to speculate on what force could have caused such damage. If he did, he would run, so he kept his mind blank. They would face whatever they found down there together.

Quinn went first, still clutching her gun. Lucius wondered how many bullets were left; he hadn't counted before and wouldn't know how many it held anyway. Hopefully there would be enough. He had grabbed a kitchen knife from the block on their way through, but he had no idea how to use it, and its handle kept slipping in his wet, nervous palms. But it had seemed like a prudent idea anyway.

The wooden stairs were rickety and loose, and they swayed alarmingly as they descended at a snail's pace. The damage was even stronger down here, cracks radiating down the walls of the enclosed stairway. At the bottom, a flickering blue light suggested some occupancy, but he could hear no movement save a faint groaning and a constant buzz like radio static.

They reached the bottom of the stairs. Quinn inched her head out from behind the wall, and Lucius could not resist the urge to do the same. An astonishing sight awaited him there. The basement was dominated by a single long room with bare stone walls and hard packed dirt floors, and the door emerged at the center of the long wall. To the right, a large blue oval hung in the air by some incomprehensible magic, crackling and spitting sparks. Within its glowing depths, flickering images of buildings came into and out of focus over and over again, as if the very air throbbed to the tune of some ancient, inaudible beat.

The empty carcasses of fish encircled this inexplicable object on the ground beneath it, their entrails pulled out into ropy strings that glistened in the lurid illumination. There were so many of them, too many to count, but Lucius instantly knew their number. It had been specified in the *Necronomicon*. He had included it in his section on divination, assuming that the entrails of eighty-eight fish would have no other possible use. But he had been wrong. This was no vain attempt to tell the future, but a ceremony designed to pierce the walls of the universe in the most unnatural, profane manner.

A groan captured his attention, and he jerked with fear, fully expecting one of the fish-people to come leaping out at him once again. But the floor was littered with bodies that appeared like normal humans. In fact, he was fairly sure that one over there was at the mahjong party. Were they all dead? A dawning horror gripped his spine until he realized one of them was sitting up – a middle-aged, paunchy gent who held his head as he groaned. The others began to stir, one by one, coming back to consciousness with a gasp. Now that he no longer had to worry about some strange mass murder in the basement of his friend's boarding house, he registered the fact that the lot of them wore sickly green robes.

So this was what a cult looked like. He had expected them to be more… aggressive. Perhaps they would be, when they hadn't been stunned by that thunderclap. If it had been loud upstairs, he could only imagine how deafening it would have been right beside it. He saw more than a few nosebleeds on the dazed faces.

"We've got to close it," said Quinn, her voice shaking. "How do we close it?"

"Close what?" Lucius asked, trying desperately to make sense out of this strange situation.

"The portal!"

As soon as the words escaped her mouth, everything clicked. The fish. The cultists. The stars painted on the ceiling. One of them would have a ceremonial dagger, and there would be glyphs…

Just as the *Necronomicon* had specified. He had dug the instructions out from the lines in which they'd hidden. All of those nights he'd spent poring over the verses, pulling out echoed language from each section and crafting an argument about the thematic meaning – that hadn't been thematic at all. They had been instructions, a recipe for opening that blue and swirling portal. With a pang, he realized that the buildings within it were quite familiar to him. He had seen them in his dreams.

Flash.

The buildings new and gleaming, the spires reaching toward multicolored skies.

Flash.

The city underwater and crumbling, clustered with luminescent green growths.

Flash.

The buildings aflame, the dark husks of its occupants crowding the streets.

Flash.

The floodwaters coming in, choking the roads.

Flash. Flash. Flash.

Each reality piled up on the previous one as if this place existed in all times and in all incarnations all at once, the veils between them as thin as paper. He stared at it, mouth open. This was his drowned city. The place that had called to him for so long, and now it was within reach. He belonged there.

Dazed, he took one single step toward the portal before Quinn's fist rocketed into his chin. For such a petite person, she packed a punch. Stars swam behind his eyes for a moment, and although his face throbbed, he felt as if some unseen cloud had lifted from his eyes. A pressure he had not even felt before lifted from his spine. He turned new eyes on the city beyond the portal – R'lyeh, she'd called it – and saw it for what it truly was.

He had no words to explain the dawning horror he felt as he looked on that strange place with its soaring buildings that defied the laws of nature. Their impossible angles twisted in his vision, forming shapes that seared his brain. They said things, those buildings. They were glyphs themselves, the very language of binding built into every stone. He did not want to know what the city had been built to contain, but he remembered with unsettling vividness the depthless chamber which he knew now to be a prison cell, just as he knew that by stepping through this portal, these cultists risked releasing whatever slept within. The thought froze the marrow in his bones and choked the breath from his lungs.

R'lyeh was a resting place, but not of an artifact like Quinn had suggested. A thing. A massive, world-ending thing with an endless hunger. What was it that the famous quote had said? Even death may die.

How could death end? Simple. If there were no living things left to die.

As he reeled with this realization, the cultists rose to their feet, crying out in what sounded like jubilation. "*Ia! Ia!*" they shouted, the strangely accented syllable grating on Lucius' ears. They gathered quickly, their over-wide eyes fixated on the portal beyond. Only he and Quinn stood in their way, and the numbers did not look good.

Quinn squeezed off a warning shot into the ceiling, driving them back, but it would not hold them long. He needed to close the portal.

"So are you here to stop us or to join us, Lucius?" asked a familiar voice.

From out of the darkest corner of the basement came Helen Berringer, her eyes burning with an unnatural light. She wore a robe as well, but hers was different than all the others. It was a deep purple, the hood and sleeves edged in glyphs woven from golden thread. The shapes swam in his vision, and he averted his eyes quickly. He did not want to know what those words said.

"No matter," she continued. "It's really too late for either."

A weight settled into the pit of his stomach.

"I thought we were friends," he said. "I came here; I braved all of this … this *terror* in order to rescue you."

"That's not Helen," said Quinn, lifting her gun, her shaking hand at odds with the firmness of her voice. "I worked with her for years. That's not her voice; this is somehow an impostor. Who are you?"

"That's not Helen?" he asked, confused. "But she's always sounded like that."

Everything they'd said and done, the laughs they'd shared, the childhood tales they'd exchanged – none of it had been real. It felt as if he'd been punched in the stomach, driving all of the breath from his body. Had she been manipulating him all this time? If she wasn't the real Helen Berringer, who was she? What inexplicable magic was at work here?

"As much as I'd love to have this chat, there's no time." Helen smiled cruelly, the expression sitting uncomfortably on her face. "To the portal!"

The cultists sprang into action at her command, crying out once again in manic joy as they streamed toward the portal. Lucius hesitated, unsure of what to do. He could not stop them all. But Helen's outfit suggested she was different, perhaps the leader of them all. If he could only keep one of them from the portal, it had to be her.

The stinging sense of betrayal he felt down to his bones had nothing to do with it.

Quinn seemed to share the sentiment. She kept the gun fixed on Helen. The old woman's face flickered, and for a moment, Lucius saw fear there before it was buried in an expression of smug confidence.

Although he had his knife, he couldn't bring himself to

stab his former friend. Even if she had no sense of loyalty, he couldn't be so duplicitous. Besides, he was no fighter; his mind was the strongest weapon he had. Something worried her. If he could figure out what it was, he could use it against her.

Think, Galloway, think!

His mind raced through the work of the past few months, searching for the nugget of knowledge that could possibly make a difference. He muttered stanzas beneath his breath, sifting through the ancient words. How did one close a portal? It wasn't as easy as grabbing the knob and shutting it down.

Then he had it: one hundred breaths.

He'd found multiple references to the hundred breaths throughout the manuscript, and he'd argued that the writer must have practiced some form of breath prayer or meditation. But there was one other thing that breath could be used for – a measure of ancient time. How many times did a person breathe in a minute? Fifteen? Twenty? The portal would remain open for a hundred of them. If it had opened with the thunderclap, the time must be almost out. All they had to do was keep Helen here for a while longer. It shouldn't be too hard. She was a tiny old woman.

He still couldn't risk it. That flicker of fear suggested that maybe she'd figured it out. There was also the possibility that the house was burning down above them, or that the fire had gone out and those things would come after them once again. They had to leave while they still could. So he made the only choice he could think of: he grabbed her by the wrist and began to drag her to the stairs.

She was even lighter than he'd expected, but she struggled with more strength than he would have given her credit for. When they reached the bottom of the staircase, she howled, attracting the attention of the remaining cultists. Quinn leveled her gun at them.

"I'll hold them off," she said grimly. "Go."

He didn't look back. If she could trust in him without question, he could offer her the same courtesy. Helen thrashed like a cat in a sack, mumbling something he didn't quite catch. The few clotted syllables he did make out writhed in the chambers of his mind. An intense urge to clap his hand over her mouth and make her stop came over him, but he had no hands to spare. Her thin wrist kept slipping loose from his grip, forcing him to hold on with both hands and tug her along behind him. Perhaps once he got her away from all this nonsense, he could talk some sense into her. Even if Quinn was right and this wasn't Helen Berringer, that didn't erase their friendship. She truly cared; he had to believe that.

Something swelled in the air, settling down on him like a dread blanket. His heart leaped into his throat, choking off his breath. Helen let out a wordless "hah!" of triumph, ceasing her struggles.

Then the pain hit. He had never felt anything so excruciating, not when he'd broken his arm as a boy, not when his appendix had burst and required emergency surgery. It felt as if his bones twisted in their sockets, their ends grinding against each other. The agony was everywhere, tearing the last of his breath out of him with a gasp. It squeezed his neck and contorted his spine. It felt like he was dying.

Through a haze of red, he looked down at himself, but there was nothing wrong. He still stood on the bottom step of the basement, frozen in the act of dragging Helen out. She stared at him with a smile of utter satisfaction stretching her lips despite the fact that her hand remained imprisoned in his.

She had done this. If he could believe all of these other things – the portal, the Marco-thing, the sheer *magic* of it all, he could believe that. She had woven some spell to force him to release her. Apparently, she didn't know him as well as he'd thought. He didn't give up that easily.

Tears of agony leaked from his eyes, but he gritted his teeth and lifted one foot. The movement sent new waves of pain rocketing through him, so severe that his stomach heaved. The stairway wavered in his vision just like the city beyond the portal, his grip on consciousness beginning to slip through his fingers. He bit down on his own tongue, hard, the very real pain of it flooding his mouth. He took another step.

"Damn it," said Helen, going limp in his arms. "You just don't give up, do you?"

It was tempting to think that he'd bested her, but until the portal closed, he wasn't letting go. In fact, he tightened his grip once again, sweat leaking from his palms.

"I don't have the time for this," she said.

The pain eased with such suddenness that it made him stagger. Then she gave him one last grin, her eyes twinkling, and she went limp like someone had pulled out some cosmic electrical plug. Her eyes rolled back in a suddenly vacant face, and she dropped bonelessly to the floor. He felt something unseen float past him in that moment, running unseen hands over his spine. Although he had never been particularly religious, in that moment, he firmly believed in the existence of a soul, and somehow hers had rotted.

Still, he leaned over her, his eyes wide with horror. An inexplicable certainty that she had died filled him, but perhaps he could bring her back. She deserved a chance, and he wanted – no, *needed* – answers. But the body crumpled at his feet began to decay at an alarming rate. In seconds, it withered before his eyes, the skin sucked of all moisture. The dry lips peeled away from the teeth, creating a leering grin that unsettled him so much he averted his gaze.

For the briefest of moments, he stood there frozen and rudderless, unsure of what to do. Then clarity struck him. He could not save Helen, but he would not abandon Quinn.

He launched back out of the stairway and into the basement only to find it empty save for a pile of scattered bodies and only two live occupants left. Dao dragged an unconscious Quinn toward the portal, grunting with the effort. The former research assistant wore one of the green robes, its hood now thrown back to reveal her contorted face. As he emerged from the staircase, she snarled at him like an animal.

"Curse you, Lucius Galloway," she said in Helen's strange, deep voice.

He had no idea how to explain that, but it didn't matter. She released Quinn's arm and sprinted for the portal. He rushed after her, his muscles somehow loose and disjointed after everything they had gone through. He tripped over Quinn's outflung arm and went sprawling on the floor. The portal crackled as it swallowed Dao's form. Before he could even consider following her, it collapsed with a boom that sent him reeling into the black of unconsciousness.

CHAPTER TWENTY-NINE

"Are you sure about this?" asked Quinn as she stood next to him on the train station platform.

His lips firmed with resolution as he considered the question. He could think of nothing else to do. The boarding house had burned to the ground, and if any of its horrific occupants had managed to escape, they hadn't bothered him over the past few days since that living nightmare in the basement. Of course, he had spent most of the time sleeping, or keeping watch while Quinn slumbered. It had given him a lot of time to think about things, and he knew in his heart that this was what he had to do.

"I'm sure," he said, patting her hand where it rested in the crook of his elbow. "I need to go to Arkham and see for myself."

"I know it's for the best that we get out of town," she murmured. "Just in case a witness does come forward to link us with... you know." She waved a hand, unwilling to say aloud that they'd been somehow a part of the unexplained conflagration which had been the talk of the town, just in case someone was close enough to overhear. "But I've gotten used to having you around. It's nice to have a partner for a change."

"Well, go handle that key thing and come join me when you can," he suggested.

She snorted. During the few waking hours they'd had together, she'd told him at length about the organization she belonged to and its quest to safely store objects of arcane power. To be honest, he was still undecided about her offer to join. A large part of him still wanted to return to his Brooklyn apartment and forget this whole sordid thing had ever happened. Write the whole thing off as a dream.

But he couldn't do that, no matter how tempting it was. Besides, even if he wanted to, it wouldn't be home without Rudi. His hand dipped into his pocket, clutching the letter he'd taken so long to read. When he had finally opened it, the contents made him shake with nerves.

I'm staying in Arkham. You wouldn't believe the things I've learned here. The world is bigger even than we'd imagined. Come join us, and you'll see.
Rudi

The missive sounded more cult-like than he could bear. Had the pilgrims gotten to Rudi? He had to get to Arkham as soon as possible. What use was there in saving the world if it meant losing the person he loved more than life itself? Besides, he couldn't deny that after everything that had happened, he needed to see with his own eyes that Rudi was safe. Some people might call that paranoia, but given recent experiences, he considered it an entirely rational approach.

"'That key thing'? Do you even listen to anything I've got to say?" Quinn was griping in mock indignation.

"I assure you," he replied in a grave tone, "that I listen to at least every third word."

She threw up her hands, unable to keep her lips from quirking. "Why do I even talk to you?" she exclaimed.

The banter reminded him uncomfortably of Helen. After he'd told her about how Dao spoke with Helen's voice, Quinn theorized that he had never met the real Helen Berringer at all, but instead some unknown entity that had possessed her body, abandoning it for Dao's once it realized that was the only way it could escape through the portal. He wasn't sure what he thought about any of it, although he could not deny that he'd felt something when Helen died. Whether it was her soul leaving her body or the waft of some sorcerous specter as it fled for another host was beyond his ken. He would probably never know, and he wasn't sure how much it would matter anyway. He had still lost something precious. Even if their friendship hadn't been real, it had meant something to him.

Quinn seemed to read some of his melancholy thoughts on his face. She squeezed his arm, waiting until he met her eyes.

"Seriously. Are you okay? I could maybe delay a day or two and accompany you to Arkham," she said.

He straightened up, trying to look reassuring.

"No, no, you need to go. You were lucky to get a berth on a ship at such short notice. Perhaps you'll get some time to sightsee? I hear Barcelona is lovely this time of year."

"This is not exactly a sightseeing kind of trip. More like a saving-the-world kind of trip."

"You might as well have good weather while you save the world, then." He offered her a thin smile. "Don't you worry about me. If Rudi has been approached by the pilgrims, I'll do whatever it takes to wrest him out, and I'll swing through town on my way back home to make sure there's no sign of our old friends from the boarding house. If there's anything out of the ordinary, I'll telegraph."

"I don't doubt you," she said quietly, her eyes locked on the approaching bulk of the train as it chugged into the station. "You've more than proven that you're capable, otherwise I wouldn't have offered to sponsor you in a bid for a Foundation position. But I've seen this kind of knowledge break strong people before. It's hard to come to terms with the fact that the underpinnings of the world don't work the way you thought they did. Please don't underestimate the effects of that."

He considered her words carefully as he scanned the crowd. There was no denying the fact that he had changed. Since the events in the boarding house, he had become the kind of person who remained always on the alert. Always skeptical. Always watching for signs that a person was not who they claimed to be. Perhaps the urge to do so would fade with time, but he didn't think so. Like Quinn had said, something fundamental had shifted within him.

"I won't, and I appreciate the counsel," he said.

Across the long length of the platform, passengers began to spill out the doors of the train. He had watched them do so many times over the past few months – he had always been a bit of a people watcher – but now it hit different. All of these people with their lives and worries and loves, scurrying off completely unaware that the rules of the universe did not work the way they thought. Up until a few months earlier, he had been one of them.

The drowned city of his poetry was real. He knew that now, just as he knew that the opening of its doors would have consequences which he could barely even begin to comprehend. That knowledge was written on Quinn's face too, etching deep lines that remained despite her smiles. There was nothing to do but batten down the hatches and wait for it to come. But in order to do that, he needed his safe harbor. His rock. His home.

He needed Rudi. Whatever happened next, he would always need Rudi.

"We'll see each other again," he said, holding out his hand. "If you ever need me, you call, and I'll come running."

"Even if it means getting on a boat?" she asked, hesitating.

His lips firmed.

"Even if it means getting on a boat," he affirmed.

She bypassed his proffered hand, squeezing him tight in a quick, somewhat rough hug.

"Well, go on now or you'll miss your train, and then I'll need to listen to your snoring all night again," she said.

"I'll have you know that I do not snore, young lady!"

"Hey, at least you're sleeping."

At least he was. The dreams had faded. Sometimes that worried him, but it was probably for the best.

He climbed aboard the train and settled into a seat alone, missing Rudi's endless chatter. When he threw open the window, he saw Ari Quinn standing there alone, clutching her hat to her head as the train emitted a gust of air and lurched into movement. She raised a hand, and he waved back until she was no longer visible.

He settled into his seat, determined to ignore his roiling stomach. Rudi needed him, and he needed Rudi. Whatever was coming, he refused to face it alone.

• • •

Abdul Alhazred stood before the Dream Gates of R'lyeh, trailing his fingertips over the arcane sigils carved into ancient stone. Finally, after hundreds of years of searching, he had reached his goal, and he soaked it in, reveling in his triumph. His cultists had all fallen on the long road, but reinforcements would arrive soon, summoned from all over the world to join him in their new home. He smiled, an expression that felt foreign on his face. He had still not gotten used to Dao's body yet, and it was not worth making the effort.

The gate emitted a low thrum of power, a constant ebb and flow that skittered over his bones, setting his magical senses alight. He could feel the presence of the great entity beyond the gate, a presence that had awaited his arrival for millennia.

Arching over the gate were the words that had been locked from his memory for so long, but now they blazed in his mind: *ph'nglui mglw'nafh Cthulhu R'lyeh wgah'nagl fhtagn.* In his house at R'lyeh, dread Cthulhu waits dreaming.

Now he remembered everything. He knew what needed to be done.

Here at the end of all things, dread Cthulhu would cease to dream.

ACKNOWLEDGMENTS

As always, thanks go to all of the fine folks at Aconyte, but especially to Charlotte Llewelyn-Wells, whose keen editorial eye and kind feedback have talked me down off many a ledge. I also owe a debt of gratitude to my agent, Kate Testerman, and her swashbuckling optimism. Marcy Rockwell deserves an award for being the best Jamie Lee Curtis and cheering on fellow writers with gusto. Lastly, I'd like to thank my friends and family – particularly Andy, Connor, Lily, Ryan, Keith, Lisa, Aunt Marian, Sarah, Lee and all the Driveway Drinkers, and Emily and Jen for always humoring and supporting me, even when I'm rambling nonstop about tentacle monsters.

ABOUT THE AUTHOR

CARRIE HARRIS has been writing professionally since the early 2000s. She writes original and licensed books in a variety of worlds including *Marvel, Warhammer 40K, The World of Darkness*, and the *Fate RPG*. Her books *Shadow Avengers: A Marvel Crisis Protocol Novel, Witches Unleashed: A Marvel Untold Novel*, and *Liberty & Justice for All: A Xavier's Institute Novel* were Scribe award finalists for best licensed fiction, and her young adult horror comedy *Bad Taste in Boys* was a Quick Pick for Reluctant Readers. She is a member of the International Association of Media Tie-In Writers and the Science Fiction and Fantasy Writers Association. Carrie lives in New York with her ninja doctor husband, teenagers, and a cranky dog named Slartibartfast.

carrieharrisbooks.com // x.com/carrharr

THE DEFINITIVE GUIDE TO THE
WORLD OF ARKHAM HORROR

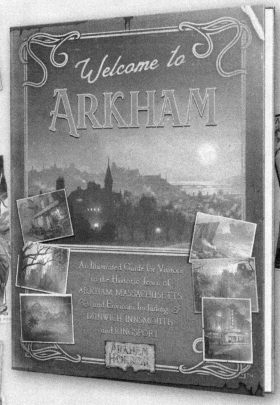

*Venture deeper than ever before into the
legend-haunted city of Arkham and its
neighboring towns of Dunwich, Innsmouth
and Kingsport. Explore 115 fabled locations
with more than 500 illustrations in this
gorgeous, full-color hardcover guidebook.*

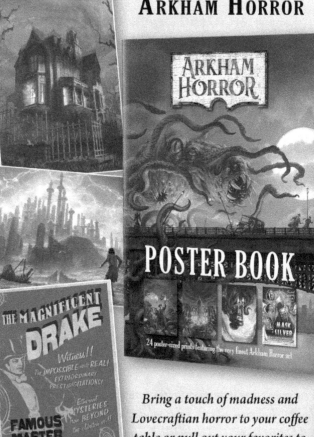

Printed in the USA
CPSIA information can be obtained
at www.ICGtesting.com
CBHW020923061224
18215CB00039B/104

9 781839 083105